# THE
# KILLING
# LIGHT

# THE
# KILLING
# LIGHT

## MYKE COLE

A TOM DOHERTY ASSOCIATES BOOK

NEW YORK

THE KILLING LIGHT

Copyright © 2019 by Myke Cole

A Tor.com Book
Published by Tom Doherty Associates
120 Broadway
New York, NY 10271

www.tor-forge.com

Tor® is a registered trademark of Macmillan Publishing Group, LLC.

The Library of Congress Cataloging-in-Publication Data is
available upon request.

ISBN 978-0-7653-9599-3 (hardcover)
ISBN 978-0-7653-9598-6 (ebook)

Our books may be purchased in bulk for promotional, educational, or business use.
Please contact your local bookseller or the Macmillan Corporate and Premium
Sales Department at 1-800-221-7945, extension 5442, or by email
at MacmillanSpecialMarkets@macmillan.com.

First Edition: November 2019

Printed in the United States of America

0  9  8  7  6  5  4  3  2  1

To Pallas Athene, in the words of Homer:

*Bright-eyed, wise, resolute,*
*Armed and armored in flashing gold,*
*Aweing the gods as they looked upon her,*
*Hail to you, Aegis-bearer.*

*Long is the way and hard,*
*that out of Hell leads up to light.*

—Milton, *Paradise Lost*

# I

---

## MARCH

*"Only have faith," sayeth the Emperor, "and I shall see thine labor bears fruit." And He stretched forth a hand, so that those most precious to Him should have power as great as the wizard, as mighty as the devils themselves. Yet they knew not the blight, the corruption. Yet they remained holy, for their power flowed from the Emperor's hands.*
—Book of Mysteries, I. 10.

At last, the iron sky cracked, pouring out a torrent of snow.

One moment, Heloise had a clear view of the gray-green wash of grass to either side of the rutted track, and the next all was driving white. She squinted as the wind picked up, driving sprays of frost through the slits in the war-machine's metal visor. Careful not to leave the safety of the war-machine, she had allowed Xilyka to climb up onto it, loosening the straps enough to dress Heloise in a thick woolen shift, but the metal frame did little to keep the wind out, and she shivered as its freezing fingers effortlessly found their way through the cloth weave.

"Too early for snow." Wolfun had been Lyse's Town Wall, the master of its sentries and the captain of its watch. He was one of the many Lysians who had declared for Heloise when she'd taken the town, but the only one whose counsel had brought him into her inner circle. Sir Steven, the commander of the Red Lords' host, had given him a horse, and he sat it awkwardly, shivering in the cold.

Barnard, the giant tinker who had built Heloise's war-machine, sat his horse nearly as awkwardly as Wolfun, but he did not shiver. "Tell the Emperor His will"—the tinker was a mountain of muscle, and his huge weight told on the animal, its ears pinned back as it shuffled uncomfortably along—"and see how He answers you."

It didn't take long for the snow to blanket the ground, and Heloise felt the war-machine's metal feet begin to slide. She could hear the troops around her slowing as their horses began to shy on ground gone suddenly treacherous. The Red Lords swatted at the snow piling on their armor, the Traveling People extended awnings over their wagon-drovers. Heloise's people, the villagers, pulled up hoods or swaddled their heads in blankets against the piercing cold.

Heloise turned to look back down the column. Her own people were few, poorly supplied and disorganized compared to the Red Lords' disciplined ranks, their well-stocked wagons. Their fine war-gear was belied by their simple appearance, plain red tabards over their armor. Plain red banners flying above them. Simple square, iron-banded shields.

Heloise swallowed, suddenly feeling very small. All these different people—all here because of her. The thought of all these lives tied to hers made her stomach clench. Some thought her a saint, others a lunatic, still others a brave idiot with a common enemy. But they were all here in the driving snow, the biting cold.

The Red Lords set a punishing pace, the serjeants shouting out the cadence. "Step lightly, lads! Pick them up and put them down!" Some of the soldiers sang marching songs. The words meant nothing to Heloise, but she could tell the rhythm was meant to keep the soldiers moving quickly. The Traveling People in their horse-drawn carts had no trouble keeping pace, but the villagers had just a handful of horses. They were believers drawn to Heloise's legend, farmers and wheelwrights and carpenters. Heloise could see children and old men among them, panting as they struggled to keep up.

Ahead of them, through the whirling flurries of snow, was the Imperial capital—the home of the Order and the Sacred Throne itself. Seated upon it was the Emperor, whom Heloise and all villagers worshipped. The thought of facing Him made her weak, but she pushed the feeling aside. *You are not marching to dethrone Him. You are marching to break the Order, who profane His holy name with their wickedness. You will free Him from their influence. You will restore Him.*

Behind them was the ruin of Lyse, the town that Heloise had miraculously held against the full might of the Emperor's army. She would probably still be there now, if the Imperial force hadn't resorted to forbidden wizardry to tear down the walls.

Barnard followed Heloise's gaze to the Red Lords' knights beside them. "I don't like it much, either, your eminence," he said. "Say the word and we'll go our own way. You are the Emperor's chosen. You don't need an army of heretics to take the capital. The Sacred Throne itself will throw open the gates to you, just as it held them shut at Lyse."

She wished she had his unwavering belief. It would be so much easier to be *certain*. But no. Barnard, like many of the villagers following her, believed her to be a sainted Palantine, one of the holy warriors of legend who had killed a devil. He was half right. She *had* killed a devil, but all that made her was lucky.

Onas and Xilyka, Heloise's "Kipti Guard," bridled. They were Traveling People, and "heretics'" themselves. Heloise spoke quickly before either of them could say something to provoke Barnard's fanaticism. "What does the Writ say about truth?"

Barnard glared at her before looking down at his horse. "That a word of it is more pleasing to the Emperor than poetry, your eminence."

"The Red Lords saved us, Barnard. The Order would have crushed us if Sir Steven's troops hadn't shown up. They fed us. They took care of our wounds. They *helped* us."

Barnard kept his eyes on his horse's mane, and said nothing. She knew it was risky to challenge him, especially in front of others, but it would have been just as risky to let his words stand. War, she was finding, was nothing so much as a series of choices between bad and worse.

"Begging your eminence's pardon," Wolfun said, breaking the uncomfortable silence, "when we take the capital, what then? Do you think the Red Lords will be content to leave? That they will simply throw down the Order and return the capital to the Imperial court?"

"The Emperor will not permit them to remain." Barnard lifted his chin.

Wolfun eased off his metal skullcap and scratched at his balding pate. "Don't see that the Emperor is going to have much of a choice, after we let an army into His city."

"He is the *Emperor*." Barnard fixed Wolfun with a hard look. "All the armies in the world are nothing to Him."

Wolfun looked away. "We had a saying on the wall. 'Trust in the Emperor, and keep your spear sharp.'"

"I . . . I will talk to Sir Steven," Heloise said. A real commander would have thought of this already, would have a plan to sound out the Red Lords' intentions. *I am only sixteen winters old. How can I lead these people?*

"That's best," Onas said. He was a Sindi knife-dancer, as agile as a cat. He could have stood on his horse's back if he'd a mind. Xilyka was a knife-caster of the Hapti band. She could throw a knife accurately enough to take a bird on the wing, but she was even more awkward on horseback than Barnard. The Traveling People used horses to pull their wagons, not for riding. Heloise felt her eyes dragged to the Hapti girl again and again, tracing the line of her shoulders where it disappeared beneath the runnels of her dark hair, gathered into copper rings set with tiny stones.

Xilyka's horse took an uncertain step, its back swaying, and she clung to its mane, her feet swinging in the stirrups, heels gently touching the horse's flanks. Heloise could see the beast take the touch as a command and it quickened its pace. Xilyka let out a cry, flailing, digging her heels in even harder.

Heloise couldn't help but laugh, and she stepped into the animal's path before it could set off into a trot. The horse nosed the shield, shied, then stopped.

"I do not," Xilyka's voice was relief and anger in equal measure, "understand how you villagers do this."

"I don't," Heloise said, "not really, but I know a little. You can't keep using your heels, Xilyka. That's how you tell it to go faster."

"How," Xilyka said through gritted teeth, "in the Great Wheel, am I supposed to stay on if I don't use my heels? This monster's back twists like a snake!"

Heloise laughed again, tried to turn it into a cough, failed. The laughter banished the worry, the weight of the column behind her for a moment, and she was grateful. "I'm sorry. Just try taking your feet out of the stirrups."

"Are you mad? They're the only thing keeping me on this animal."

"Just trust me, Xilyka. If you take your feet out, your weight will hold you in the saddle and your heels won't touch it. Please just try? If it doesn't work, you can put them back in."

Xilyka held her gaze, her jaw still set, but Heloise could see the laughter behind her eyes. She was learning that there was little the Hapti knife-caster did without laughter. Xilyka slowly slipped her feet out of the stirrups, letting them dangle at the horse's side.

Heloise nodded, and stood aside, giving the horse its head. The animal walked placidly forward a few steps, then lowered its head to nuzzle the snow in search of forage.

"See?" Heloise asked as she began walking again, the horse moving alongside her, Xilyka much more stable in her seat now.

"This is doubtless some form of what you call 'wizardry,'" Xilyka groused.

Heloise laughed again, and gave herself permission to watch the Hapti girl now, letting her eyes linger.

Xilyka squinted against the driving snow, wrinkling her nose as the ice drove against her face. Heloise watched the flakes turning to water on the girl's cheeks, and felt her heart melt with them. Xilyka glanced her way suddenly, and Heloise looked away. *Don't be stupid. You're just looking at her. She can't read your thoughts.* But Xilyka's wry smile left Heloise with the odd feeling that she could.

"You're cold," Heloise heard herself say. "You can ride in your mother's wagon . . . if you want to." *Why are you saying this? You know you don't want her to leave.*

Xilyka took a moment to answer, and Heloise's heart sank with the thought that the Hapti girl might agree, but at last she shook her head. "My place is with you."

"It's all right." Onas sounded hopeful. "I can look after Heloise until you're warmed up." Heloise knew the real reason Onas wanted to be alone with her. In Lyse he had cornered her and asked for her hand, and in her panicked belief that refusing his suit would drive the Traveling People from her cause, she had agreed to put off discussing it until after the battle. And here they were, the battle a day behind them, with nothing said. *I'm not ready for this now.*

Xilyka rescued her. "Not the first time I've been snowed on. You'll do well enough if an assassin comes on her close, but what'll you do if they've a bow?"

Onas laughed, spinning one of his knives on his fingertip. It was doubly impressive in the wind, on the shifting back of the horse. "Oh, I've done for archers before."

"Still," Xilyka grunted, "I'm staying. Mother wouldn't abide me coming back in the wagon if she knew it meant leaving Heloise."

*Is that the only reason you're with me?* Heloise thought. *Because your mother promised you would? Why should that reason matter?* Xilyka was her guard, not her friend. *Because I want you to choose to be here because you want to be.*

"Yes," Onas said, "I suppose that's best." But his eyes were fixed straight ahead, color rising in his cheeks.

Heloise was grateful when her father kicked his horse and drew even with them, interrupting the tense silence. The days since they fled their village had been hard on Samson Factor. His big belly no longer overhung his belt, and the last defiant streaks of brown in his hair had been overwhelmed by the rising iron gray. His eyes were the worst, red-rimmed and puffy. Purple shadows hung beneath them, bruises left by grief. The Order had murdered Heloise's mother, Leuba, before the fighting at Lyse, and her father grieved her sorely. It was easier on Heloise, she supposed. With both the villagers and the Traveling People looking to her to lead, she hadn't time to mourn. Like the conversation with Onas, it was a thing she would put off as long as she could. The hurt and exhaustion so plain on her father's face cut her, but she swallowed the urge to speak soft words to him. She knew what Samson wanted more than anything: for Heloise to come out of the machine, to abandon her quest and be his little girl again. One glance at the shivering villagers behind her reminded her that she could never let that happen, no matter how much she might want it.

"Heloise," her father's voice was like his face, bruised, drawn. He alone didn't call her by the Palantine's honorific of "your eminence," but neither did he call her "dove" anymore. "We can't keep up this pace." As if to underscore his point, the wind howled, and the entire column hunched as it drove the stinging snow into their faces.

"The men march well enough," Samson went on, "but many brought their families. Children, the old and sick. Do the Red Lords plan to run all the way to the capital?"

Heloise fought against the frustration rising in her throat. "I know." *But what can I do? I did not ask for children and graybeards. I did not ask for anyone.*

"You are a Palantine," Barnard said. "All who serve the Emperor's will, all who hold the Writ sacred, are drawn to you like a moth to a flame. You must not refuse their homage."

"We could fall back," Samson said, "catch up to the Red Lords later."

"The Red Lords have the food, Father." Heloise tried to keep the frustration out of her voice. "The snow will make it hard to glean in the woods." Heloise left unspoken that the Red Lords were more than double the number of the villagers. If she was going to have to fight again, she wanted to do it in their company.

Villagers from every settled place in the valley had walked for leagues to join her, carrying their few belongings on their backs. Only a few had come mounted, riding plow-horses or ponies barely broken to the saddle. Most of these were riding double, mounting up a child or an old man too weak to make the long march. But there were far more on their feet, stumbling in the snow as they tried to keep up.

"There aren't enough horses," Heloise said. "I can carry two or three on the machine's shoulders."

Samson waved his arm at the line of creaking wagons. "The Traveling People will take them, if you will ask it, I am sure of it."

Xilyka and Onas stiffened at the words, and Barnard narrowed his eyes at them. "What's wrong with that? We all work the Emperor's will, and if it is His will that the weak ride in your carts, then it'll bring no harm to you."

Onas spoke through gritted teeth. "The Traveling People do not work your Emperor's will, and those are not *carts*." He stabbed a finger at the line of wagons. "Those are our *homes*."

"Aye, so?" Barnard asked. "They've still got wheels and shelter from the cold. Plenty of room for you to take on extra charges for a time."

"That is not our *way*," Onas said. "You do not just tell a band Mother who she must take into her home. She must invite them of her own will." Xilyka nodded agreement.

The wind picked up again and Wolfun shivered under the saddle blanket he'd drawn around his shoulders. "Well, they don't seem to be in the inviting spirit just yet, and the snow don't care either way. That's children and old folks there. They'll fall behind, they'll freeze."

Xilyka turned to Heloise, reaching into the machine's metal frame and touching her hand, sending a thrill racing through her. "Please, Heloise. Onas is right. You may ask the Mothers, but it will anger them. What we give must be given freely."

"We cannot wait for them to decide it is right," Samson said. "We lose families, and we will lose the fighters that came with them. Some may think better of their decision to march with you. I've seen folk desert, back in the Old War. It's like ice melting in spring. At first it's just a few pieces dropping off, then suddenly the whole sheet goes."

"I'll talk to Sir Steven," Heloise said. "Maybe the Red Lords have room in their supply wagons."

She turned the machine and set off with long, clanking strides toward the Red Lords' column. They were at least twice the number as Heloise's troops, stretching back so far down the road that she could only just hear the creaking of their supply carts at the column's end. Xilyka and Onas spurred their mounts to keep up with her. That she was too important to ever be left alone should have made her feel mighty, but it only made her feel unworthy.

Sir Steven rode at the head of his column, a huge, plain red banner snapping above him. His face was clean-shaven, his hair cropped so short that it stood up in gray spikes, like a bushpig's quills. He wore the same plain armor as his troops, the same simple red surcoat. The only nods to his rank were the red enameled chain around his neck and the white band, marked with three red stripes, cinched tightly around his right arm.

His knights looked nervous at Heloise's approach, but they kept their lances up, reining their horses back to let her come close. "Heloise Factor"—Steven jerked his thumb at the gray sky—"this is an unpleasant turn. Snow is a rare thing on the Gold Coast. How are your people faring in it?"

"They can't keep up," Heloise said. "They brought their families. Children and graybeards. Some are falling behind."

Steven frowned. "An army on the march is no place for children and graybeards. They should go home and sit by their fires. We will make the valley safe for them once we have taught the Order a lesson."

"If they go, their fathers and brothers and sons will go too."

Steven looked past her at the line of wagons and people, straggling and tangled. "This is the problem when an army marches by its faith, rather than its will. War is the work of captains, not saints."

"I never said I was a saint."

"Heloise, the armored *saint*." Steven smiled.

"That is what *you* say," Heloise said. Sir Steven was a powerful man, with an army behind him. Heloise didn't like disagreeing with him, but she couldn't let his words stand any more than she could Barnard's. *All these friends, always testing me.*

"And if you think I am the only one, you are fool and saint both. At this pace, we will reach the capital in four days. Your people will have to find a way to keep up. Four days is not so long a march."

"Why can't we go slower?"

"Because even now, word of our victory at Lyse is making its way north. Once it does, the Imperials will dispatch their army to meet us before we reach the city."

"We just beat their army."

Sir Steven looked at her like the child she felt she was. "Heloise, this is the Empire. Did you think you'd beaten every fighting man they have?"

*Stupid.* Steven was a war leader. She knew she couldn't match his experience, but someone had to speak for her people. Whether she wanted it or no, it was her. "What difference does it make if we fight them in the field or at the capital?"

"Because, Heloise, the Imperial army are *riders*. Their strength is in their Order and their knights. Horsemen all. If we bottle them up in a city, they are near useless. If we face them in the field . . . I will admit I do not like our chances."

"We already beat their knights and the Order at Lyse."

"We beat them," Sir Steven said, "when they were *surprised*, Heloise. We beat them *after* their knights and their Pilgrims both were exhausted by assaulting the walls. Facing them fresh, mounted, and in a field battle is another matter entirely. We *must* reach the capital before they have a chance to deploy."

Heloise looked back over at her column. Sir Steven could have been lying to her, she had no way to know. But while she couldn't tell the truth of his words, she could see the truth of her own people, shivering, stumbling, desperate to keep up with the pace of the Red Lords' troops. "We have to do something. They can't go on like this."

Sir Steven threw up his hands. "What would you have of me, Heloise Factor?"

"Let the children and the old ones ride in your carts. You said yourself it's just for four days."

"Urchins and beggars to plunder my stores? My carts are for supply, not for carrying children."

Heloise's stomach tightened as she met Sir Steven's eyes. What if she angered him and he left her behind? *No. If I don't stand up for them, no one will.* "You told me we could march with you, and you would care for us as long as it took us to reach the capital. Did you mean it?"

Steven exchanged a look with one of his captains and then let out a long sigh. "You will not rest until I regret those words."

"I will not rest until you do what you said you would. And my people will fight. We may not be so many as you, but you saw us at Lyse. We're not cowards."

"I hope you are right, Heloise," Steven said. "Very well, I will tell my baggage master to take on your stragglers, but you will answer if they loot my stores. And I know I can rely on you to remember the kindness the Free Peoples have shown to yours when the time comes."

Heloise bridled at his tone, but she swallowed her anger. "Thank you, Sir Steven. And . . . I wanted to ask you a question."

Sir Steven folded his arms across his chest. "Yes?"

"When we beat the Order, what will you do?"

"What do you mean?"

"Will you leave? Will you stay and try to rule us?"

Sir Steven held her gaze in silence, and then finally broke into a smile, spreading his hands. "My charge, Heloise, is to ensure the Empire never threatens my people again. When we have broken their army, I will leave observers and advisers in your court and take my army back to the Gold Coast. You have my word on that."

*He is lying.* Heloise thought of Sigir, of the love in his eyes, his sad words as he plunged the knife into her. *Men do what they want when they are in charge, and they tell themselves it's right.*

She was almost grateful when Xilyka interrupted them, pointing back over the long train of the army. "What is that?"

Heloise squinted. The snow had stopped falling, but the wind whipped what remained about so fiercely that it settled in the army's tracks, covering all trace of their passage. "I see nothing."

"Look harder, Heloise," Xilyka said, "on the horizon. Back by Lyse."

And now Heloise could see it, a thin green cast to the light, a sick shade, the color of pond slime or a toad's skin. It shimmered far in the distance. "What . . . what is that?"

But she spoke the words as a reflex. Her mind was screaming at her, the color of the wavering glow was too familiar. She'd seen light like this before, ripping through the fissure in her old friend Clodio as his body split and the devil emerged, screaming, into the sunlit world. But this couldn't be the same, could it? It was so . . . vast, lighting the whole horizon over Lyse. Perhaps it was some trick of the snow, and her fear was turning shadows into monsters.

"I have never seen a light like that," Sir Steven said, shading his eyes. His captains followed his gaze, and she could hear them whispering to one another, fear plain in their voices.

"I . . ." Heloise began, "I think I have."

Sir Steven turned to her. "What?"

"When . . . when my friend . . . when the devil came out of him."

"What you call wizardry, no doubt," Xilyka said. "Perhaps something to do with what the Order did when they took down the wall."

Heloise felt her stomach turn over. She had deliberately not told Sir Steven of the Order's use of wizards to break the walls of Lyse, but she couldn't order the Traveling People to do the same.

"Wizardry?" Sir Steven was as shocked as his captains. "What wizardry?"

There was no point in trying to keep it from him now. "The Order had three wizards," Heloise said, "as prisoners. They forced them to use their power to take down the wall. You arrived just after."

Sir Steven looked at Heloise over steepled fingers. "And why, pray tell, did you keep this from us?"

Heloise faced him. *This man is not my lord.* "Because I didn't know if you think of wizardry as the Order does. If you did, you would have killed us all. And because you saw the wall. You could see the rot. What did you think happened to it?"

"We thought it a ruin," Sir Steven said, "and this is another mark in your ledger with us, Heloise. You have kept information from me. You ride my horses. You ask to place your weakest with my baggage and put upon me for provisions for the rest. Your debt to the Free Peoples grows greater with each passing day."

"I don't owe you anything." Heloise struggled to keep her voice even. "You said you would help us to thank us for helping you to surprise the Empire's army. You said we would work together."

"And what work have you done so far? Let this be the first work you do—send a rear guard down the road. I will provide you with fast horses. Ride back and find out what . . . that is."

"Ride back?" Heloise asked. "The capital is the other way."

"Aye," Sir Steven said, "and when you have had more time in command of an army, you will know that no war leader leaves an enemy unchecked to his rear."

"How do you know it's an enemy?" Heloise asked.

"You say that's the light you saw when your so-called devil came forth."

"Yes, but this is much bigger . . . maybe I'm wrong. Maybe it's not an enemy."

Sir Steven looked back to the greasy smudge of light wavering on the horizon. The snow had begun falling again, looking gray where it passed before the light.

"Whatever it is," he said, "it is not a friend."

# 2

## COUNCIL

*Captain-General held a nightly council. Gathered us all to-gether in his tent, big as a palace. Well, the serjeants, at least, with the men all huddled together outside the flaps, pretending they could hear. Built a great fire in the middle, and said that any man could come before it and speak plain without fear of punishment. Said the council fire was an ancient tradition going back before the Emperor closed the veil. But we saw the Pilgrims standing beside him, flails in their hands, eyes daring us to test the limits of tradition. I held my peace, and so did every other man.*

—From the journal of Samson Factor

"You cannot go," her father said. Heloise could see him almost adding *I forbid it*, but he stopped himself. The last time he'd tried to command her, Barnard had knocked him in the dirt.

Samson fumbled for a moment, and then his eyes lit. "These people follow you, Heloise. They won't march if they don't see you at the front of the column."

"He's right in that, your eminence," Barnard said. "We cannot spare you."

Samson's argument made her sick with both anger and love. *You don't care about the march. You just want to protect me.* She was furious that he undermined her command, but warmed by the knowledge that there was *someone* in the world who saw her as something other than a saint.

"Don't see why he can't send his own riders," Samson said. "He's got more than enough men."

"He gave us food, clothing, tents, horses," Heloise said. "He took our people on his wagons like I asked. We have to do something too. Isn't that what you always taught me, Father? That good people repay their debts?"

"Still . . ." her father muttered.

"There . . . it just looks like the light that came from Clodio," Heloise said. "What if there is a devil? I am the only one who can fight it."

"All the more reason you shouldn't go," Samson said. "I'll not see you pick a fight with a devil."

"Who will fight it then? You?"

"That's not the point. It's . . . it's as I said. You're needed here."

"I will go in your place, your eminence." Barnard's son Guntar broke the tense silence. He was the spitting image of his father. Nearly as big, his shaven head gone to stubble over the long march. His beard was patchy and matted, but Heloise could see the beginnings of the fine red thatching he would share with his father someday. His brother, Gunnar, had been much the same, before Brother Tone had killed him. "If there's a devil, we won't run afoul of it. Just spy it, then ride back quick as we can to summon the army."

"You're no horseman," Barnard said.

"None of us are," Guntar replied, "but you are at the Palantine's side every step of the way, while I am in the column with Mother. I am nearly a man grown, Father. I have fought the Order at your side. Let me do this."

"I have lost one son already," Barnard said. "I will not lose another."

"Look around you." Guntar waved an arm to take in the columns. "We are an *army* marching to war, Father. There is nothing but danger all about us. You cannot keep me safe, but you can let me work the Emperor's will. We labor in Heloise's cause, and that cause is holy. No harm will come to me."

Heloise could see the pain in Guntar's face. *He has no task to take him from his grief.* Heloise had the command of her troops to keep her mind from the loss of her mother. Guntar had only leagues of walking and endless time to brood. "You promise you will only look, then ride straight back to us as fast as you can?"

Guntar nodded so quickly his chin nearly tapped his throat.

"Let him go, Barnard," Heloise said, ashamed of her relief. If there was a devil in the world again, she had no wish to see it.

The huge tinker raised his eyes to her, sputtering. "Your eminence, you cannot . . ."

"Good!" Samson folded his arms across his chest. "I'm pleased you'll listen to sense."

Her father's smug words made the anger surge so hot that Heloise's scalp burned. She locked eyes with her father, but spoke to Barnard. "I won't ask your family to do something mine won't do. My father will go with him."

Barnard stopped his sputtering, his eyebrows rising. "Your eminence?"

"Heloise," Samson said, "I am no rider."

"Didn't you hear Guntar, Father? None of us are."

"My place is with you."

"I am in a war-machine, with an army. Onas and Xilyka are great fighters. I am safe enough."

"Still." Samson looked stricken. "I don't like leaving you."

Heloise regretted the words as soon as they tumbled out of her mouth. "I am not your little girl anymore, Father."

"Come, Samson." Guntar clapped his shoulder, breaking the tense silence that followed. "I will be glad of your counsel."

"Take another," Heloise said.

Guntar turned to Xilyka. "Do you think the Traveling People will spare one of their own to help?"

Heloise's heart warmed that Guntar would even ask a "heretic," and Xilyka smiled. "I cannot speak for the Mothers, but you lose nothing by asking."

"Good," Heloise said, not wanting to give time for either Barnard or her father to protest. "Get your people and horses. Stick to the road so you can find us again. Sir Steven will not slow the army for anything. He says we have to reach the capital in four days or the Order will beat us in the field."

"No matter how fast you march, you are on foot mostly. We will all be mounted. We'll catch you up, don't worry!" Guntar beamed. "Thank you, your eminence!" And then he was off, running down the column toward the Traveling Peoples' wagons. Samson held Heloise's eyes for what felt like an eternity before turning his horse to follow.

"Are you all right, Heloise?" Xilyka asked.

"I'm fine," Heloise said. "I can't have him trying to hold my hand all the time. I'm supposed to be a leader. It's better this way."

"Better." Xilyka didn't sound convinced.

"Yes."

"Then why," the Hapti girl asked, "do you look like you just drank a pail of sour milk?"

·    ·    ·

Samson set out a quarter-candle later, with little more than a sad look and a grunt of "We should be able to make it back by nightfall." He rode out on one of Sir Steven's fine chargers, a broad-shouldered animal that Heloise could tell would eat up the road despite the snow. With him rode Guntar and a Sindi knife-dancer. Heloise watched her father bouncing awkwardly in the saddle as he shrank in her vision, felt a surge of love for him.

"Well," Xilyka asked, "are you glad he is gone?"

"I am," Heloise said, "and I miss him. It's . . . it's like being two people at the same time."

She winced as she spoke, worried Xilyka would think her childish, but the Hapti girl only nodded knowingly. "It is always thus with love."

"What if there is a devil? What if he's hurt?"

Xilyka didn't answer, and after a while Heloise said, "I only sent him because he made me angry. Because he was treating me like a little girl. I . . . Maybe I shouldn't have."

Xilyka shrugged. "Do you remember what my mother did on the wall of Lyse?"

"Her . . . talent. She saved us."

Xilyka shrugged again. "She swung the battle for a time, at least, yes. Just that morning I yelled at her for making me repeat myself. She . . . she doesn't hear as she used to."

Heloise looked down at her. Xilyka's eyes were on the snow, her hands making useless circles at her sides. "I told her she was old."

"She . . . she is old. We all get short with our parents sometimes, Xilyka. It doesn't make you bad."

Xilyka shook her head. "It was unkind. And then that very afternoon, she . . . did what she did on the wall. It was the Wheel, turning up a lesson."

"What lesson?"

"To have faith in our own. Even when they seem weak. Especially when they seem weak."

Heloise looked up again. Even through the blinding snow, she could still faintly make out the sick shimmer of the strange light. Her father's figure dwindled slowly toward it, until finally the gale swallowed him.

It was well before nightfall when the snow finally forced a halt. Heloise kept thinking the driving wind might finally break, but the gusts came closer and closer together, until they ran into a single gale that whipped the powder into whirling white funnels that blotted out the sun, leaving the column in a gray-white haze. The horses stumbled, unable to pick their footing in the thick drifts.

Mother Leahlabel, Onas's mother and one of the leaders of the Sindi band, at last ordered her wagons drawn into a line across the road. The Sindi set to piling snow beneath them, until at last they formed a wall that shielded them against the worst of the wind. The column huddled up as close to the wagon-wall as they could, shivering miserably against one another. A few tried to light fires, but gave up as the wind and the soaking snow fought a winning campaign against them.

The wind blew harder and the snow closed around them, until Heloise could barely make out the figures of Onas and Xilyka, shivering in their saddles, so close that their horses' necks brushed against the machine's metal arms. At last, a blob of red pierced the storm, trudging to Heloise's side. One of the Red Lords' heralds, shivering in his metal armor, his plain red surcoat soaked with snow. "Heloise Factor! Sir Steven summons you to the commander's tent."

Barnard loomed over the man. "Heretics do not presume to summon Palantines."

Heloise raised an arm, the machine groaning and shedding ice as it matched her movements. "It's all right, Barnard."

The twist of the herald's mouth was petulant. "A request, then. Will you come?"

"Yes, but my guard will come with me."

The herald nodded. "The First Sword requested representatives be sent from among the Kipti. They will suffice."

"They are the *Traveling People.* 'Kipti' means 'homeless.'"

The herald ignored her. "It is the custom of the Free Peoples to take petitions when our leaders meet. May I cry this through your camp?"

"Yes," Heloise raised her voice to be heard over the strengthening gale, "but I can't find your tent in this storm."

"It's there." The herald pointed into the unbroken white behind him. "Walk that way no more than one hundred paces. You cannot fail to find it."

He was right. In less than fifty paces, Heloise could see the tall red canvas of the commander's tent, a scarlet wound on the white expanse of the landscape. The drifts had grown deep enough to drag at the machine's metal legs, and with each step she could feel the cracking of the thin crust of ice beneath the powder. The entry flaps faced away from the wind, large enough to admit a man on horseback. Heloise still had to duck the machine's metal head to step inside.

A tiny fire burned under an iron grill in the center, utterly failing to warm the huge tent. Sir Steven sat in a simple camp chair, red cloth stretched over painted rods, surrounded by his captains. All wore their armor even though dismounted and with no fight threatening. A simple table, painted red like everything else in Sir Steven's army, sat to one side. It was piled with plain fare—hard bread and cheese, nuts and dried fruit, all untouched.

"Heloise Factor." Sir Steven inclined his head, not rising. "We speak twice in one day. Such a pleasure. My man tells me you have sent your riders out, my thanks for that."

"Father says good people always pay their debts."

Sir Steven's mouth twitched. "I hear that you sent him."

"So?"

"It struck me as an unusual choice."

"I can't give someone special treatment just because he is my father."

Sir Steven nodded. "Spoken like one of the Free Peoples. It is our custom to hold council at the end of each day's march. I would ask that you attend each evening, to speak for your people."

"I can only speak for the villagers." Heloise nodded to Onas and Xilyka. "The Traveling People keep their own counsel. How are our graybeards and children?"

"They were taken in the carts, as you asked. The baggage master will be seeing them back to their families now, I expect. How are your people faring?"

"Suffering."

Sir Steven spread his hands. "Suffering marches with an army."

"We're the leaders. Isn't it our job to take care of our troops?"

"I have been a fighting man since my naming day, Heloise. It is interesting to be instructed on the nature of war by a girl in a machine."

"I took Lyse. I have fought in battles. I have an army. I have just as much right to talk about war as you do."

Sir Steven stiffened, leaned forward on his stool. "More battles, more sieges, and more time at the head of an army will teach you how little you know, girl."

Heloise swallowed the part of her that wanted to agree with him. "Is that what you want to talk about? How little I know about war?"

"There is no need to discuss your warcraft, Heloise. You march beside a veteran army, and we have warcraft enough for all. We will hear petitions first. I do not doubt that some in your number will have them."

He looked beside Heloise, and she turned to see the herald

bowing slightly from his waist. "There is one, First Sword. A woman, from the village of Seal's Rock."

"Just one?" Steven asked. "I am surprised. Show her in."

The herald pushed back the flap to admit a tiny old woman, so swaddled in seal skins that Heloise could barely see her face. Her eyes were plain enough, widening in shock as she found herself face to face with the sainted Palantine. She bowed, averting her eyes. "Savior," she said. "Your eminence."

"Stop that." Heloise reached out to straighten her, remembered she was in the machine, and stopped herself before she accidentally crushed the old woman. "Come in out of the cold."

"Your eminence," the woman said again, bowing her way through the flaps. She held her bow, eyes darting around the room, quickly settling on the table of food.

"Please." Sir Steven gestured to the table. "Help yourself."

The old woman gave him a nod of thanks and raced to the table, stuffing bread into her mouth as quickly as she could. Her eyes continued to rove as if she expected one of the Red Lords to take it from her.

Heloise winced. "So hungry . . . ?"

"Begging your eminence's pardon," the woman said through a mouthful, "but we up and came as quick as we could. Most didn't think to bring vittles more'n a night's worth."

"Why not?" Heloise asked.

"You're the Emperor's chosen, ain't ya? Folks' figurin' you'd tend to us."

Heloise swallowed her shock. She would have to discuss feeding them with Sir Steven, and it was probably best spoken of after the woman had left.

"How are you called?" Sir Steven asked.

"My husband is—"

"How are *you* called?" Heloise cut her off. She knew that the women of Seal's Rock took their husband's names, but if she could lead an army with just sixteen winters behind her, then this woman could petition under her own name.

The woman blushed, bowed again. "I am called Helga, if it pleases your eminence."

"Thank you, Helga." The bowing and honorifics grated, but Heloise knew if she spent her time correcting everyone who called her "your eminence," she would do nothing else. Still, knowing the woman's name helped Heloise feel less like a lord, and more like a person. "I will find food for you." *Somehow.* "Is that what you wanted to ask?"

"The Kipti, your eminence," the woman said, glancing up at Onas and Xilyka. "They need talkin' to."

Heloise's bodyguards stiffened.

"They are the Traveling People, Helga. 'Kipti' is an insult." Heloise swallowed her frustration.

Helga didn't look like she'd heard. "As you say, your eminence. Only it's that one of their menfolk's taken a shine to my daughter. Took her on his wagon, given her food, promised her a new dress."

"What," Onas's voice was ice, "is wrong with that?"

Helga responded to Heloise. "She's seen but seventeen winters, your eminence."

"She's a woman grown," Xilyka said. "Is she promised to another? If not, she may do as she wishes."

Heloise looked down at her guard, the frustration rising in her throat again. It would take time to make Xilyka, to make all the Traveling People, understand villager ways, to know that at seventeen winters a woman was still considered the ward of her parents, and that giving herself to a man before she was married would bring shame upon her. "Please, Xilyka," she said, "it's not our way."

"It's not," Helga agreed, "an' even if it were, I'd not promise her to a heretic."

Onas opened his mouth to reply and Heloise silenced him with a wave. "The Traveling People have different ways from ours. This man didn't know . . . how we do things."

"As you say, you eminence," Helga said, "but they're here followin' you, ain't they? We all is. And you're a villager. You hold to our ways, and you're the saint, so we think that it's our ways, villager ways, that should hold for all."

"Not while the Free Peoples lead this army," Sir Steven said. "We have our own ways as well."

Helga ignored him, still speaking to Heloise. "Nobody leads nothin' but you, your eminence.

"You're the saint that shines brighter'n all."

Sir Steven finally stood. "Your petition has been heard, Helga of Seal's Rock. You have leave to go."

Helga didn't move. "You need to speak with the Kipti, your eminence. Folks from the village are whisperin' 'bout those two." She pointed at Onas and Xilyka. "Say you love the Kipti more'n your own, since you have them with you like shadows."

"They are my bodyguards," Heloise said, the frustration boiling over into anger. "They protect me."

"A Kipti bodyguard," Helga said. "Plenty of your own folk be glad to have that duty."

"Stop," Heloise growled, and immediately regretted it as Helga cowered, bowing so deeply that she nearly pitched forward on her face. "I will talk to the Mothers . . . but these are my friends. You can tell your people that from me."

"Seal's Rock's villagers, your eminence," Helga said, "they're your people too."

"Get out!" Heloise barked.

Helga bowed her way back to the tent's entrance, muttering

apologies as she went. She paused at the flaps, shivering, and Heloise felt a stab of guilt as the old woman finally went back out into the cold and driving snow.

"I'm sorry," Heloise said to Xilyka. "We . . . we tell stories about the Traveling People—"

"That we are child thieves," Xilyka interrupted her. "That we steal children and raise them on the road. That we can turn into birds. That we dabble in wizardry. That we cannot control our lusts and lie with whomever we will, whenever we will. The Traveling People trade in stories. We have heard every one told about us, and more besides."

"We're fighting the Order," Heloise said. "We can't fight each other."

Xilyka swallowed. Anger still burned behind her eyes, somehow making her even more beautiful. "And to that end, I would present my petition."

Sir Steven arched an eyebrow. "To Heloise?"

"And to you, First Sword," Xilyka said, reaching beneath her cloak and removing a bolt of red cloth. She shook out it out before her, the scarlet fabric unrolling to reveal a forked pennant, edged with gold. In its center was a winged wheel, the wingtips unfurling almost to the banner's edge. Beneath it, embroidered in gold thread, were the words THE PEOPLE.

"My mother stitched it as we marched. We've need of unity," Xilyka said. "We are Free Peoples and Traveling Peoples and villager peoples. All people, one way or another. The red is for the Red Lords, the wheel for us, and the wings are those of a Palantine."

Heloise felt her throat close and tears prick at the corners of her eyes. She reached out with the machine's metal fist and gently raised the banner on the back edge of her knife. "I'm not a Palantine."

"Maybe not," Xilyka said, "but the villagers say you are, and the wings are for what they believe."

The envy was plain in Onas's voice: "I do not think all will agree to march beneath that."

"They will if she accepts it." Xilyka kept her eyes on Heloise. "And that is my petition, and that of Mother Florea and all the Hapti band. Fly this banner as your own."

The heat of Xilyka's eyes set a warmth blazing in Heloise's chest that felt so good she was loath to look away. The title of Palantine was a weight on her, heavy with demands. Looking at the banner in Xilyka's hands, Heloise felt the strength of the symbol— the others, the Traveling People and the Red Lords, lifting that weight from her a little. *Thank you.*

"I accept it," she said, failing to keep the heat from her voice.

"The Free Peoples march under no banner but our own," Sir Steven said. "We do not adorn ourselves with geegaws. We are a plain folk, and we will not fly that."

"I don't see why you need to give a sop to malcontents," Onas said. "You are the great Heloise, liberator of Lyse, bane of the Order. What does it matter what anyone thinks of you? The villagers follow you. My people follow you. You don't need to unite them, only command them."

"You have much to learn of why soldiers follow commanders," Sir Steven said, "and of how to lead."

But Heloise ignored them both, her eyes moving from the banner to Xilyka and back again. "It's beautiful," she said. *You're beautiful.*

She hadn't spoken the words aloud, but feeling Onas's eyes burning into her, she wondered if, somehow, he'd heard them anyway.

"We shall see what—" Sir Steven began, stopping as shouts

rose from outside the tent. The herald ducked outside, reentered a moment later.

"It's the villager outriders, sir. The ones who rode to scout the weird light."

"What?" Heloise and Sir Steven asked at the same time. Heloise ran out of the tent so quickly that she forget to duck the machine, and nearly tangled herself in the huge canvas flap before ripping free. Guntar was on his knees, panting. His shirt was stained with blood, though Heloise couldn't see its source.

He was alone.

"Where is my father?" Panic strained her voice. She knew she should take a moment to calm herself, but the urgency of her father's absence was like a storm, driving her helpless before it. "Where is he?"

Guntar shook his head, sobbed. "They were waiting for us, your eminence. They fell on us as soon as we were out of sight of the column."

Sir Steven turned, bellowing at his captains, "Whoever is responsible for the rearguard pickets will answer for this!"

"Who did this?" Heloise asked.

Guntar spat, sucked down a whooping breath. "They took our horses. Would have taken me as well, but the Kipti . . . bested two of them, cut their traces, and rode off on their beast. I doubled up with him. He rode the animal until it dropped, then he . . . fell. He had taken a wound. I tried to revive him, but he was gone. I ran the rest of the way."

"*Who?*" Heloise bellowed.

"Brigands, I'll wager," Sir Steven said. "They follow an army as surely as flies follow a herd."

But Guntar was already shaking his head. "Black-and-Grays. The Emperor's Eyes. They were making sure of the length of your column, I'll wager. They're riding back to their army now."

"Remnants of the army at Lyse," Sir Steven said. "There's no way fresh troops could have arrived from the capital by now." But he did not sound certain.

But Heloise scarcely heard him, her eyes fixed on Guntar as if they could bore answers out of him. "Guntar, where is my father?"

"Gone," Guntar sobbed.

"Gone?!" Heloise's stomach shrank, her throat closed. *I told him to go. I sent him away.* "Dead?"

"They took him," Guntar said, stumbling to his feet. "They took them and rode north. He's gone, Heloise."

# 3

## THE PEOPLE

*The wound Mahesh had made was great, and the Emperor's strength began to fade. But His eye was ever fixed upon the veil, and he reached out and plucked a nightingale from a branch and set her on the right arm of His throne. And behold! The nightingale did make a joyous music, and the veil was entranced, and held fast. Then the great music wore upon the singer, and the nightingale's voice did falter, until the Emperor set a congregation of the faithful upon the left arm of His throne. The congregation lent their voice to the great music that the nightingale might rest her head beneath her wing, and the veil was shut for all time.*
—Book of Mysteries, III. 5.

Even Heloise was not so foolish as to try hunting for her father in the dark, but neither did she sleep, her eyes locked on the opening between her tent flaps, scanning the black horizon for the first shreds of dawn.

She emerged as soon as she saw the dimmest glow, even before the serjeants had roused their soldiers. She found her inner circle wrapped in their cloaks, huddled around the smoldering remains of a feeble fire. Clearly none of them had slept, either. Wolfun had drowsed in the saddle, lying across his horse's neck. He lifted his head and blinked at her.

"Thought you might do this." Guntar sat on a frozen rock with his mother, Chunsia, bent over him. One of the Black-and-Grays had managed a lucky shot on his arm as he'd ridden off, but the wound wasn't deep. Still, Heloise did not blame her for fussing over it. She had lost one son to the Order already. "If anyone's to blame, it's me."

"I know what you're planning, and I don't see the use of it, your eminence," Wolfun said. "If the boy speaks true, then they've ridden back to their main force. You want to find your father, that's where he'll be."

"I speak true," Guntar said. "They rode off north. Capital's too far for them to have ranged all the way to our rear."

"What do you know of how far a man can range?" Wolfun said. "Brave lad's still a lad. You've never even mustered to a levy, I'll be bound."

"And you've never faced down the Black-and-Grays on a scout, and lived to report back," Barnard growled at him. "We could try to track them, now that it's light."

"In this snow?" The Lysian gestured at the white drifts. "It's coming thick enough to fill a man's tracks faster'n you can blink."

Heloise felt sick, her mind playing and replaying her father's face as she volunteered him for the scout. *My place is with you.* She turned to Xilyka, trying to keep the desperation from her face, failing utterly. "Can your people track in snow?"

Xilyka shook her head, but Onas laughed. "Now there is a story of the Traveling People I've yet to hear. We've been called child-thieves, pot-menders, wizards, but never storm-trackers."

"I am going," Heloise said, swallowing the ball of terror and grief in her throat. "Guntar, if you can guide me to where they found you, maybe I can pick up some . . ."

"Your eminence," Barnard said. "I grieve for your father the same as all of us, but we cannot lose you, too. Whatever you feel, your people need you here."

"I cannot just do nothing!" Heloise could not keep her voice from rising to a shout. "I lost my mother, I cannot . . ."

Wolfun kicked his horse to Heloise's side, gripped the machine's metal leg. "You can. You can and you *will*, your eminence. We have *all* of us lost someone. Most of us more'n one. Running off in the storm like a fool won't bring him back to you. It's not what he would want, and you know it. He'd want you to be smart. He'd want you to be careful."

Wolfun's words were a punch to her gut. *You cannot find him. You cannot track him. There is nothing you can do.* Suddenly, the world felt much as it did when she contemplated leaving the machine—the sky was too close, the sounds too loud. She felt her skin itch, a desperate need to run in any direction. Heloise swallowed hard, looked over at Barnard. He had lost two children in less than a turning of the moon. If he could keep his head, then so could she. "What do I do?" she pleaded.

"Might be Wolfun's right, your eminence," Barnard said. "They took Sigir before, and we got him back."

"And then he turned traitor." Heloise could feel herself sweating despite the cold. *I will never get him back. I will never see him again.*

"Not because they made him a captive," Barnard said. "I was shocked as you to find how rotten that bastard's heart was, but it wasn't the Order what made Sigir that way. If they've got your father, they'll want to trade him."

"Trade him for what?"

"For a truce," Wolfun said. "Or for gold. Or for prisoners of their own. Or some other advantage. Happens all the time in parleys, your eminence. We may yet restore your father to you."

"If they figure out who he is," Barnard said, "they may come to us with an offer. For now, the best thing to do is wait."

"What if they figure out who he is and kill him? I shouldn't have sent him." Heloise cursed. *I only wanted him to let me be.* "So stupid."

Xilyka set a hand on Heloise's leg through the machine's frame. "You did what you thought you must, which is all any of us can do. We cannot know which way the Wheel will turn. I know it is hard, Heloise, but for now it seems the best thing to do is wait and see if Sir Steven's outriders can find the Imperial army, or at least pick up the trail of these men who stole your father."

"Sending out another small scouting party might just mean we get the worst of another skirmish, your eminence," Wolfun added. "Won't do us, or your father, any good. Do not forget that we must march quickly. It's the dawn of the second day. We must reach the capital by the fourth or the enemy will take us in the field and destroy us."

Heloise's stomach clenched, the sob rising up her throat, so strong that nothing she did could choke it back down. It bubbled out of her mouth, almost a howl. "You're right."

Because in her heart, she knew that they were. *Your father is one man. You are responsible for an entire army.* Even if it were safe to hunt for her father, it was true that she would never be able to find him.

The thought sent the panic surging, and Heloise was powerless before it. She needed away from these people, from this camp. She had to do something. "Might I be alone? Just for a moment."

Wolfun ignored the question, touched the machine's elbow. "Do not cry, your eminence. It will be all right. You'll see."

She barely heard him. Her mother was dead, and now she would lose her father, too. "Please. I just need to be by myself."

It was Onas who answered. "No, Heloise. It isn't safe."

"It's all right." Xilyka appeared, tugging on Onas's arm. "I will go with her."

"You can't . . ." Onas began.

"Give us one quarter-candle. Let me . . . She needs to be alone. We won't go far. Just a little ways into the woods."

Onas flushed. "You are not the sole guard of—"

"Onas!" Mother Leahlabel's voice rang out loud enough to make even Heloise stop. The Sindi woman was barely bigger than a child. Her gray-red hair was piled atop her head in a bun, wrapped tightly around a short iron dirk. Heloise had seen the tiny woman kill with that slim weapon, and knew Leahlabel was not to be underestimated. Of far more importance than her skill at arms was her wizardry. Leahlabel could heal wounds at a touch, and had saved Heloise's life more than once. "Stand aside before she flattens you."

Onas blinked up at his mother. "Mother . . . I cannot just—"

"You can do as you're told by your band Mother. She is in a war-machine, and with a guard besides," Leahlabel said. She turned to Xilyka. "A quarter-candle. Swear it."

"I swear it," Xilyka said. "No harm will come to her."

Leahlabel nodded as Onas, still stammering, moved just far enough to let Heloise pass. She didn't hesitate, the fear gripping her, the tears coming now, her father's face in her mind as she walked the machine forward, moving into the woods, the sound of Xilyka's feet padding on the snow behind her.

．　　．　　．

Heloise remembered when she had last gone into the woods, fleeing from her mistake with Basina, her friend breaking their embrace, pushing Heloise away, her hands coming up.

But as with Basina, the woods could not save her from her mistakes for long. No sooner had she cleared the tree line, branches shaking off snow as she pushed through them, than the thoughts came crowding in. *You cannot find him. He is gone.*

And as with Basina, tears came with the thoughts, breaking like the onset of the snow, when it cracked the gray clouds and poured out on the shivering army. Heloise managed not to scream, at least, for fear that her people would hear. She slipped her good hand free of the control strap and held it over her mouth while she sobbed.

Heloise slowly mastered herself as she heard Xilyka's footsteps crunching in the snow. The knife-caster looked up at her, eyes huge with concern. "Will you be all right?"

*No, I will never be all right again.* "Yes." Heloise swallowed, painfully conscious of how stupid she must look. "I'm sorry. I know it's useless. I just . . . I couldn't stand there anymore."

"I know, Heloise. You don't have to explain anything to me."

Heloise took a deep breath, felt her heart steadying. "Thank you. We can go back now."

Xilyka smiled, shook her head. "Didn't you hear Mother Leahlabel? I have a quarter-candle to bring you back, and I intend to use it."

She turned, moved deeper into the woods.

"We can't," Heloise began, "the army has to march. We have to . . ."

"I am no great commander"—Xilyka beckoned—"but I can't think of a war that turned on the space of a quarter-candle. You can't lead if you are driven mad by that pack of brooding beards. Come, we won't go far. I promise."

Xilyka's smile made Heloise's heart race again, and as with Basina, her body betrayed her, feet moving almost of their own accord, following her bodyguard.

The canopy was thick deeper in, the interlocking branches tangled so tightly that they kept much of the snow off the ground.

Heloise hadn't realized how much the relentless blinding white of the road had drained her until she found her eyes drinking up simple sights—the tips of pine needles pushing up through the snow, a cluster of blueberries clinging to an exposed shoulder of rock.

It was just a handful, but Heloise looked at the plump fruit and thought of the hungry look in Helga's eyes as she devoured the bread from Sir Steven's table. "Can you take those?" she asked Xilyka. "I can't, with the machine."

Xilyka gently pulled up the bush, tucking it into a pocket in her cloak. "You may as well eat them, Heloise. It's just a handful."

"I can't eat the first fresh growing food in leagues when everyone else is hungry. What if someone saw?"

Xilyka made a great show of looking around, turned back with what Heloise was learning was *her* smile, one corner of her mouth higher than the other, eyes narrowed as if she were sharing a joke with Heloise and Heloise alone. "Looks like I am the only one to see."

Heloise snorted a laugh in spite of her worry over her father. The sudden mirth felt so good, and was followed by a surge of gratitude so profound that she had to resist sweeping Xilyka up into the machine's metal arms. "Thank you," she managed.

"For what?" Xilyka cocked her head to one side.

"It feels good to laugh."

"It does. You villagers need to laugh more."

"Seems wrong . . . laughing now."

"Not wrong. It is just the Great Wheel turning. It turns as it will, whether we would have it or no. So, why not laugh?"

*Why not?* Heloise silently agreed, and the laughter threatened to come bubbling back.

Xilyka turned suddenly, looking back the way they had come. Heloise froze, listening, but all she could hear was the snow whispering against the frozen leaves above them, the gentle stirring of the wind across the undergrowth. Xilyka looked back, the smile rising until it made her eyes crinkle at the corners. Heloise had never seen anything so beautiful in all her life.

"It's your menfolk," she sighed. "I knew they would follow."

"You can hear them? Are you sure it isn't—"

Xilyka raised a finger to her lips. "I can, and it isn't. The Order clanks so loud with their chains and their armor I can tell them from a league off. Villagers are quieter, at least. Come on! I said a quarter-candle, and we are getting a quarter-candle!"

She moved past, gesturing for Heloise to follow.

And she did follow, though she knew it would worry Wolfun or Barnard or whomever else was following her. She moved after Xilyka, watching the Hapti girl's curls bounce, the snow reflecting the light from the brass rings about them, and she forgot for a moment that she was in a war-machine. She forgot that her father was gone. She forgot her eye, and her hand, and the lurid scars across her face. She felt like she had on the day she'd chased the kite with the tinker-engine, Basina running at her side. Lutet had stretched out before her, as it was before wizardry or the Order had come to it, pristine and safe and bounded only by the shadows of the gloaming coming on.

They walked and the woods rose around them, the trunks coming closer together as they forged deeper. Heloise knew she should be afraid, but somehow, in the company of the Hapti knife-caster, she wasn't.

At last, Xilyka stopped and Heloise brought the machine to a clanking shudder at her side. Xilyka listened for a moment before nodding. "We've lost them. For now, at least. Tiresome. Everything with men is a great care."

"Xilyka, my father is taken. We are marching to attack the capital. That's . . . that's all . . . serious."

"It *is* serious, Heloise. But that doesn't mean you have to wear it so heavily. We have this quarter-candle. Setting your burdens down now and then doesn't mean you won't take them up again when it is time."

And now that she knew they were alone, Heloise was suddenly shy. She was surprised to see that Xilyka seemed the same, looking at her feet, the trees, the dusting of snow around them, anywhere but at Heloise. Heloise looked down at herself to avoid staring at Xilyka. She immediately regretted it; her body was filthy where it peeked out from beneath the heavy shift, and she could just glimpse the pink puckered edges of the scars on her face where the shining metal of the machine's frame reflected them back at her. She felt so unspeakably ugly. "So . . . so what do we do now?"

Xilyka looked up at her and smiled. "We glean."

"Glean?"

"You know Xilyka the knife-caster. But you've never met Xilyka the *forager*. The girl who could feed the whole band for a fortnight with only her nose and enough baskets to carry her find."

Heloise looked around. "In this? There's snow on the ground!"

Xilyka put her hands on her hips. "How easily the great war leader admits defeat! Did we not just find a handful of berries?"

Heloise felt her scars stretching with her smile. "That's just a handful."

"Where there's a handful, there's a bushel," Xilyka said, "lots to eat under snow. Roots, nuts, onions of all sorts. Horseheads . . ."

"You can't eat horseheads!" Heloise said, "they're for when you're sick. They make you . . . you know."

"The *leaves* make you . . . you know," Xilyka imitated Heloise's voice, "but you can eat the hearts and the branches both, if you boil them first. They're delicious."

"You . . . you can't. You're mad!" Heloise laughed.

"Maybe, but be mad with me for a time. We won't go any

farther in. Your menfolk are nearby. If there's trouble, we'll raise a cry. The column could hear us from here."

The words made Heloise feel so free, as if Barnard and Wolfun were not coming to find her, as if there were no army waiting for her return, no column of villagers, expectant eyes waiting to fix on her back. Xilyka's eyes were sweeping the ground, hands brushing the tree trunks she passed.

At last Xilyka stopped, clapped her hands together. "There." She knelt, dusting the snow off what looked to Heloise like a patch of withered brown stalks.

"Don't be silly," Heloise said, "that's just a bunch of frozen grass . . ."

The words died on her lips as Xilyka produced one of her knives, thrust it into the ground, and popped up a plump white bulb at the far end of one of the withered-looking stalks. She held it up triumphantly, still trickling clods of frozen earth. "Nikolae's onion," she said. "They grow on the lee side of rocks, where there's enough shade. You pick them in winter. Don't eat 'em raw unless you want your backside to sing, but if you cook them in a stew, they're delicious!"

"How did you know where to find them?"

"My mother taught me. Well, at first, anyway, but I took to it, I suppose, and when you do a thing enough, you master it. Was the same for me with casting. I threw a blade at the side of a tree a thousand times a day for a season."

"That must have driven you mad."

"It did . . . but it also felt good, once I started getting better, anyway."

"I was the same with my letters. Father made me practice them every night, and at first I hated it, but then . . ."

". . . but then you mastered it. And it feels good, being good at something."

"It does!" Heloise said.

"Of course"—Xilyka looked at her feet—"you're good at everything."

Heloise was so shocked that it took her a moment to answer. "How can you say that? You can take a bird on the wing with your knives. I couldn't hit the side of a barn."

"Of course you could. I told you I spent a season throwing the blasted things. Anyone can do that. You do a thing enough, it becomes a piece of you. That doesn't take anything more than mule-headedness. Mother always said once I got the bit in my teeth, there's no stopping me."

"I suppose. But look at you. You're so free, and you don't even worry about being promised."

Xilyka cocked an eyebrow. "Why would I worry about that?"

"It's just . . . it's what girls do. You live with your father and then you move into the house you make with your husband."

"It's what *villager* girls do. Traveling girls take what lovers they will, and one day, if they find one they like they promise one to the other."

"They don't have to?"

"No . . . but most do."

"Why haven't you?"

"Why haven't you?" Xilyka shot back, color rising in her cheeks.

Heloise's stomach tightened. *You've ruined this.* "I just . . . even in villages, the girl gets some say in how she's promised. I just . . . I was never ready." *Because there's no boy in the world I'd want.*

Xilyka looked apologetic. "I'm sorry, Heloise. It's just that . . . I didn't want to promise, either. There's plenty of boys who asked my mother, or tried to make time with me."

Heloise felt as if the conversation were skirting something important, a bigger question that both of them wanted to ask. It made Heloise excited and afraid at the same time, as if she balanced on the edge of a knife, and could either slide to safety or cut herself badly, depending on her next words. "Oh, well . . . I guess we're . . . I guess . . ." *Are we the same, Xilyka?*

"Anyway," Xilyka said, "you missed my point," and suddenly the moment was gone, leaving a tiny feeling of relief, swamped in a sense of loss. Something important had passed them by, and Heloise didn't know how to get it back.

"My point is that you're amazing, Heloise. Any woman can learn to cast, or to glean. I'm riding a horse now!"

"Riding a horse is—"

"Not for Traveling People, Heloise. My point is that anyone can do these things, but only you can do what you do. I've seen seventeen winters come and go. I've plied the road from the Argint almost to the Gold Coast. I've never met anyone like you."

Heloise felt her cheeks burn, and she dropped her eyes, unable to hold the heat of Xilyka's gaze. "I don't . . ." She couldn't finish the thought, stared at the tops of the machine's metal knees, waiting for Xilyka to rescue her.

Fortunately, Xilyka did. "Can't you see, Heloise? The world is changing around you. Your village is marching to war. My people are beside you. Beside a *villager*, Heloise. We, who have sworn ourselves to the road. We, who only trade and look to our own. We are *with* you, Heloise. And the Red Lords, too."

"The Red Lords don't care about me," Heloise said.

"Don't they?" Xilyka asked. "Then why aren't they marching on their own?"

Heloise searched for an answer, found none, felt her cheeks burn hotter. "My people follow me," she said at last, "because they think I am a Palantine."

"But the Traveling People do not believe in Palantines, Heloise. *I* don't believe in them. We are with you because we believe in *you*. Because we believe that you, and only you, can change . . .

this"—she swept her arms in a wide circle—"and that is greater than the finest knife-casting in the world."

"Please, Xilyka," Heloise said, suddenly biting back tears. "Stop."

Xilyka's expression shifted. "Heloise, I'm sorry, I didn't mean . . ."

"No, it's fine. It's just that . . . I have my father trying to make me into his little girl. I have every other villager trying to make me into a Palantine. Everyone wants me to *be* something, Xilyka. And . . . I just don't want you to . . . I need someone with whom I can just be . . ."

"Heloise," Xilyka finished for her, "and that is who you are. Enough lofty talk, then. Let's gather up these onions. They'll be glad of them back in camp, and might be we find enough out here to direct other foragers."

"I'd like that," Heloise said, "but I'm so thirsty."

"Don't eat snow," Xilyka said, "only makes you more thirsty, and if you're not careful it can make you sick."

"Any stream out here'll be frozen."

Xilyka brightened. "Have you ever licked an icicle hung from a silver oak?"

"I don't think I've ever licked an icicle at all."

"You must! In winter, the bark weeps sweet sap into them. Come on!"

She turned and led Heloise on again, and Heloise followed, grateful for the sudden return of the light feeling, for putting that heavy talk behind them, even though she had not had the answer she sought.

Xilyka went to the base of a tree that looked much the same as any other, reached up for a fat icicle hanging from a sagging branch.

"It doesn't look silver . . ." Heloise ventured.

"It isn't now. I will bring you back here in the moonlight someday, when the snow is gone, and you will see."

Heloise warmed at the thought. "I'd like that."

Xilyka searched around for a fallen leaf, then reached up, wrapped it around the icicle's base, and snapped it off. "There you are." She passed it through a gap in the machine's frame. Heloise released the shield's control strap and slid her arm free, took hold of the icicle by the leaf. It was so clear that Heloise could see right through it, Xilyka's beautiful face suddenly layered with the tiny white flaws in the ice, as if she lay at the bottom of a river.

"Give it a taste," Xilyka said.

Heloise let herself sag in the chest strap, bringing her head down far enough to allow her to reach the icicle up to her mouth. The cold was sharp against her tongue, almost painful, but so refreshing that Heloise didn't mind. It was much sweeter than Heloise had expected, nearly as cloying as the sugar candies her father had bought her on market days, mixing with the cool water as the ice melted and began to drip into her mouth. She pulled the icicle back to swallow . . .

. . . And found she couldn't. She tugged, gently at first, then harder. "Thilyka!"

"What's wrong, Heloise?"

"My thongue! Ith sthuck!"

Xilyka laughed so hard that she doubled over, leaning against the machine's leg. "By the Wheel, I am sorry, Heloise. I forgot that can happen. I'm a fool."

"Halth! It won leth gah!"

"Wait a moment, sometimes it just takes time."

Heloise waited as long as she could stand. "Thilyka. Ith wonth leth gah. Wat thoo I thoo?"

The words sent Xilyka into another gale of laughter. "I'm sorry, Heloise. You just sound so silly!"

"Sthtop lathing ah me an halth!"

"We need hot water."

"Were ah we goinh a geth hah waher?!"

Xilyka was quiet for a moment. "I have an idea. Can you come down a bit?"

The thought of exposing herself outside the machine made Heloise's heart race, and she froze.

"Heloise, it's all right. I am not asking you to come out. Just get as low as you can, all right? I think I can help."

Heloise swallowed the panic and slumped down, bending her knees and letting the chest strap climb into her armpits, the machine bending slightly at the waist in response.

"Perfect," Xilyka said, "here I come."

She scrambled up the machine's knees and wriggled under the breastplate, forcing herself into the driver's cage. She slowly wormed her way up, Heloise pressing herself into the leather pad behind her to make room. She could feel Xilyka's hips pushing against her own, their shoulders touching, as the Hapti girl pressed herself into a driver's cage built to hold a single person. At last, Xilyka's face was level with her own, pressed so close that Heloise could feel the soft curls brushing her cheeks, could smell the sweet tang of her breath. Their foreheads pressed together so tightly that Heloise could feel a dull ache forming there. Her heart raced again, much faster than it had at the thought of coming out of the machine. Her legs felt suddenly weak; she was painfully conscious of how she must smell, searched Xilyka's face for signs of disgust, but Xilyka only grinned back at her. *What is she doing?*

"Now, hold still, Heloise," Xilyka said. "This is going to be the funniest thing if we *both* wind up getting stuck."

And then she was pressing forward, stretching out her own tongue, running it over Heloise's own.

The world vanished. Heloise was vaguely aware of a tide rushing up from her toes and engulfing her entire body. It was urgent and hungry and it devoured all her senses, leaving her aware of only the tiny point where Xilyka's tongue touched her own, shining in her mind like a single, glorious star.

She had no idea how long she stood there, her legs liquid, her body held upright by the machine's chest strap, her head foggy and spinning, drowning in delight. When at last she emerged, blinking, back into the sunlit world, her tongue had returned to her mouth, freed from the icicle's grasp. "Oh . . ." she managed. "It worked."

"Yes," Xilyka husked, still painfully, deliciously close. "I suppose it did."

They stood like that, staring at one another, Heloise too frightened to speak, worried that if she did it would be stupid and would ruin the moment, would make Xilyka climb back out of the machine.

Xilyka looked as if she might say something, but stopped at the sound of voices calling, feet crunching on snow. Her face twisted. "It seems your menfolk have found us."

"Yes," Heloise said, "I . . . I suppose you should climb down now."

Xilyka had an easier time climbing back out, her hair brushing Heloise's lips as she went. When, at last, she emerged from beneath the breast plate and back onto the snowy ground, Heloise shivered. Though the canopy held off most of the snow and the tree trunks broke the wind, she was somehow colder than she'd ever been on the open road.

# 4

## CAUGHT OUT

*Beside the Order is the Imperial court. They are nobles born and bred, rich and titled families going back to before their so-called veil was drawn shut. The Order and their Pentarchs are the supreme authority in the Empire, but the nobles of the court truly rule alongside them. The Order is busy with their mad rituals, their obsessive hunts for wizards and the devils they supposedly let into the world, leaving most of the day-to-day administration of the Empire to the secular court.*

—Letter from the Third Sword
to the Exchequer of the Free Peoples
of the Gold Coast

Heloise walked back in silence. She did not blame Barnard, Wolfun, and Onas for following her, but their arrival brought back all the hardship she had briefly left behind, as surely as if they had carried it with them. She could feel the hint of joy she had just known drifting further and further away with each step they took back toward the army, and she grappled with a sudden, insane desire to turn and run back into the woods again.

Sir Steven was waiting for them when they emerged from the

woods, arms folded across his chest. Leahlabel stood before him, making wide gestures of her arms as she argued with him.

Sir Steven spurred his horse toward them as soon as they appeared. "What were you thinking?"

"Are you all right?" Leahlabel asked as she hurried after.

Heloise nodded, but not before Onas said, "She is fine, Mother." *As if you had anything to do with that.*

"Fool of a girl!" Sir Steven pounded his fist on his saddlehorn. "Were you not listening when I told you we must make haste?"

"They were gone less than a quarter-candle," Leahlabel said. "If we cannot spare even that, then we are truly lost."

Sir Steven purpled. "I'll not be lectured on warcraft by a Kipti trader. If the Emperor's cavalry catch us out on open ground, you will be praying to your precious Wheel to save you, and all because this girl"—he stabbed an angry finger at Heloise—"needed a moment alone."

He was right, Heloise knew, but the loss of her moment with Xilyka made her angry. "You didn't have to wait for me," she said. "I would have caught up."

Sir Steven opened his mouth to say more, but Barnard shouted him down. "You are addressing a sacred Palantine, and you will keep a civil tongue in your head."

Sir Steven's knights stirred at that, hands moving to their sword hilts, reining their horses around to face the huge tinker. Barnard hefted his hammer, widened his stance. One of the knights lowered his lance, and Sir Steven slapped it up. "There is no time!" He spun his horse and began trotting back toward the army, bellowing at the serjeants to get the men marching. He spared a glance over his shoulder at Heloise, and shouted, "You're all mad!" before disappearing into the throng of his troops.

"You must not let him yell at you," Barnard said. "Do not forget that you are a Palantine."

Anger spiked, so hot and sudden that Heloise struggled to form words. "What is the good of being a Palantine if I can't find my father?"

"Even Palantines yield to the Emperor's will," Barnard said. "You will find your father in His time, your eminence. That, I promise."

They walked toward the head of their column. Heloise could feel the eyes of the villagers on her. Had they seen her panic? Flee into the woods? What would they be thinking of her now? The snow had let up during the night, leaving a landscape of glittering diamonds. Heloise would almost have had the snow back, if it meant the wind would stop. It scoured everything, sending the canvas tops of the wagons flapping, stripping the soft snow from the frozen crust and sending it stinging into the villagers' faces. Heloise watched them shivering, felt her stomach twist at the sight.

"Look at them! They don't have enough food. They don't have the right clothing. The woman from Seal's Rock said her people thought that I would feed them, because I was a Palantine."

"You are a Palantine," Barnard said. He stood stiff-backed and straight, his eyes blazing. The fire in them made him look a bit like the Order fanatic who had taken her eye, Brother Tone. The thought chilled her.

"What good is that? Tell me, how do I feed these people? How do I get them clothes? Do I pray the Emperor makes it rain bread?"

Barnard locked eyes with her, as if through the force of his fanaticism he could make her believe. "I hope, your eminence, that the day will come when you see yourself as all of us see you."

*If that day comes,* Heloise thought, *then you will have traded the Order for something just as wicked.*

The horn sounded from Sir Steven's column, and Heloise could hear the serjeants shouting at their men to get moving. With an audible crunching of snow, the Red Lords' column stepped off to resume its punishing pace.

"Your eminence," Barnard said, "we must go."

Heloise's eyes fixed on the shimmering light in the distance behind the army, her heart pounding. "What if he's back there, somewhere?"

"The boy said they rode north, your eminence," Wolfun said.

"You must trust Sir Steven," Barnard said. "He knows his business."

"You just called him a heretic yesterday," Heloise said. "Asked if we should go our own way."

Barnard spread his hands. "Aye, and the Emperor spoke through you to correct me. His will is in all things, your eminence. As the wind stirs the flower, sending its seeds forth to take root, it is an easy thing to miss if your eye is not fixed on it. I was wrong, and I am glad to be given this chance to learn and to be better."

He cast a nervous glance toward the Red Lords' column. Already the knights at the fore were disappearing into the wind-driven sprays of snow. "Your eminence, we must go."

It took an act of will for Heloise to rip her eyes from the light on the horizon and turn them to her waiting column. Most did not know that her father had been taken, and if they did, what difference would it make? They followed her to fight the Order, not to protect her family. *My family is my army now, and it will be until we have finished this.* The thought made her chest tighten, so she added a new one: *I will find you, Father. I am so sorry.*

Heloise met Xilyka's expectant gaze. The Hapti girl had made a petition of her, and Heloise had promised to honor it. She nodded and Xilyka raised a spear to unfurl the banner on its end, letting the wind take it, the forked pennant tails snapping in the strong wind. Heloise turned back to Barnard now, feeling the fire in her single remaining eye. "If we win, if we stop the Order and free the Emperor from their wickedness, then we will do it not because I am a Palantine, but because we came together to fight as one people."

Barnard looked up, the color draining from his face. "What . . . what is that?"

"It's us," Heloise said, then turned to the column, raising her voice. "We come from all across the Empire, and even from beyond its borders! We are from Lutet and Lyse and Frogfork and the Shipbreakers! We are from the Gold Coast! We are from the road, with no home save where we build our fires! But we all have this one thing—that we have had enough of the Order! We are red people and Traveling People and settled people—all people. *One* people. *The* people. Forward together!"

Silence.

Had she expected them to cheer? Their spines to straighten like Barnard's? The crowd did indeed look like Barnard, their faces just as shocked, their eyes just as angry. The villagers cast hateful glances at the Traveling People, who huddled in the drovers' chairs of their wagons, shivering against the cold. Heloise spied Helga at the front of her village, all swaddled in their snow-dusted sealskins. The old woman shook her head and looked at her feet. Heloise heard the low growl of the Red Lords' horn again, the thundering of footsteps and hoofbeats as their column lurched forward.

Time to go.

Heloise turned, the silence buffeting her like a wind, and began to march. Behind her, the creaking of the Traveling People's wagon wheels, the crunching footsteps of the villagers on the snow, even the dull hoofbeats of the few horses sounded sullen.

She heard brief snatches of muttering borne on the cold wind.

". . . not march beneath a Kipti wheel." ". . . red as Old Ludhuige's blood!" She wanted to turn and shout at them, but what good would it do? They might revere her as a saint, fear the power of the war-machine, but neither fear nor reverence could banish their distrust of one another.

She could feel the ill glow of the light on the back of her neck, the absence of her father like a phantom limb. She was shocked to find herself missing Sigir, the Maior of her village who had turned traitor and tried to kill her. She hated him, of course, but he had known how to lead, both a village and an army. He would have been able to counsel her on what to do about her father without employing Barnard's blinding faith.

They had marched in silence for no more than half a candle when one of Sir Steven's outriders galloped up and reined in beside them. His horse was lathered and his surcoat torn. A long cut ran from his temple to the corner of his mouth, still bleeding. "Heloise Factor, the First Sword summons you to his . . . Apologies, he *asks* that you attend him at the head of his column."

As he spoke, the horns sounded and the Red Lords' army drew to a halt. She could hear blades clearing scabbards, archers stringing bows.

"What is it?" she asked the outrider.

The man looked around her. "Apologies, but it is a war council, and it is not our custom to . . ."

"Tell me!"

He swallowed. "We have found the Imperial army. They are reinforced, dug in on the road north, and offering battle. We must decide how to engage them if we wish to win through to the capital."

Her stomach turned over. "But . . . but Sir Steven said we had four days . . ." She remembered the First Sword's words. *Their strength is in their Order and their knights. Horsemen all. If we bottle them up in a city, they are near useless. If we face them in the field . . . I will admit I do not like our chances.*

But the sinking in her gut competed with a second, more ur-gent emotion. Relief. *Father.*

The man reined his horse around and pointed toward the head of the Red Lords' column. "Attend Sir Steven there with your ad-visers as quickly as you can. We must decide the order-of-battle." He dug in his spurs and galloped away.

Heloise gestured to the banner snapping in the wind above her head. The news made her feel hope for the first time since the council in Sir Steven's tent. "We fight as one people. I will take two advisers and two guards: one each from the villagers and from the Traveling People." She raised her voice as everyone around her began speaking at once. ". . . And I am *not* arguing. For my advisers, I will take Wolfun and your mother, Onas."

Xilyka did not speak, but Heloise could feel her anger. "I will bring Mother Leahlabel at once," Onas said.

"Thank you," Heloise said. "For my bodyguards, I will bring Xilyka and Barnard."

"Heloise, no—" Onas began.

"I *said* I am not arguing," Heloise cut him off. "The Sindi will be represented by Mother Leahlabel, and the Hapti by Xilyka."

Onas's cheeks colored. "What of the Brock? What do I tell Mother Andrasaia?"

"You know your own people . . ."

"The Brock are not my people! I am of—"

"Barnard, Xilyka, come on." Heloise cut Onas off and turned, driving the machine toward the head of the Red Lords' column. She heard the footsteps and hoofbeats as her chosen guard moved to comply. She could hear Onas cursing under his breath as he turned his horse. That was good. She could deal with his anger later. For now, at least, he was obeying. It would take time for the army to get used to Heloise's expectation of unity, but they *would* get used to it. Everyone was constantly saying how they followed her and would work her will. Well, this was her will.

There was no tent this time. Sir Steven and his captains had formed the same circle around the same fire-grate, with the same board of food, but now it was open to the sky, with the relentless wind carrying the thin flames crackling across the pitted metal to threaten their ankles.

Wolfun was riding just behind her, and Heloise could see Mother Leahlabel picking her way through the packed snow toward them, her red cloak whipping around her.

The Sindi Mother came into the circle, panting from the exertion of forging through the snow. "Heloise, thank you for calling on me. What's the matter?"

"My outriders van have found the Imperial army," Sir Steven said. "They have cut the road north."

"So soon?" Heloise asked. "I thought if we kept up the pace . . ."

"If you had wanted to keep pace, then perhaps you should not have gone running off into the woods . . ."

"Do you mean"—Leahlabel's voice was calm—"to tell us that the Imperial army has outpaced us because Heloise took *less* than a quarter-candle to tend to her grief?"

The juxtaposition of Sir Steven's strong voice with his worried expression frightened Heloise. "I had *hoped* the pace of march would be enough, but I misjudged. Perhaps they had pigeons, or relay-riders stationed on the road. There's no way to know. But if my outriders have made contact, then there's nothing to be done."

"But . . . but you said . . . if we fought them in a field battle, we would lose."

Sir Steven raised a hand, looked over his shoulders. "Mind your tongue! Talk like that can be the death of an army. This isn't

what I wanted, but neither will I beat my breast and rend my gar-
ments. We will give battle, and see if . . ."

"Give battle?" Heloise asked. "Why can't we retreat? Why are
we fighting them in the field if you said they will . . . if you said
you didn't like our chances?"

Sir Steven winced at the words, sucked in his cheeks. "This is
my punishment for taking council of war with a girl. We cannot
retreat once we have made contact, Heloise. An army in retreat
is at its most vulnerable. If we'd had better warning, we might
have been able to withdraw, but we are too close now. If we retreat, they will follow, and they will fall on us from our rear, which
will make matters even worse than they are already. And where
would you have us retreat to? Lyse is an indefensible ruin. The
road is wide and open all the way back. There is no ground
we could take and hold to make good our defense. No. Our best
hope is to stand here, while our people are fresh, and make the
best fight we can."

"And how good is our best hope?" Leahlabel asked.

Sir Steven did not answer, and he did not meet her eyes.

Heloise thought of the Pilgrims and knights charging her across
the field left open by the collapse of Lyse's wall. She had been so
brave then, so resigned. She turned inward, tried to find that same
strength, but it eluded her.

"I will have need of your strength now, Heloise," Sir Steven
finally said, "and whether you call it a debt or no, you cannot deny
that the Free Peoples have been friends to you, though we had
no reason to be. I hope you keep this in mind when you hear what
you must do."

Her heart pounded, her breath coming fast. *What of parley?
What of Father?* "What is it?"

Sir Steven reached out a hand. One of his captains placed a slim
stick in it, capped in red-enameled iron. The First Sword leaned

forward and began drawing in the snow. "They've cut the road straight across, and dug in. Trained bands, well-formed, all with pikes. It'll be hell's work fighting through them. There's forest on their wings, screening their cavalry. If we've any hope to stop their charge, and we *must* stop their charge if we're to have any chance at winning this, we have to hold those woods. Fighting horsemen in a thicket is a far easier fight than out on the plain."

"They won't just let us do that," Heloise said.

"Unless I miss my guess," Sir Steven said, nodding, "they've put their Black-and-Grays there, waiting for us to try to take them. What we need is a skirmish line to pepper their ranks. Soften them up. And we need people as skilled at moving through rough terrain in loose order as the Black-and-Grays."

"You need Traveling People," Leahlabel said. "Knife-casters to weaken the enemy line, and dancers in the woods."

Sir Steven nodded. "Not just you, Mother. We need the villagers, too. Heloise, your people have hunted with slings and bows in these woods for generations. The Free Peoples are fisher folk, for the most part. My archers are good massed, but not at skirmishing. And we've precious little light foot. My infantry are trained to fight in armor in the field, not for running battles around trees. This is your terrain, and you are best suited to take and hold it." The First Sword clenched his fist as he spoke, his voice pitched to a low growl that she knew was intended to inspire her. "I can have my armorers distribute . . ."

Heloise raised her knife-hand. "What about my father?"

Sir Steven blinked. "What about him?"

"The enemy army has him."

"Heloise, we do not know that for certain. It's just a theory from one of your villager boys."

"I grew up with Guntar. He's not stupid. Unlike you, he saw my father taken. He saw which way the riders took him."

"That means nothing. Heloise, the enemy is not sending heralds. They do not fly the flag of parley. We have no Imperial prisoners to exchange. This is foolish."

"You want my help? You negotiate for my father."

She could feel her advisers stiffening beside her, but she ignored them.

"Heloise, I know you love him and are grieved by his loss, but he is just one man, and your army must do their part."

"'Our part.' You mean 'go first.' The Traveling People and the villagers, while the Red Lords hang back."

"We will only hang back until you have done enough damage to give us the advantage. Then, we will break them."

"And how many of us will die, I wonder, before you decide to come and break them? We aren't 'light troops.' We are *villagers*. We have almost no soldiers among us. We will fight, but we will do it *beside* you, not *before* you."

Sir Steven's cheeks colored. "Heloise, you are not a commander . . ."

"I am also not a fool."

Sir Steven turned to Barnard. "You're a veteran. Surely you can speak some sense to her."

"Why are you talking to him?" Heloise could feel the anger rising. "I speak for my army. You're saying that you want the villagers and the Traveling People to fight and die, and then the Red Lords will come once the enemy is weakened. Like you did at Lyse."

Sir Steven looked to Mother Leahlabel, his jaw clenched.

"That is also what I hear." Mother Leahlabel crossed her arms. "The Traveling People will not be fodder for crows. Our people will advance with yours or not at all."

"And we won't fight at all unless you send someone to talk to them, to try to get my father back," Heloise added.

Sir Steven looked to his captains, then back at Heloise. "This is madness. I only present sound strategy . . . If you had any knowledge of war at all you would . . . You must trust me!"

"The last man I trusted," Heloise said, "let my mother die before he put a knife in my chest."

Sir Steven's face went from red to white. "Now, you listen to me—"

A scream sounded from the woods, loud and long, rising until it was suddenly cut off with a wet ripping sound. The entire column turned, and Heloise heard shouting as several of the Red Lords' infantry raced into the tree line. She heard a booming, the splintering of branches.

"What in the Peoples' name is going on?" Sir Steven began walking toward the tree line. "Color Serjeant! Plant a banner and muster the vanguard on it. Get me a report!"

Heloise's mouth went dry. She heard the dull crunch of a heavy tread crushing down on snow, watched the swaying, splintering treetops. She could feel the sick glow far behind them, hovering on the horizon over the ruins of Lyse.

She knew what was coming.

Her anger, her bravery fled her, drained away as if a plug had been opened in her heart. Suddenly she was a little girl again, cowering inside the Tinkers' vault as the roof came crashing down on her.

"No," she called after the First Sword, "we need to run."

She took a step back. She wasn't ready to see this.

There was a sound of crunching metal and two of the Red Lords' infantrymen came flying out of the tree line, thrown as easily as child's toys. They rolled end-over-end in the snow, shedding bits of armor as they tumbled, leaving long red streaks behind them.

Sir Steven drew his sword, knelt over the fallen men, reaching out to touch one of their bruised faces. "What the . . ."

"Run!" Heloise's paralysis broke, and she found her voice. "First Sword, you have to run!"

Sir Steven looked up at her. "What are you—"

"Devil!" Heloise screamed, as the tree trunks shuddered and the thing she had named stepped out into view.

# 5

## RENT

*Hell's hands are they, knowing no master and no law, as wicked as the forked lightning, as strong as the mountaintop in winter, as numerous as the stars in the summer sky.*
—Sermon given in the Imperial Shrine
on the centennial of the Fehta

The devil that burst through the trees could have been the twin of the one she had killed. It stood taller than the giant machine, at least twice the height of the tallest man, covered in spade-shaped scales the unhealthy purple of a fresh bruise. Black horns corkscrewed above the clustered white stalks of its eyes, its mismatched nostrils, its slim black cut of a mouth.

It spread its six arms, hooked claws still dripping the blood of the men it had killed, and screamed. Heloise had forgotten how piercing the eagle shriek could be, how painful.

The color serjeant had been mustering infantry around a plain red banner. He clapped his hands to his ears now. The few men he'd managed to muster stumbled back, dropping their swords or spears.

The devil took a single step toward them, huge clawed foot crunching down in the snow. Where it touched, the fluffy white turned to sick black, melting and steaming. Runnels of black-gray shot out from around the footprints, misting the cold air.

The trees shivered and another devil appeared. Then another. The canopy was still shivering behind them, resounding with the crackling of splintering branches. *There are more.* The thought tore through Heloise's mind. *There are more in the woods.*

The infantry abandoned their weapons wholesale now, throwing them down in their haste to flee. The color serjeant did his best to stop them, but after the second man struck him he gave up and turned to face the devils, his long halberd looking ridiculous in the face of the giants. The devils made a low clicking sound, advanced slowly, calling to one another, clearly enjoying the terror of the fleeing troops.

Heloise wanted nothing more than to join them, to give the tinker-engine rein and let it carry her as far and as fast from this place as it could. She had been so brave for so long that now, looking at the devils, she had no courage left to her.

But there was Sir Steven, alone, his men melting away behind him. For all his faults, a man, alone, in the shadow of devils.

She remembered Basina's flashing smile as they'd rode in Poch's cart to the Knitting of Hammersdown. *Father says being brave isn't not being frightened, it's doing a thing even though you are.*

Heloise had no courage left, but the machine was just a thing of metal and leather. It felt neither fear nor bravery. So she moved it, let it carry her back to Sir Steven, putting it between the First Sword and the devils. "Get back," she said.

"I have an army to fight them!" Sir Steven began bellowing at the fleeing infantry.

"Heloise!" Wolfun had reached her, was pulling on the edge of her shield. "Come away, you can't fight them all yourself!"

She jerked the shield free of his grip. "I am the only one who can."

A company of archers raced along the tree line, then froze, gaping up at the devils. The color serjeant ran toward them, waving his halberd. "Don't just stand there, you great pills! Loose! Loose!"

A few of the archers ignored him, struck dumb, but the rest began nocking arrows to their bows, drawing and loosing in no particular order. The arrows found the leftmost of the devils, plinking off its purple scales, spinning harmlessly into the snow. It turned with a sudden speed that shocked Heloise, one moment moving toward her, and the next spinning into the archers. It swept its long arms through them, snatching one up to thrust into its tiny mouth, stretched suddenly wide enough to swallow the man to his hips. With another hand it grasped a second archer by his head and flailed him against the ground. With its remaining arms it scooped archers up or batted them aside, sending the men flying through the air like the remains of a puddle where a boot has stamped down.

The other devils shrieked at the sight of the slaughter and lurched into a run, angling straight toward the column's head. The color serjeant moved aside, deftly avoiding being flattened by the devil's foot, swinging his halberd at its knee. The blade struck the target squarely, sparking off the scales before turning flat, and the devil reached down with its two closest arms, grabbing the serjeant by his neck and leg. Heloise could see the color serjeant's free leg kicking madly before the devil tugged the man into two pieces, his leg ripping away, blood fountaining from his trunk, then hurled the pieces at her.

She raised her shield, felt the meaty thump of flesh striking it hard enough to send her back a step. Sir Steven moved clear of her, ludicrously tiny, his flimsy weapon even smaller than the serjeant's halberd. Barnard was at her side a moment later, carrying his two-handed forge hammer, and Wolfun with one of the Lysian

levy spears. They tried to move out in front of her, and she shep-
herded them back with her shield. "No!"

Xilyka sprinted past them all, racing toward the devils, the first
of her flat-bladed knives flying. Two more followed it, so fast that
Heloise couldn't even follow the girl's arm. All three slammed into
the devil's knee where it had turned the serjeant's halberd. The
first two drew sparks, spinning off, but the third found a gap between the scales and stuck fast, quivering. A trickle of black blood
leaked down the creature's shin and it screamed again, stumbling.
She let another knife fly, just wide of the devil's stalked eyes, thud-
ding against the monster's cheek. The devil winced, jerking its
head back.

Heloise saw her moment, rushed in to meet it.

The devil only had time to raise two of its arms before Heloise
dropped the machine's shoulder, hooked its elbow up, and sent
the knife-hand bursting through its chin. The blow lifted the
monster off the ground, arms pinwheeling. It went sprawling on
its back, leaving a slick black track through the snow.

A cheer went up from the troops behind her, and Heloise felt
herself smile through the terror. The devils were strong, huge. But
they bled like men, and that meant they could die like men. She
had seen it before, and now the Red Lords had seen it too. Hope-
fully, they would believe it.

And then the second devil was upon her.

She barely had time to get the shield up before the creature
slammed into it, throwing its full weight against the machine. It
snaked one of its arms behind the machine's helmet and yanked
forward, slamming the visor into the shield's edge hard enough
to rattle Heloise's head against the leather padding. Her vision
went black, filled with stars. She shook her head, her sight coming back into focus just as the devil took a step back and wrenched
the machine forward. Heloise watched the purple scales rush past

her as the machine toppled face-first. The fouled snow rushed up, glistening at first, going flat black as the machine fell against it.

With it came the fetid stink of the devils—the rot smell of swamp muck, of twisting roots and river slime, of wet places that never saw the sun. Heloise felt the machine shudder as the devil fell across it, heard the scrabbling in the snow as it dug with its claws, trying to reach down and around the metal frame. It wouldn't take it long to find a gap and reach inside.

She pushed off with her shield and knife-hand both, heard the engine roar, the frame groaning as it struggled against the devil's weight. The frame lifted, handspan by handspan, moving faster as the engine built momentum. Light crept in, the stink lessening as she pushed herself up from the rancid snow. At last, the machine shot upright, and Heloise gave a shout of triumph.

It turned to a scream of frustration as the devil held on to her, tipping the balance backward, and the sky replaced the snow in her field of vision. Heloise threw her weight forward, but it was too little and much too late. The machine overbalanced and fell again, this time on its back, pinning the devil beneath. She twisted, slammed her elbows behind her, but it was no use. The devil held on, its six arms wrapped around the machine's torso. It squeezed with all its strength, and Heloise felt the metal frame shudder.

She could hear more eagle screams, shouts of pain and alarm from the army behind her. More devils, raising havoc among the ranks. "Xilyka!" she shouted. "Barnard!"

And then the sky vanished behind a huge bulk covered in sharp purple scales. A devil leapt onto the machine, pinning its shield arm to the ground. Heloise strained to lift it, but the devil had three arms on it, holding it by the wrist, elbow, and shoulder. It reached up with one of the remaining fists and punched the machine hard in the metal visor.

Heloise could feel the metal buckle under the blow, barking hard against her face, her head rebounding against the leather cushion behind her. She felt fresh blood trickling from her scarred cheek. She blinked, relief flooding her as she realized her remaining eye could still see.

The devil was shrieking now, a sound somewhere between its clucking growl and the eagle scream. It shook its hand, one of the knuckles twisted, black blood leaking from where it had broken against the machine's metal plate. One of its remaining hands rose to soothe the wounded one, but the last snaked forward, probing with a clawed finger toward the visor's eye-slits.

The devil beneath her had given up squeezing the frame, was flailing to get out from under her.

Her knife-arm was free.

She shrieked, swinging the blade up, punching it into the devil's neck. Once, twice, three times. The creature screamed, knocked her knife-arm away, and she punched it again lower, plunging the blade into its side. She felt the hard scales flex, then break beneath the machine's relentless strength. Drops of the creature's black blood fell through the faceplate to spatter across her face, filling her nose with the swamp-stench. Somewhere to the north was her father, held prisoner by the Imperial army, and this thing was stopping her from saving him. She stabbed and stabbed and stabbed, and the devil's struggles grew weaker, until at last she ripped her shield arm up, slamming the corner into the devil's head, sending it rolling off her.

She rolled the machine onto its stomach, then levered it to its feet. The devil that had been beneath her sprang to its feet, reached for her.

And then Barnard was between them, hauling his huge hammer over his head, swinging it down with all his might. Its massive head was a brick of black iron nearly as heavy as an anvil. It landed square atop the devil's foot. The scales were good enough at turning an edge, but they crumpled under the weight of the hammer blow, the metal sinking deep as it shattered the bones and bit into the meat beneath.

The devil wailed and its charge turned into a stumble, all six arms flying toward its crippled foot, head bowing. Xilyka appeared, snarling. She reached up with her throwing knife, thrusting it into the center of one patch of stalked eyes. She spun out of the way as the head hurtled toward her, weaving between the long black horns.

Heloise rolled her shoulder, bringing her knife-arm up and then hurtling down, driving the point into the top of the devil's head, the weight of the fist snapping the horns, pushing the creature face down into the dirt. She leaned into the strike, felt the devil's skull hold, then flex, then break. She thought of Basina, pressing down until gray-black jelly squirted out to coat the metal frame to the elbow. The creature stiffened, kicked, and was still.

Heloise braced herself on her knife-hand, feeling the breath rush in and out of her.

She looked up. The devil she had stabbed so many times lay still, sprawled on its face a few paces distant. At the head of the Red Lords' column, the infantry had formed up into a hedge of spears, were slowly driving forward, pushing three of the monsters back. One of the devils gathered itself to charge them, but then it ducked under a hail of arrows fired by the Red Lords archers, formed up behind the spearmen.

Behind them, the dead lay in heaps. Heloise marveled that so many could have been killed so quickly.

There were too many to count, all wearing the red tabards of the Free Peoples. Heloise knew she should feel horror, pity. But instead she found herself battling the relief that her own people were spared. *No one deserves this. The Red Lords are your allies. Help them win.*

She gave a final push against the pulp of the devil's head, lurched to her feet, driving the machine at the devils. "The Throne!" she shouted.

Her war cry echoed from the throats of hundreds of villagers, arriving to assist the Red Lords at last. The people she had known all her life, who had followed her this far, through battle after battle. Heloise saw Chunsia and Danad. Even old Poch Drover with a spear in this thick fingers. The sight made her heart swell. "The Throne!"

The devils gave a final hiss, turned, and ran, leaving trails of gore and the black, fetid slime they had made of the snow. They were answered with cheers so loud that Heloise felt carried on them. A shower of sling stones, javelins, and arrows followed the devils, most falling well short. Some infantry pursued the monsters a few steps, but Heloise could tell it was half-hearted, a show of terrified men, conscious of their place in the songs that would be spun around this day.

Heloise let the machine slow and finally stop. The cheers had set her blood alight, but she heard them grow fainter behind her, and knew she was alone. The devils had been run off by an army, but that didn't mean they wouldn't turn to fight if she came after them by herself.

The treetops shuddered as the devils pushed into the woods, the sounds of breaking branches receding. The cheering and shouting subsided, until an eerie silence blanketed the column, broken only by the dripping of the rotten slime that the devils' touch had made of the trees, the hoarse sighing of the wind, and the cries of the wounded.

They were gone. The heat in her blood faded, and Heloise

shivered. Devils. So many devils. *Sacred Throne, what is happening? Where did they come from?*

Wolfun ran to the machine's side. "Are you all right?"

"I'm fine," Heloise panted, her head still spinning. Xilyka was still turning, knives fanned out in her hands, watching for threats. She slowly backpedaled, moving closer and closer to Heloise, ready to strike should the devils return, or some enterprising assassin try to take their chance now that chaos reigned.

Heloise tried to count the dead, stopped at one hundred. At last Xilyka stopped turning, stood beside her. Heloise could hear the tremor in her voice. "So, these are your famous devils. They are . . . daunting."

But Heloise wasn't listening. "It all happened . . . so fast."

"The Great Wheel turns as it will. Sometimes quickly. They died well, at least."

There was an emptiness in Heloise now, so great she thought she might never feel whole again. "They still died."

"A moment ago, that Red Lord was going to throw us all at the enemy while his precious roses held back. Perhaps his arrogance spun the Great Wheel thus."

Wolfun let go a shaking breath. "Sacred Throne. Six devils. Six!"

"There were more," Heloise said, "in the woods." She remembered Clodio's body splitting in half, the bright light shining through him, his skin sloughing off like a crumpled bedsheet, the devil climbing through. She remembered what Leahlabel had said to her of it. *That is not a portal, Heloise. That is the reflection of the world beyond. You are seeing a tiny sliver of what the wizard sees. Sadly, by the time you can see it, there is no saving them.* Had there been many wizards? Could so many devils come through one person?

"And you would have killed the rest, if they hadn't run." Barnard's voice alone did not shake as he admired the black blood dropping off his hammer's head.

"I didn't kill them alone." Heloise blinked at the devils' corpses. They seemed so much smaller now that they lay twisted in the snow. "Xilyka helped me. And you."

"We are the Emperor's instruments," Barnard said. "We do nothing but that which is according to His will. You are His Palantine, His hand in the world. You are the tool he uses to deliver us from the enemy."

"Tell that"—Heloise gestured at the heaps of dead—"to them."

Barnard reversed his hammer to wipe it off in the snow. "I do not rejoice in their deaths, your eminence, but they were heretics. The Emperor protects His own."

Heloise knew she should correct Barnard, but she could not stop wrestling with the enormity of what she had just seen. So many devils. "Where . . . where did they come from?"

Wolfun opened his mouth to answer, but a wailing cut him off, so grief-stricken that it froze Heloise's heart. She had cried like that when she'd had a moment to accept that Basina was gone. Her father had cried like that when he thought no one could hear him, standing over Leuba's corpse.

Onas and Giorgi were on their knees, sobbing over a crumpled form. At first, Heloise thought it was one of the Red Lords, but then she saw the subtle difference in the shade of red, that the scarlet cloth was not a tabard, but a cloak.

Like the devils, Leahlabel looked smaller in death. Heloise couldn't see the wound that had taken her life.

Onas gathered Leahlabel in his arms. The boy looked so much bigger than the fragile doll that was his mother's body that Heloise couldn't believe he was her child. He buried his face in her hair, shrieked out his sorrow.

Her father was taken because Heloise had insisted he ride out.

Now, Leahlabel was fallen because Heloise had insisted she come with her. The Sindi Mother had been the first person Heloise had seen when she'd awoken in the Traveling People's camp, the fiercest advocate among her people to give Heloise and her village shelter. Heloise swallowed her tears. It wasn't her place to weep. This was Onas's mother. Heloise had already lost her own.

Sir Steven broke her from her reverie, bellowing at one of his captains. "Get pickets set up! I want eyes all along the column! Put out outriders! Get these dead cleaned up, counted, and prepared for the pyre!"

He strode around in front of Heloise, ignoring Onas and his grief. "I don't suppose"—he stabbed an angry finger up at her— "that you can tell me what in the name of the People just happened?"

"Devils," Heloise managed. Over Sir Steven's shoulder, she could see the other Sindi Mothers weeping, placing comforting hands on Onas's shoulder. The young man was still sobbing over his mother's corpse, but Giorgi had mastered his tears and stood with arms folded, looking down at him, eyes hollow and red-rimmed.

"Devils," Sir Steven nearly spat, "are stories. Fables sown by your false Order to frighten the Emperor's subjects into submission."

"They are real," Heloise said. "I killed one."

"You killed three, your eminence," Barnard said, gesturing at the monsters sprawled in the snow.

"Where did they come from?" Sir Steven's face shook, and Heloise realized that his anger was a fragile screen, scarcely covering the terror beneath.

"I don't know," she answered, trying and failing to pry her eyes away from Leahlabel.

"I do." Giorgi's voice was stricken. He waved in the direction of the sick-colored light that hovered over the horizon in the direction of Lyse. "Someone was Veilstruck. Enough to tear a hole through the veil so wide it stayed open."

"There is no veil!" Sir Steven fumed. "It's a damned story!"

Heloise remembered the wizards the Order had savaged, beating them until they worked the most powerful wizardry she'd ever seen, strong enough to collapse one of Lyse's walls. She remembered the censer the Red Lords had found, burned with such heat that the metal had melted. *Of the rags, there was little more left than ash*, the Red Lords had said of the wizards' clothing. Something powerful had consumed them. She thought of the blinding white light that had emitted from Clodio as the portal opened within him. She hadn't gone back to check his remains, but it had certainly looked hot enough to consume what remained of her old friend.

"The wizards," she said, "the ones that took down the wall."

"What are you talking about?" Sir Steven asked.

Heloise turned to him. "The Order did this."

"Nonsense," Sir Steven said. "Why would the Order bring devils into the world? I thought their whole purpose for being is to keep them out."

"I don't think they meant to," Heloise said. "I don't think they knew this would happen."

"What? What are you talking about—" Sir Steven began.

"You!" Onas cut him off. Heloise turned to see him striding toward her. He had laid Leahlabel back down in the snow, where Mother Tillie was busy wrapping her in her own cloak.

"You"—Onas's hands were white knuckled on his knife handles—"you let my mother die."

Xilyka stepped between them, her eyes fixed on Onas's hands. "Be careful, Sindi."

"You are every bit as guilty," Onas spat. "Where were you?"

"Right where I was supposed to be." Xilyka's voice was calm. "Fighting the devils. Protecting Heloise, as our mothers charged us."

"You couldn't protect a stone!" Onas seethed.

"I am the finest caster in the Hapti band."

"Are you? Show me the wounds in the devils made by your hand. It was Heloise who laid them low."

"Onas, I had help . . ." Heloise began.

"Not the right help. Not the help that would have kept my mother alive. You should have taken me." His voice broke. "Why didn't you take me?"

Heloise's mouth worked. She'd had good reasons. She didn't want to bring too many people to the council. She was trying to be true to Xilyka's vision for them—to be one people. And the ugly truth beneath it all—that she'd wanted Onas away from her ever since he'd pressed his idiot suit back in Lyse.

The thought brought the rage hot and quick. "Because *I* lead here, Onas," Heloise said. "*I* decide who guards me. Because I do *not* belong to you."

Onas's face turned purple, then white. His hands flexed on his knife handles, and Xilyka tensed. Heloise's throat tightened at the thought of him harming Xilyka. She moved the machine forward, raising the knife-hand. Barnard advanced as well, hammer coming off his shoulder. Wolfun came with him.

Onas held their gazes, eyes trembling. Then he turned and scooped his mother up, carrying her back toward where the Traveling People's wagons were lined up, pale smudges in the snow. Giorgi held Heloise's eyes for a moment before he turned to follow, the Mothers in his wake.

"Giorgi," Heloise called after them, "Analetta, Tillie!"

But none of them turned, and none of them answered.

# 6

## BREAKS THEM ALL ALIKE

*The sword, the spear, these are the instruments of the sol-*
*dier. The Emperor's hands succor and provision, heal and*
*mend. They bear the threshing flail, the only weapon that*
*may make bread as readily as it may take life.*
— Writ. Imp. XXI. 17.

The Traveling People circled their wagons at the head of Heloise's column. When all three bands disappeared inside the circle, the villagers were wise enough not to follow.

Xilyka had been as reluctant to leave Heloise as Heloise was to have her go, but Heloise insisted. Wolfun and Barnard had shadowed her from the moment the Hapti girl had gone, eyeing the circle of wagons with undisguised worry.

Heloise knew the Traveling People were sending Leahlabel "up the wheel," the Traveling People's custom of honoring their dead. Heloise had seen the ceremony once before, and that time, too, the Traveling People had held her responsible for the deaths. Leahlabel had healed Heloise and her father, but even more, she had been a friend, the latest in a long line of them lost to her. A sob rose in her throat, so sudden that she could not choke it back entirely.

"I . . . I am sorry for your loss, your eminence," Barnard said.

"Which loss?" she asked him. "My mother, my father, Leahlabel?" She knew she was being cruel. Barnard had lost as many loved ones as she had, but she was too drained by the worry over her father and the grief of losing Leahlabel to apologize.

Barnard spread his hands. "Whichever you wish, your eminence."

Heloise swept her eyes across the circled wagons, picturing the hundred-odd Traveling People inside. She looked across the long line of villagers, at least triple their number, shivering in the snow, waiting for orders.

Heloise's orders.

"I don't think"—Heloise pointed with her knife-hand, taking in all the assembled people—"that it matters what I wish anymore."

Sir Steven trotted into view, his horse stepping awkwardly through the thick snow. "What are you doing?"

"Waiting," Heloise said.

"For what?"

"For the Traveling People to finish saying goodbye."

"How long will it take?" Sir Steven was clearly losing his struggle to keep the impatience out of his voice.

"What do you want, Sir Steven?" Heloise didn't bother to keep it out of hers.

"I need their knife-dancers. My riders have been out longer than I'd like, and I want to cover more ground. We have the Empire to our fore and those . . . things off our flank."

"They are called devils," Heloise said.

Sir Steven ignored the correction. "Can you not speak with them?"

Heloise finally turned to look at the First Sword. "They are sending one of their most honored Mothers up the wheel. If you want to interrupt them, go ahead. I would take your guard."

Sir Steven looked as if he were seriously considering it, then his face brightened, and he waved one red-gloved hand over his head. Heloise turned to see a rider in a red surcoat galloping toward them. The man's horse began sliding as it tried to forge through a high drift, and he finally leapt off, finishing the rest of the distance on foot. He bowed, a stiff incline of his head. "First Sword."

"I hope you have a report for me," Sir Steven said.

"Aye, sir. We've found them. A great slaughter. I've never seen the like."

Heloise's heart leapt. *Father.* The emotion warred with rising dread. The Imperial army, deployed to meet them in a field battle. One they would likely lose.

"A slaughter? The Empire or . . . or the creatures?" Sir Steven asked.

"They are together, sir. Or, at least, they were."

"What do you mean?" Sir Steven frowned.

"The devils, sir . . ." The man caught Sir Steven's glare and hastily corrected his words. "I mean the creatures, sir, it looks like they went on up the road after the young lady ran them off." He nodded toward Heloise.

"The Empire is dug in across the road," Sir Steven said.

"Not anymore, sir. The monsters did them worse than they did us."

Sir Steven's shoulders sagged with relief, and Heloise knew she should have been happy. But all she could feel was hope curdling in her gut. *No. Perhaps Father wasn't with them. Perhaps some survived.*

Her mouth was suddenly too dry to speak, and she was grateful when Sir Steven asked the question burning in her mind. "How many dead?"

"Didn't stay to count, sir. Just a squadron of us, and we didn't want to risk getting caught out on our own. It was . . . it looks like a great slaughter."

"That is not an answer. How many Imperial troops were slain?"

Heloise realized how haunted the scout's eyes looked, how hard he was working to keep his voice even. "Well, hard to tell, sir. But I think all of them."

"All of them," Sir Steven's voice cracked.

"Sir." The man looked at his feet.

"You mean to tell me that those animals slaughtered every single Imperial soldier, levy, and knight in their army? Reinforcements as well?"

"Couldn't say, sir. But they were . . . the dead were piled higher than my shoulder."

Sir Steven took a moment to master himself, slowly exhaled. "That is . . . fortunate."

"Did you see any captives?" Heloise asked. "Did any survive at all?"

The man glanced nervously at Heloise. "Begging your pardon, miss, but there were too many dead and too far off for us to tell who was a fighting man, and who a cook, and who a captive."

Sir Steven's face was pale with relief. "Well, it seems we will not have to fight a field battle after all, may the People be praised. Did you . . . were you able to tell how many creatures set upon them?"

"Hard to tell, sir. Their tracks turn the snow . . . well, you seen that, I know. Serjeant was saying it had to be a score, more maybe."

Heloise's swallowed a sob. A score. Maybe even more. Six had nearly been too much for them. How could her father have survived that?

"Did you see any . . . any of the creatures dead?" Sir Steven asked.

"No, sir, though perhaps they take their fallen with them."

Heloise knew it wasn't so. There were no dead devils because the Imperials had been powerless to kill any of them.

"A siege engine might do for the monsters," Wolfun offered. "Scorpions, or catapults."

Sir Steven shook his head. "We haven't the time to fell trees and quarry stone for siege engines. And I haven't the means to haul them once they're built."

He looked back up to the rider. "From one boiling pot to another, then. Thank you, trooper. You may return to your squadron with my thanks. Get yourself fed and rested. We'll have work before nightfall, I'm sure."

The man saluted and returned to his mount, struggled to catch his stirrup in the uncertain footing, and finally trotted away toward the Red Lords' column.

"Well, Heloise, it seems you will get your wish of parley, if there are any left to parley with. We will need another council, I think," Sir Steven breathed, "and soon."

"I will ask the Mothers as soon as they are finished."

· · ·

They marched north split in three.

Heloise marched in the center with the villagers behind her. The Hapti band continued along with them, wagons struggling in the heavy snow.

To their right, the Red Lords column marched in dressed and disciplined ranks, but Heloise could see their losses plainly. Worse, she could see the toll the devils' attack had taken on the soldiers' courage. Shoulders were slumped, eyes darting fearfully toward the woods.

The Sindi and the Brock bands held themselves apart now, breaking the snow in sullen silence, some fifty paces to Heloise's left. Onas did not return to his post at Heloise's side. She could see him in the drover's seat of his mother's wagon, bent over the reins. Xilyka remained at Heloise's side as always, but Heloise could catch her stealing glances at the Sindi and Brock wagons when she thought Heloise wasn't looking.

"If . . . if you want to go to them," Heloise ventured.

Xilyka cut her off with a curt shake of her head. "My people are there." She pointed to the Hapti wagon where Mother Florea still handled the reins expertly, despite her age.

"I'm . . . I'm sorry . . ." Heloise said.

Xilyka looked up at her, puzzled. "For what?"

"For . . . for Leahlabel." *For everything. For dragging you along on this march.*

Xilyka waved a hand. "The Wheel turns. We cling to it as it rises and as it falls. Wasn't you who killed her. Onas knows that. They all do."

Heloise swallowed her relief. *She wants to stay.* That thought was followed by another. *Stop testing her, you fool. Sooner or later she will get sick of it and decide to leave after all. You are a woman grown and the leader of an army. Act like it.*

The split in the Traveling People and the constant threat of the devils hung over the army. They marched in silence, eyes wary, the stumbling gallop of the Red Lords' picket riders circling them. Heloise was beginning to feel tired, not just of the march, but of the tension, of her body always ready for the dozens of conflicts in bloom around her—Onas and his suit, her villagers and their condemnation of the Traveling People's "heresy," her battle against the Order. Heloise glanced up at Xilyka's banner snapping overhead, a symbol of the one people she doubted they would ever be. Heloise shook her head, remembering spring days in Lutet, fishing in the river with Basina. Her biggest worries then had been mastering her letters and which boy her parents would choose for her betrothal. She could scarcely believe those things had worried her at all, that they had ever seemed more than laughably small.

Heloise was lost in her reverie as the light began to fail, sinking into the rhythm of the march, feet up, feet down. The monotony helped drag her mind from worry, soothed by the sound of the snow beneath the machine's metal feet. *Crunch. Crunch. Crunch.*

*Squish.*

Heloise froze, looked up.

The sheet of unbroken white had given way to sudden, slick black, a river of rancid muck that cut across their path, then matched it, moving steadily up the road toward the capital. All around her, the army had frozen mid-step, staring at the ground.

The earth was churned to mud beneath the slime, here and there refrozen to leave a massive clawed footprint in stark relief. *Sacred Throne*, Heloise thought, taking in the vast landscape of rancid black, stretching out past her field of vision. *How many devils must have passed through here?*

Wolfun pointed with a spear. "We seem, your eminence, to have found the Imperials."

"Sacred Throne," Barnard breathed, as Heloise squinted into the deepening dark.

The Imperial troops had thrown up earthworks, long ramparts of dirt piled as high as a man and set with sharpened sticks. There was no doubting they would have meant death for any person attempting to scale them to reach the defenders behind.

Death for people, but not for devils.

The earthworks were smashed clean through in places, stomped flat in others. Here and there, Heloise could make out broken banner-poles, their pennants trailing in the mud. The line of mounded dirt spanned the entire road to the woods on either side, and of it all, only a single banner still flew—a triangle of black fabric embroidered with the image of a winged and armored Palantine in the traditional pose, arm extended, palm outward to ward off evil.

Heloise stared at it. "It did them no good."

Barnard snorted. "Just a geegaw of stitched silver. The real Palantine has three devils to her tale, so far. There'll be more before you're done, your eminence."

Heloise searched for words to respond, but her breath was stolen as they moved farther up the road and the earthworks came into clearer view.

Not earthworks.

Some of the ramparts were built from corpses, piled as high as Barnard was tall.

The Empire's vaunted cavalry, the fearsome riders who Sir Steven feared would crush them in a field battle, all dead. Horses and people mingled together, their broken limbs entangled, their heads shorn off or their bellies opened. Armor was cracked or dented, weapons snapped off at their hilts. It looked as though a storm had ripped through the Imperial line, so mighty that it had torn living men asunder, leather, metal, and flesh as if it had been nothing more than the paper that had been her family's stock-in-trade since she was a girl. Heloise didn't try to count, there were thousands of corpses at least. She was surprised at how quickly the shock of seeing all the corpses faded. *I am getting used to this.*

"Sacred Throne," Heloise said. "They tried to build walls from their own dead."

"For all the good it did them," Xilyka added.

"Thus to the false servants of the Emperor," Barnard said. "Thus to all who stand in the way of your righteous path."

"No," Wolfun breathed, "it was devils who did this."

"All things serve the Emperor," Barnard said. "Even them."

And at last the panic she had struggled so hard to swallow bubbled up. *Father.* There was no way he could have survived this. No way anyone could have. She gritted her teeth to keep the sob from escaping her throat. Xilyka looked up and placed a hand on the machine's knee. "We will find him, Heloise."

"But will we find him alive?" Heloise whispered.

"Wolfun"—she tried and failed to keep her voice from breaking— "take riders and search the field. I want to know if anyone survived." She avoided direct mention of Samson. She was the commander of an army, and he was just one man.

But Wolfun was no fool. "If he's here, we will find him, your eminence."

Wolfun tugged his forelock and reined his horse around. A moment later, three of the Red Lords' horsemen detached from their column and raced off after him.

They rode across the front of the grisly barricades and around, and Wolfun reined in sharply, waving his hand over his head. Heloise began jogging toward him without waiting for the others.

Xilyka managed to outpace even the machine's long strides, her head turning as she raced past the piled dead, scanning the trees, hands on the hilts of her throwing knives. Wolfun was already speaking as she slowed. "There are survivors."

He turned and trotted off without waiting for her to follow, but Heloise could already see where he was going, toward a line of squat shapes in the distance, outside the swath of black slime that marked the devils' passage.

Heloise jogged the machine after him, hope suddenly hot in her chest, squinting at the sudden whiteness. Xilyka cursed the thick snow before finally giving up and leaping on the machine's arm, clambering up it to seat herself on the reliquary box on its shoulder.

The line of shapes slowly resolved into a circle of supply wagons, piled high with earth and brush. The Red Lords' riders had pulled back out of bowshot.

Behind her Heloise could hear the crunching of horses breaking trail through the snow, the pounding of feet. The army was coming. She could hear the Red Lords' serjeants bellowing at their men to stay in formation as some broke off from the rearguard to loot among the dead in the earthworks.

Before long, Sir Steven was at her side, his knights forming a wedge behind him. The lighter armored Red Lords' archers were busy stretching out in a skirmish line beside them, planting sheaves of arrows head down in the snow. Heloise's villagers formed a tight knot behind her, all three bands of the Traveling People driving their carts into a circle beside her.

One of Sir Steven's outriders galloped over to them from the supply wagons. Wolfun galloped beside him.

"How many?" Sir Steven asked his outrider.

"Less than a hundred, maybe half that many," Wolfun answered, speaking to Heloise. The Lysian tugged his metal cap off his head, scratched at his bald pate, whistle-spat through the gap in his brown teeth. "And those left're done hard, and no mistake."

"Will they fight?" Sir Steven asked, as if Wolfun had spoken to him.

Wolfun slowly canted an eye toward the First Sword, paused for a long moment before answering. "Aye, I suppose so. They've just stood off all the devils from hell, so I don't imagine they'll be cowed by men in red dresses."

Sir Steven ignored the man's disrespect and spurred his horse forward. His bodyguard spurred after him, calling him back out of bowshot.

"Xilyka, come with me," Heloise said, following him. "The rest of you stay here."

She strode to the First Sword's side just as he was cupping his hands about his mouth and shouting, "I am Sir Steven! First Sword to the Senate of the Free Peoples of the Gold Coast! Who commands here?"

The wind whipped his words across the blowing snow, echoing them about the wagon tops. Silence. A few arrows arced toward them, but they were half-hearted shots, carried wide by the gusting wind. Heloise could hear shouts and clanking metal behind the barrier of wagons.

The hope and terror mixing in her chest bubbled up through her throat until it formed into a shout. "Father? Father, are you there?"

"Well?" Sir Steven shouted again. Silence. "Shall I bring my army to you to demand my answer? Who will treat with me?"

Another long moment, with only the howling of the wind for a reply. *Enough.* Heloise shouted, "I am Heloise Factor of the village of Lutet. I am the one you call the 'Queen of Rats and Crows.' I killed the Emperor's Song with my own hands. Send out my father if you want to live."

All sound behind the wagons ceased. The silence dragged on so long that Heloise was about to speak again when the thumping of iron-shod boots on boards announced a man clambering onto a wagon's top. He straightened, his gray cloak flapping back from his leather armor. He held a long-hafted flail in his hands, its black iron head swaying at the end of its short chain.

He raised his head, the wind sweeping back his cowl, revealing his flashing blue eyes, his cruel mouth. "I am Brother Tone, the Emperor's Own. I lead this noble company, we who have thrown back the very tide of hell in the Emperor's name."

# 7

## THE ENEMY

*And the devils knew that they could not triumph over Him, and strove instead to bar his passage. They were thick upon him as a cloud of flies. And as they could not overcome Him, neither could they impede Him, and soon he came to grips with the enemy.*
—Writ. Ala. XII. 4.

And there he was, the man who had taken everything. She had expected to lose herself to anger, to charge in screaming.

Instead, she remembered the Song's eyes, going blank as she pushed the knife-arm home. The thrill of revenge had been brief, and bright, and over the instant the Song breathed his last, leaving her with only his broken body. When life was stripped away, all people were the same limp meat. You couldn't feel triumph over a side of beef, couldn't crow victory over a leg of mutton.

Looking at Tone, she knew it would be the same. Her mother would still be dead. Sigir would still have betrayed her. She grasped for the hatred, conjured the memory of every wrong he had done her since she had first met him on the road to Hammersdown. It was no use. He was flesh and blood slowly making its way to the grave. She could hasten that journey, but it wouldn't give her justice.

Wolfun trotted to her side. "Keep Barnard back," she said to him.

The Lysian nodded and reined his horse around. The ambush against the Order outside Lutet had been utter chaos, and Heloise couldn't be sure if Barnard realized it was Tone who had killed his son Gunnar, but she couldn't risk him going mad with rage when there was a chance her father might still be alive.

She had imagined demanding Samson in a commanding roar, but her words came out in a strangled croak. "Where is my father?"

Tone met her eyes silently. The last slivers of hope pulsed, slowly drifting away.

And then, a shout from behind the barricade. "You bastard! We had a deal! Let me go!"

The world shrank to a tunnel between Heloise and the barricade cart. She took a step and Tone held out a hand. "Come closer, and you lose him."

"Lose me!" Two more Pilgrims clambered up onto the cart's top to stand beside Tone. They held Samson between them. Her father looked much the same as when he had ridden out, save a gash across his forehead, old and badly healed. His hands were unbound.

"We had a deal," Samson spat. "You swore in the Shadow of the Throne. I kept faith. Now stand here in front of what's left of your people, and in the full view of my daughter and her army, and cry false. Do it, so all can see just what you are."

Heloise started to take another step, but she could see the Pilgrims' flails, held at the ready mere handspans from her father's head. She froze, eyes moving from her father's face to Tone's and back as the two locked gazes.

At last, Tone looked away. "Release him."

"Holy brother!" began one of the other Pilgrims.

"I said release him! He plied arms against the devils! He made no effort to flee, and I seem to remember him saving your life, Brother Althred, or have you forgotten so quickly?"

The Pilgrim reddened and looked at his feet.

"Go, Samson Factor," Tone said. "Go to your precious daughter before I change my mind. My debt to you is paid. When I meet you again, it will be as an enemy."

Samson leapt from the cart, sprinting the distance to Heloise. She dropped the machine to one knee, opening the shield arm to receive him, terrified that an arrow would find his back before he reached her. He collided with the machine's metal knee, wrapping his arms around it, and Heloise folded the shield across his back to cover him.

She struggled to keep the tears from her voice, failed. "Oh, Father. I thought I'd lost you. Are you hurt?"

"I'm fine, Heloise." Samson wept openly. "Oh, Sacred Throne, it is good to see you again."

Heloise choked back a shuddering sob, keenly aware of the eyes of the entire army on them. "I should never have sent you . . . I should . . ."

"Peace, Heloise," Samson said. "No harm came to me, we are together again."

"What happened?"

"They fell on us as soon as we left you. Brought us here with them. Tone recognized me, wanted to bargain with me, but the Sojourner was for sending me on to the capital. They were still arguing when the devils came."

"And you fought?"

"Not at first. They had me tied up in their chapel tent, but once they started getting the worst of it, they armed every groom, page boy, and sutler. At last they cut me loose and gave me a spear, promised me freedom if I'd fight. Looks like the bastard made good on it."

Heloise looked back up at the Pilgrim. His cloak was little more than stained rags hanging off his battered armor. Only his eyes matched the man Heloise knew, and even they were . . . changed somehow. Moving too quickly, trying to see everything at once.

"Heloise Factor." Tone's voice was still haughty, but Heloise could hear the strain in it. "I see you have taken service with the Emperor's enemies. I should not be surprised. Heretics are all the same."

She knew she should step forward to face him, but she couldn't bring herself to move away from her father. "We're not heretics." Heloise gestured to the banner Florea had made. "We're just people, tired, hungry, sick of this cold. Same as you."

"You are not the same as us," Tone said. "You are still a dog of hell, and I am still the Hand of the Emperor."

"If you are the Hand of the Emperor, then tell me, why are the devils here?" Heloise asked. "Tell me what happened."

"Do not presume to—"

"Tone!" Heloise's shout stopped his words. "The devils attacked both of us. Answer me. *Help* me. Why would the Emperor let this happen?"

Tone was silent for a long time. At last his shoulders sagged, and he leaned heavily on his flail. "I do not know. I must return to the capital to ask Him. I have restored your father to you. For that alone, you must let me go."

"Your cloak is gray," Samson said. "Will the Emperor speak to a mere Pilgrim?"

"He may," Tone replied, "but if He will not, there is the Congregation of the Faithful."

"The who?" Heloise asked.

"He is a lying brigand," Samson hissed. "Do not listen to him."

Tone gave a short bark of a laugh. "Even before you succumbed to heresy, Heloise Factor, there were mysteries of the faith you did not know. You prayed to the Emperor before you slept at night. I devoted my every waking moment to His service. There are reasons why the veil might be torn, and means to Knit it. Heretic though you are, whatever you think of me and my Order, the devils are much worse. Your father is with you. He is unharmed. Let me go and I will do what I can to repair this."

"Barnard, no!" She heard Wolfun's shout from behind her, turning to a grunt as the huge tinker ripped free of him and came racing for Tone.

Heloise stood in a rush, blocking his path. Barnard's eyes were shining, his breath coming in tight gasps that left no doubt he recognized the man who had killed his son.

"Your eminence"—Barnard's hands were white knuckled on his hammer's haft—"you know who that—"

She had no time to make Barnard understand that killing Tone would no more restore his children to him than her mother to her. She thought of Sigir, kicking as he burned, of the Song, gurgling as the light left his eyes. She thought of the yawning gulf the first death had opened, and how the second one had only made it wider. "I know who it is, Barnard."

"He dies!" Barnard shouted, then took a step toward Tone. Heloise moved the machine to intercept him.

"Your pet tinker is right." Heloise turned to see Onas approaching with the Mothers of all three bands. "We place the lives of more than twenty Traveling People at that gray-cloaked bastard's feet. We did not agree to quit our ways and fight the Order only to let them run. He owes for what he has done. They all do. We are agreed on this."

"We are *not* agreed," Mother Florea said, "and it is for the Mothers to speak on this, not some boy." The Sindi and Brock Mothers looked uncomfortable but said nothing.

"You speak now of the old ways?" Onas sounded every bit as

haughty as Tone. "Look around you, Mother. Everything has changed. We are no longer traveling. We move like villagers, fight like villagers. Who is to say a man cannot speak for the band, as villagers do?"

Xilyka went to her mother's side. Her voice was a bare whisper that was still somehow loud enough to be heard by all. "You are no man."

Onas ignored her, drawing one of his hooked, silver-handled knives and pointing it at Tone. "He dies. All the cloaked ones do. We can let the soldiery go once we have plundered their goods."

Tone raised his flail. "This is how you repay the release of a prisoner in good faith? Come, then. You heretics love dancing and drinking and rutting like dogs. The Emperor's Own love only death."

Barnard advanced again and Heloise moved to block him, watching helplessly as Onas approached the Pilgrim.

"Let me go, your eminence!" Barnard shouted.

"Onas, no!" Heloise shouted, but the Sindi boy ignored her, eyes locked on Tone as he moved toward him.

"I regret I must deprive you all of the brawl you so clearly desire." Sir Steven's voice was long-suffering, exhausted. He waved his sword and a line of his infantry spread out between the army and Tone's circle of carts. "Captain, both parties will keep to their sides of your skirmish line. Should either attempt to cross, kill them."

One of the Red Lords' knights trotted his horse to take up a position on the right of the line. "Aye, First Sword."

"That man's life is forfeit!" Onas gestured fiercely with his knife.

"It is," Sir Steven said. "He will most certainly die in the full-ness of time, as we all do. But he will *not* die at this moment. And if he does, then so will you. Heloise Factor, a word."

Heloise turned to her father. He was safe now, but the thought of leaving him after he had just returned to her . . .

Sir Steven saw the direction of her eyes and shook his head. "A word *alone*, Heloise. You bested an army in that machine. You have nothing to fear from one man."

Xilyka made to follow as Heloise turned away, but Florea clutched her elbow and she reluctantly stayed put. Sir Steven walked his horse just out of earshot and awaited Heloise.

He studied her face for a moment. Heloise was surprised to see that he looked every bit as exhausted and wan as Tone. *War is a sickness*, she thought. *Even in victory, it eats you slowly from inside.*

"When first we met," Sir Steven said at last, "you asked for a man, presumably to dispose of him as you did the Emperor's Song. Here he stands, nearly close enough to touch. Your people are calling for his blood. Why do you not press to the attack?"

"He gave my father back to me."

"He gave your father back to you after taking him in the first place. I would not call that a kindness."

Heloise searched her heart. The numbness, the fatigue, threatened to overwhelm her, and it was a moment before she could master it enough to speak. "I have had enough killing."

Sir Steven frowned. "You have more killing ahead of you, I think."

"I know," Heloise said, "and I'll do it when I have to."

"And now?"

"And now I have a choice. I'm fighting to bring down the Order."

"Tone is of the Order," Sir Steven said.

"He is," Heloise sighed, "but he can't hurt anyone now."

"Until he returns to the capital and is reinforced."

"Then we fight him at the capital. What's one more flail?"

"He took your eye, Heloise."

"Killing him won't grow it back."

Sir Steven shaded his eyes, looked off to the north. Somewhere just beyond the horizon, the capital squatted astride the Imperial Way, what folk still called the "old king's road," over which all the trade wagons bigger than a Traveling Person's cart must travel sooner or later. At last, he shook his head. "You are wise beyond your years, Heloise. I have known many great commanders with less patience than you."

"Last council, you said I wasn't a commander."

"War is a great teacher, and a quick one. I agree with you, Heloise. The enemy are the monsters now. I cannot say how many there are exactly, but it is enough to be more than a match for us, with each one of them strong enough to take on any ten of our warriors." He pointed to the banner Florea had made. "It's as your Kipti girl says: we are all *people,* and there are precious few of us to face this threat. How much weaker will we be if we bloody ourselves against one another now?"

"Are you sure there are so many devils?"

"I am," Sir Steven said. "My outrider spoke true. A score, at least. You saw what a handful of them did to our combined force. And even more of them were here. And they have gone north. If we want to reach the capital, we are going to have to fight our way through. Alone, I'm not sure that we can do that. But together, we might have a chance."

"What good will a few more men do?"

"This is no mere few. These are the ones strong enough to fight off a horde of those things. Far more than assailed us. As hard done as they look, they are not to be lightly turned aside. And if they are with us when we reach the capital, they may be our strongest advantage if we wish to parley with the garrison."

"Why?" Heloise asked. "If the devils are free and the Order smashed? What's the point of taking the capital now?"

"Because if the Imperials somehow win out," Sir Steven said, "things will go back to the way they were. And because my people charged me with the task, and I will see it through. And lastly this: Tone may be right. He may be the one person among us who knows how to close the veil. And if that's true, we need to keep him with us."

"I thought you didn't believe in the veil, or in the devils."

Sir Steven was quiet for a long time. "After all I have seen"— he would not meet her eyes—"I do not know what to believe."

"All right." Heloise exhaled a shaking breath, looking back at Onas and Barnard. "Barnard might listen to me, but Onas will not."

"Then he will die," Sir Steven said.

Heloise nodded, walked back to where Tone stood atop his cart, still crouched and awaiting an attack, eyes darting between her and the angry crowd around Onas and Barnard. Her stomach churned. Between Tone's, Onas's, and Barnard's gazes, she felt as if a weight lay across her shoulders, heavy enough to challenge even the machine's great strength.

"We will not let you go," Heloise said.

Tone tensed, and she could hear mutters of approval from the army behind her.

"But you gave me back my father, so you will not be harmed," she went on. The mutters turned to gasps.

Tone frowned. "What then? Will we sit here swapping stories? Shall we stare at one another until we freeze?"

She shook her head. "We march north. To the capital. Together."

Shouts rose from both sides now. She heard Onas take two

steps toward her, draw up short as Xilyka interposed herself between them.

"Do you think," Tone's voice was tight with rage, "that I will have my people unlock the gates for you?"

"We're going to the capital. So are you. The Traveling People have a saying"—she glanced at Onas—"that there is no place so safe as the road when it is taken in company, and no place so perilous, when it is taken alone."

"Your eminence," Barnard said, low and dangerous, "you cannot ask me to travel with that man."

Onas brandished one of his knives, pointing at Tone. "That man dies!"

"No!" Heloise bellowed, facing him. "He lives! He and all his men! There are a score of devils between us and the capital! Maybe more! It's not a fight between us and the Order anymore! It's a fight between people and the armies of hell! I do not like these men"—she pointed to Tone—"any more than you, but if we're going to win, we need everyone able to hold a weapon."

"They are a rabble," Onas seethed. "Not enough to make a difference."

"They made a difference to an army of devils," Heloise said. "Enough of a difference that they're still alive."

"Your eminence," Barnard began.

"You are always calling me a Palantine!" Heloise spun on him. "You go on and on about how the Emperor speaks through me! Well, He is speaking through me now. He is telling you to obey me and leave Tone alone!"

Barnard gritted his teeth so hard that Heloise feared they would crack, but he made no move toward Tone.

Onas, however, advanced on the cart, forcing Heloise to move the machine between him and Tone.

"Get out of my way!" Onas shouted. Xilyka stepped forward, stopped only when Heloise raised her knife-arm.

"How can you stop me?" Onas shouted at Xilyka. "Have you become a villager already? That man murdered your people!"

Onas made to move around Xilyka. The Hapti girl flicked one of her throwing knives at his feet, sending him dancing back a few steps. A cry went up from the Sindi behind him, and a few of their knife-dancers moved forward, stopping at a gesture from Onas.

Onas backed away, spreading his hands, and Xilyka retreated toward Heloise. But Heloise could see the calm in his eyes, the set of his mouth. "Xilyka, no!"

But it was too late. Onas reversed himself, leaping forward. Xilyka's hand flashed to her waist, snatching another knife, but Onas was as fast as a lightning strike, already kicking out, catching her in the hand hard enough to send the blade spinning. Xilyka cried out and fell back, clutching her wrist. Onas leapt, vaulting clear over her head. He landed behind her, dodged past the Red Lord infantryman who tried to intercept him, then sprang again, landing on the cart's edge as nimbly as a cat on a branch, crouching, hooked knives glittering before him.

One of the Pilgrims beside Tone rushed him, flail held high over his head. Onas kicked the man in the chest, sending him tripping backward into Tone, who in turn knocked the third Pilgrim off the cart. Tone righted himself and snarled, swinging his flail crosswise at Onas. The Sindi boy danced sideways, so close to the cart's edge that his heels were out over empty air, sweeping down with his knives, knocking the iron head away. Tone twisted his wrists and the chain jerked, entangling one of the hooked blades, ripping it out of Onas's hands.

The Red Lords troops surged on the cart, but Heloise pushed

through them. "Get back! Don't hurt him!" They looked to Sir Steven, who raised a hand, gesturing them back.

The remaining Pilgrim tried to rise, and Tone stepped over him, raising his flail. "What will you do now? With only one of your little knives?"

"I don't need two knives to kill you," Onas said, reversing his grip on the blade and crouching. Heloise raced to the edge of the cart and froze. The machine was incredibly strong, but it was not subtle. She didn't know how she could intervene between the two fighters without harming either one.

And then a shape vaulted past her and landed on the cart, sending both Onas and Tone stumbling back. The figure turned, giving his back to the Pilgrim. "That's enough."

Samson, a spear in his hands.

"Get out of my way!" Onas hissed, raising his remaining blade.

Samson leveled the spear at Onas. "You heard my daughter. She leads here, not you. We will march north together. The Pilgrims *and* you. All of us."

"Why is your back to him?" Onas pointed his knife at Tone. "Do you love the Order so much?"

"He didn't attack you, boy," Samson said. "Get off this cart, and I'll give you my back too."

"I said get out of my way!" Onas launched himself at Samson, slashing with the knife. Heloise's father raised the spear haft, parrying the blow, overbalancing and falling backward, toppling into Tone and the remaining Pilgrim and sending them both over the cart's edge. Onas seized the spear with his free hand, kicked Heloise's father in the knee. Samson grunted, falling onto his back. Onas ripped the spear from his hands and threw it away, seizing Samson by the throat. "Stupid old man!"

Heloise launched herself at the cart, heedless of hurting

anyone now, sending the bottom of her shield skidding across the top, packed earth flying. She felt the shield's bottom collide with Onas, heard the Sindi boy yelp as he caught the full force of it, sending him tumbling into the snow on the cart's far side.

Heloise leapt after him, vaulting the cart easily, and caught a glimpse of the handful of Imperial soldiers who crouched inside the ring before she landed astride Onas, the machine's metal feet planted a handspan's distance from either side of his head. The metal creaked as she bent the machine at the waist, bringing the visor as close to Onas's face as she could. "Touch him again," she said, "and I will kill you."

Onas scrambled back from her on his hands, and Heloise straightened. He leapt to his feet as Samson reached her side. "Are you all right?" Heloise asked, not taking her eyes from Onas.

"I'm fine." Samson rubbed his knee. "Some fight in these old bones still."

Samson stabbed an angry finger at Onas. "The Order didn't kill your mother, the devils did that. And even if it had been Tone what took your mother, killing him won't bring her back. Won't bring my Leuba back, either. Or your boy, either, Barnard. Might make you feel fine for a moment, but only for a moment, and then we're down a pair of hands that can swing a stick against the real enemy."

Heloise looked over at Barnard. The giant man stood on the other side of the cart, arms folded across his chest, tears running down his face.

"I'm sorry, Barnard," Samson said, "but you know I speak true. This isn't a war between the Order and the villagers and the Kipti and the Red Lords anymore. It's a war between people and devils, and from what I've seen, we're going to need everyone fighting if we're to have a chance of hanging on."

Onas gestured at Tone, who leaned on his flail, watching

Samson in shock. "Hanging on for what? To see animals like this walk unpunished?"

Samson shook his head and straightened, some of the fire coming back into his eyes. "To save the ones that are left to us. I have a daughter, and a village. Barnard still has a wife and son. You have your band. Would you throw all that away just to sate your grief?"

And now Onas's rage and shock melted away, to be replaced by a grief so keen that it stole Heloise's resolve. As he turned to her, he said, "I *loved* you. Is that so little?"

*At last you speak true.* Any sympathy Heloise had felt for Onas drowned in the rising sickness in her stomach. "I never asked for it."

She remembered Clodio's words in the roundhouse, before she'd known devils were real. When the thought of driving a warmachine or leading an army would have seemed poor jests. *Love is good, and those who love are good.*

*No, Clodio,* she thought, *you were wrong. How can this be good?*

Onas took a step toward Heloise, and three knives sprouted in the earth just in front of his feet. "Don't," Xilyka said, appearing on the cart's edge.

And at last, Onas's face melted into tears, and he turned away, walking back toward his band's wagons. The Sindi followed in his wake, Giorgi throwing an arm around the boy's shoulders as they went.

Sir Steven trotted to her side. "That . . . that did not go well."

"No, it did not," Heloise said.

Heloise looked for Barnard, but he was gone, disappeared back into the knot of villagers. In the distance she could see the Sindi checking their horses' traces, chipping frost from the wheels of their wagons. Some of the drovers were already greasing the axles with the blocks of hardened animal fat they kept for the purpose, even though no order had been given to depart.

# 8

## HOW WE LOVE WHEN WE ARE FREE

*Mahesh fixed his kingdom as a shadow of the Emperor's glory, dark unto light. Where the people of the sunlit world toiled in the fields, the devils lay in repose. Where the people broke animals to the plow, the devils slaughtered all. Where the people set a table, the devils would have none. Where the people joined, husband to wife, the devils lay like with like, in defiance of the order of the world.*
—Writ. Lea. III. 2.

Just thirty Imperials had survived the devils' assault. They were mostly levy, with a single knight and one squadron of uhlans. Tone and his two fellow Pilgrims were all that remained of their chapter. All were hard-bitten types, scarred, silent, and steel-eyed. They camped beside the columns, far enough away that they would not be seen, and even then Sir Steven ordered a canvas wall to be erected.

"It is best," the First Sword said to Heloise, "if your people do not see them." He stationed a picket of red-caparisoned archers around them, in case Barnard or any of the villagers or Traveling People decided to finish what Onas had started, or in case Tone tried to escape.

Sir Steven erected a series of canvas walls for Heloise as well, so that the wind might keep off her, but she stood resolutely outside it. The wind bit at her, but she wanted to bear witness as the Sindi and Brock bands flicked the reins and started their wagons rolling, cutting fresh trail to the east. The Hapti alone remained behind.

"I should stop them," Heloise said. "We need them."

Xilyka shook her head. "Let them go, Heloise. You do not want the faithless at your side in a fight. They will do more harm than good."

But the words did nothing to cure the sadness and fear curdling in Heloise's gut, the certainty that she'd made a horrible mistake. "I've traded two bands of the Traveling People for a handful of Imperials who hate me."

Xilyka shrugged. "It's a fair trade."

"I cannot believe they will risk travel at night."

"The Traveling People are not found when they don't want to be. Night or day, makes no difference. They're going."

"They aren't the only ones." It was Poch Drover, approaching at the head of a knot of villagers. Many were from the villages that had joined after Lyse, near-strangers whose names she did not know. But there were others she did. Danad and Ingomer. Sarah Herber. People who she'd grown up with. Helga stood at the front of what looked like all the people of Seal's Rock. They had bundled together what supplies they had gleaned from the countryside, or had looted from the corpses on the battlefield while Heloise had parleyed with Tone.

"I stayed with you when Sald took his leave," Poch said. "I was shamed by what your mother said, but now I wish I'd had the courage to go with him. More shamed it took a heretic to show me what's what. But we've seen the way now, and it's not with you."

Heloise's stomach dropped. "You will follow this boy you call a 'heretic'?"

"He can't lead us worse than you," Poch said. "You have played the Palantine for too long. We're as glad as you are that Samson has been returned, but that don't mean we should take Tone into our bosom. If your place is with the Order, then ours is on the road."

Samson spat into the dirty snow. "You break faith with Heloise now? When the devils are among us?"

"We never *made* faith with her." Poch reddened. "The village went mad, and we had no choice but to come along. But all choices are equally bad now, so we will make the one in our hearts."

"And what will you do when the devils find you?" Samson seethed.

"The devils are there." Poch pointed north, in the direction of the capital. "We're not going there."

"Do you remember what Onas said when the Sindi band joined the fight at Lyse?" Xilyka asked. "You should. You were there."

"That doesn't . . ." Poch stammered.

"He said," Xilyka spoke over him, "that the Traveling People were through running. He said there was a new way now. And he was right. Running just delays the reckoning."

Poch stabbed an angry finger at the Sindi and Brock wagons, creaking their way slowly through the thick snow and into the darkness beyond. "Then what in the Shadow of the Throne are *those* Traveling People doing?"

Xilyka spat. "Those are not Traveling People. Those are villagers on wheels."

"Well, if they're villagers, then we're in good company." Poch spun on his heel.

Samson took a step toward Poch, but Heloise raised her shield to stop him. "Let them go. I don't want a single person with me who doesn't want to be."

But as she said the words, she watched the line behind Poch. In the gathering dark, she had missed how very long it was. She watched it snake out, twenty people, forty, sixty, more.

The last of the renegades marched out of the camp and into the trail left by the Sindi and Brock wagons. Heloise surveyed the remnant of the people with her. They were much fewer now.

Barnard stood beside her, silent, watching them go.

"Do you want to go with them?" Heloise asked. "You can, I won't stop you."

Barnard's voice was raw. "You are a Palantine. Whatever you decide is right."

"And now I am a Palantine with half my army gone."

"The Emperor tests us, your eminence. When he went alone among the devils, when all his saints and his knights had fallen away, he too doubted. The Writ tells us that he cursed the old gods who had abandoned him."

"I'm sorry, Barnard. I know how this hurts you, but the fight has changed."

"You've done right, Heloise," Samson said. "Look at all you've done already. If you will not remember the Writ, remember what you said to us at Lyse. You told us that freedom is an impossible mountain that we are already climbing. It was impossible that we should survive a wizard, that we should face a devil and live, that we should ambush the Order and escape, that we should travel with the Sindi, that we should take Lyse. It was impossible that we should defeat the Order when they came for us. We did all of those things, Heloise. And we will do more. Without Poch and his mumbling ingrates. Without the Sindi and the Brock."

"It is the Emperor's will," Barnard said, and Heloise knew he wasn't referring to Samson's speech.

"Maybe," Samson said, "but it is also *our* will, and that has proved to be a force to be reckoned with."

Barnard shook his head and left, wandering back toward the remains of the army. Heloise watched him go, her father's words keeping the despair at bay.

She turned to him. "Thank you, Father."

Samson's smile was so sudden and so grateful that Heloise felt a pang of guilt. Had it been so long since she'd given him a kind word?

"I am . . . I am so glad you are back with us," she began.

"When they first took me"—he cuffed away a tear—"I will admit that I lost hope, but then I remembered that I had you to come back to, and that kept me on. I prayed to the Emperor to bring us back together, and He answered me. I have made another prayer, that He will give us back our lives as they were in Lutet, when we were at peace."

"Lutet . . . Our lives seem so . . . long ago," Heloise said.

"We are still living our lives, my sweet girl. It is just . . . different now, is all."

"It's less."

"Life is not a thing that is more or less, Heloise. It is just a thing that is. That is what we mean when we speak of the Emperor's will, what the Kipti mean when they talk of their Great Wheel."

"It is less," Heloise said. "Look at me, Father. *I* am less. I have lost my eye, my hand, my teeth. There is no Sigir, no mama, no Basina. Now, there is no Leahlabel."

"Those are different things, Heloise."

"They are not. They are all . . . parts of me. Parts that keep getting . . . cut away."

Samson wiped his eyes again. "There was a time, you know, when I thought I could protect you. I would have seen you safe and happy, with a fine husband and children of your own. But

that was not the Emperor's will. His will was that you should sur-
pass me, and be a woman grown before your time, and lead an
army. And now, there is nothing I can do to keep you safe. I cannot spare you the horror of war, and I cannot give you the comfort that will see you through it. I may be a factor who knows his
letters, but I am no sage. I keep . . . scrambling my fool brains for
a way to help you, for a way to get you out of that Throne-cursed
machine and back home where you belong. But there is . . . nothing. What kind of a father am I now? I cannot rear you. I cannot
teach you. All I can do is follow you, and help you win . . . whatever it is you decide you want."

The need to give him what he wanted, to climb out of the machine and into his arms, was so great that it nearly overwhelmed
the terror that gripped her at the thought of leaving the machine,
the anxiety that if she embraced her father, she would be Heloise
again, not the armored saint she needed to be.

Nearly, but not enough. *You have him back. Tell him you love
him. Tell him right now.* She looked at him, feeling the words building behind her lips.

Samson looked up. "Perhaps there is one thing I can do for
you."

The words twisted in her mouth, came out as "What do you
mean?"

Samson gestured at the canvas wall behind him. She could
hear the crackle of a fire and the soft bubble of water, see the
steam wafting over the top. "Hot water," her father said, "and pri-
vacy. Come out of the machine, just for a moment, and wash."

All thought of love and family vanished. The world outside the
machine was too close, the sky too vast. The devils could be anywhere, or more assassins. Maybe Onas or Poch had left someone
behind and . . . Heloise could feel sweat breaking out on her neck
and forehead despite the cold. Her heart raced.

Samson touched her foot through the machine's frame. "Heloise, please. Just for a moment. I can call some of the wives to assist you if you like."

"I . . . can't." She couldn't breathe, couldn't think.

"Of course you can." He reached up to undo the buckle around her thigh. "Let me help you."

*No*, Heloise thought, but her throat had closed. Her muscles felt liked fresh-forged iron thrust into water. *Sacred Throne, he is going to take me out and there's nothing I can do . . .* She watched her father work the buckle as if she were floating outside her own body, powerless to do anything other than observe.

And suddenly Xilyka appeared, seizing Samson's wrist gently, but firmly. "I'll see to her, Master Factor."

Samson stared at the Hapti girl. "She's my daughter."

"Just so," Xilyka agreed, "but I'm sure you'll agree that she's a bit old now to be undressed by a man, even her own kin."

"I'm not going to undress her, I just want to take her out of the—"

"All the same, best to let a lady see to it."

Samson sputtered, but Xilyka ignored her, leading Heloise behind the canvas sheet wall. A small wooden tub had been placed there, filled with steaming water from an iron cauldron that had been returned to a small fire burning in a clearing in the snow.

"It's all right," Xilyka said.

"You don't understand." Heloise's voice shook so hard that she had to bite off each word. "I. Can't. Come. Out. I. Just. Can't."

"Heloise, listen to me. You don't have to come out now, but I am sworn to protect you from dangers, even yourself. If you never leave the machine, it will kill you as surely as an assassin's blade. You must get clean. Loosen the straps, don't take them off. I will see to the rest."

"What are you going to . . ." She could feel the tears sliding down her cheeks, going cold in the chill air before they reached her chin.

"Heloise." Xilyka clambered onto the machine's knee, touched Heloise's cheek. "I am your friend. It's all right. You can trust me."

Heloise leaned into Xilyka's hand, warm and soft. It wasn't just that it was beautiful Xilyka who had fought for her. It was that it was a *person*. Another person, and not her father, touching her. "Thank you."

A camp stool beside the tub had been piled with old red surcoats. Xilyka ripped two strips off of one and dunked one in the hot water. She climbed back onto the machine's knee and scrubbed at Heloise's foot. The touch of hot water was wonderful. Xilyka alternated the wet cloth with the dry one, wiping away the water before it could go cold. Heloise winced at the dry cloth's touch, looked down, saw the red welts there. "Bedsores."

"I will clean you this way until you are ready to come out."

Xilyka's touch, the chance to be alone with someone, to just be herself, was so overwhelming that Heloise wept, great hiccuping sobs that wracked her whole body. For her mother, for Sigir, for the return of her father, for Barnard, even for Onas and Poch and those who had turned on her. She was so tired of fighting. "I will never be ready."

"The Wheel turns," Xilyka said. "You will see."

She worked her way up Heloise's legs, lifting her shift to expose them. Wiping wet, then dry, returning to the tub to soak the rag in fresh water before starting again. Heloise's relief and sadness began to change as Xilyka worked her way toward her cleft and her belly, sliding into the same melting, floating sensation she'd felt on the night she'd kissed Basina. She looked down at Xilyka, watching her black curls cascading over her shoulders as she worked, brass rings clacking together. Heloise admired the fading light sliding off the muscles in her shoulders and neck, the shadows pooling in the hollow of her throat. She was so different from Basina—dark where Basina was light, mischievous where Basina was frank, and most of all, free, where Basina walked the same path as all villager women—husband, family, the soft prison of home and hearth.

The Hapti girl looked up, and Heloise's breath caught. She had thought it was safe to kiss Basina, to tell her that she loved her as she truly did, and she had been repaid in lashing thorns, a head-long dash through the woods in the dark. *That was when all this truly began. The fighting and the Order and the devils.* She knew it wasn't true even as she thought it, but that was the way with some ideas. They planted in your mind, and nothing you did could un-seat them. She wanted to give in to Xilyka's touch, to let herself feel what she felt, without shame, without fear, but she remem-bered Basina's hands coming up, the look of shock and anger on her face. *You said you loved me. Not like friends. Like a girl loves a boy.*

Xilyka stood, running her hands up under the shift and over Heloise's breasts. She pressed her forehead against the metal visor and looked into Heloise's eyes through the slits.

Heloise's head was stuffed with clouds, her stomach floating up into her throat. When she did speak, it was nonsense that came out. "I am not beautiful."

Xilyka laughed, a soft, warm sound that reminded Heloise of the hollow wooden chimes Deuteria hung outside her door. She reached under the gorget and ran her thumb over the scars that lifted the corner of Heloise's mouth, that puckered around the place where her eye had once been. "This face has been ravaged, I will not lie, but it is *Heloise's* face. This body has lost teeth and an eye and a hand. But it is *Heloise's* body and Heloise lives in-side it, just as you live inside this machine. I do not look at the machine when I want to see you, and I do not look at your body when I want to see you, either. You are Heloise, and Heloise is so beautiful that she shines like winter stars.

"Do not doubt your beauty, Heloise. That is why Onas left. Because he loved you, and you would not have him."

"How did you know?"

Xilyka laughed. "I may not be a Mother yet, but that doesn't mean I am a fool. It is always this way with men. They seek to own a woman, and when they cannot, they go mad."

Heloise thought about that for a moment. "Clodio said love was this and love was that, and he wasn't wrong, but he left things out. Love is rage, too, and madness."

"Love is like the Wheel—it turns as it will, and rolls over everything. If we are lucky, we ride the spokes as they rise, and if we are unlucky, we are crushed beneath the rim as it falls."

*Now*, Heloise thought, *we are talking of love. Now is the time.*

She was elated and sick with terror at the same moment. Her stomach felt as small as a pebble, her head as big as a boulder. "I . . . I loved someone," she began, "and I never told her. I mean, I whispered it once. But I never really *told* her. Not when she could listen . . . not when it mattered." *There, I said "her"; if she will hate me, she will do it now.*

She pushed the terror down again. *You have been terrified every day since the night you fled Basina. What's one more thing?* "I'll never get the chance to say it to Basina," Heloise went on, "but I have the chance now."

Xilyka froze, drying rag suspended inside the metal frame over Heloise's shoulder.

Heloise swallowed again, stepping fully off the cliff. The fear finally lapped itself, and Heloise found herself suddenly serene. It freed her to speak, and the words came rushing out. "I love you. I love you and I would do the same thing Onas did. I would go mad, and I would fight and scream and do what's wrong, and I would do it all gladly, because even if Clodio was wrong about what love was, he wasn't wrong that without love, life is just a shadow. And I don't want to beat the devils and save the world if shadows are all that are left to me."

Her words trailed off, and she froze as still as Xilyka, waiting for the girl to look up, to scream at her, to strike her. It would be worth it. With the words said, she already felt so light she wondered if she would float out of the machine and into the sky.

But Xilyka only returned to her cleaning. "How did she die, this great love of yours?"

Heloise swallowed grief at the memory. "She died fighting to protect me."

Xilyka scrubbed at a stubborn smudge of dried blood. "Against your famous devil?"

Heloise let the audible hitching of her throat stand as a reply.

Xilyka nodded. "Then it is no wonder that you loved her. A shame she was born a villager. It is the place of women to fight. Sindi Mothers leave it to their men, and they are wrong to do so."

"I know that now," Heloise said, "and it's why I love you."

Xilyka looked up, and her smile took Heloise's breath away. "And is your love so fickle? Are you so eager to forget your Basina?"

"I will never forget her, and I would never want to."

Xilyka returned her hands to Heloise's hip, though she had already cleaned it once. "Because she is what you have lost. Because the pain of it lifts you up to lead."

"Because the pain of it is all that's left of her. Even now, my memories of her are . . . I'm losing them. I can't hold it all in my head. There's only room for so much, and . . . I need other memories more, like how to fight, and how the machine works, and . . ."

Xilyka reached inside to touch Heloise's hand, and Heloise

realized that she was crying. *Stupid*, Heloise thought. *You've ruined the moment.*

But Xilyka twined her fingers with Heloise's. "It's all right, Heloise. I understand."

"I don't want to lose the memories," Heloise went on. "I have nothing of her, not a lock of hair, not a drawing of her face, not a ribbon from her dress. But memories . . . they're like water. No matter how tight you try to hold them, they just run through your fingers . . . But the pain, Xilyka . . ."

Xilyka's eyes were knowing, "The pain is eternal. And after a time, it no longer hurts. After a time, it is the sweetest thing left of those we wish were still with us."

"How do you know?"

"I have not lost as you have, but I am the daughter of the sole Mother in the Hapti band, and I have learned at her feet. I would restore your Basina to you, if I could. But since you must endure her loss, remember this: loss can curdle, it can break a woman. Not all can . . . use it as you have."

"Use it for what?" Heloise asked.

Xilyka gestured, the sweep of her arm taking in the army camp beyond the canvas walls, fires beginning to dot the landscape as villagers, Traveling People, and Red Lords troops settled in for the night. "Do you not see the change you have wrought in the world?

"No, Heloise," she husked, "you are lucky in your loss."

And now a tear tracked its way down Xilyka's cheek. "And how lucky am I to be loved by one such as you?"

Xilyka leaned in and planted a long kiss on the war-machine's visor, as close to Heloise as the metal would allow.

When she finally spoke, Xilyka's voice was thick. "When we have beaten them, and we will beat them, then you will be ready to come out from there, and I will show you how people love when they are free."

# 9

## COME TOO LATE

*All acolytes doubt. It is the flick of Mahesh's wrist, his flail-*
*ing for the soul as it passes out of his grip for all time, before*
*we finally close up the mind, fortify it against hell's grip.*
*And do you know they always doubt in the same way? If the*
*Emperor is so great, if in Him alone can we be redeemed,*
*why does He not just make us happy here and now? While*
*we still draw breath? Why not just draw the dead from*
*their graves, and make the ones we love live again? They*
*do not understand that this would be the greatest cruelty,*
*far worse than any fate the devils could imagine. To take a*
*redeemed soul, to allow it to bask in the light of the Throne,*
*to know the Emperor's holy presence, and then to snatch it*
*away, and force it to walk the world again? Only a devil*
*could ever wish for such a thing.*

—From the lecture notes of Father Winaclos

They left the next morning. Heloise's column could scarcely have mustered more than a hundred villagers, tiny beside the Red Lords host. They had both lost many people, the Red Lords to the devils, and Heloise to desertion, but Sir Steven's column could far better sustain the losses than hers.

The devils had left a wide avenue up the old road to the capital, a lane of slick black, wet and stinking. Fresh snow had fallen during the night, but it could find no purchase in the mire of the devils' passage. Most of the Red Lords' troops pulled their surcoats up over their mouths and noses, and Heloise saw her own people follow suit.

The Imperial troops marched in an uneasy knot between the two columns, weapons at the ready. "Can't believe we're letting them keep those," Wolfun said.

"We'll be glad we did if the devils come," Heloise said. "There are too few of them to fight us anyway."

"With respect, your eminence, are they the hard-bitten fighters we need with us? Or are they too few to count?"

Heloise turned the machine to regard the old Lysian. The suit groaned with the movement, and Wolfun shrank into the blanket he'd draped over his shoulders as its shadow fell across him. His horse shied away a step.

"Both," Heloise said, and flashed him a smile that she knew her scars made terrifying.

Looking over at Tone and his people, she saw the truth of the statement. They were few, indeed, prisoners behind the bars of two armies. But they also looked ready to fight, alert, gaze darting from the villagers to the Red Lords to the woods beyond, where the devils might emerge at any moment.

But she knew that would be no comfort to Barnard. The huge tinker's eyes were fixed sullenly forward, as Onas's had been when he had left Heloise's side and returned to his band. *Seeing Tone out of the corner of his eye is hurting him.*

"Barnard." She turned to the huge tinker. "You will lead our column. Father, come with me." She made no mention of Xilyka, knowing that the Hapti girl would never leave her side.

Barnard said nothing, only stared straight ahead.

"Where are we going?" Samson asked.

"We are taking Brother Tone, and only Brother Tone, to the head of the army. He can't cause trouble if he is separated from his people."

She set off toward the knot of Imperial troops, who stiffened at her approach. "Brother Tone," Heloise said, "we are three armies now, and so the three leaders should march out front."

The other Pilgrims immediately began whispering to him, and the looks on their faces and the few words she did catch made plain what they were advising. Tone raised a weary hand. "If they want to kill me, there isn't much I can do about it now," he said to them. "Lead the way, Heloise Factor."

Sir Steven didn't appear at all surprised when Heloise and her entourage arrived, and he sent his groom to bring a horse for the Pilgrim. Mounted, Tone fell in between the First Sword and Heloise, riding in silence. His flail remained at his shoulder, the links draped across it and the head hanging down his back. Heloise could feel his presence as when she stood beside a raging fire, the heat of it making itself known even when she looked away.

After a while, Tone closed his eyes and began muttering quietly under his breath. It drew uncomfortable stares from Sir Steven and his bodyguard, but Heloise recognized the words of the Writ. All Pilgrims memorized them, and Sojourners took pride in their ability to recite the entire work from beginning to end, word for word.

At last Sir Steven could take Tone's quiet chanting no longer. "Pilgrim, you spoke before of the Congregation of the Faithful. If dealing with these creatures depends on it, I would know how it works. Will you tell me more about it?"

"I will not." Tone did not open his eyes. "I am not in the habit of discussing the mysteries of the faith with heretics."

"We are riding to the liberation of your capital," Sir Steven said. "You might show a little more gratitude."

And now Tone did open his eyes. "I am no fool. Devils or no, you are riding to the conquest of my capital."

Sir Steven gave no reply.

"The Order," Heloise said, "always talks about knowing the Writ. Here we are, trying to learn . . ."

"The *Writ*," Tone snapped, "not the mysteries. That is the nature of heresy. Always needing to understand how things work. Have you ever stopped to consider that asking questions does you no good? You don't need to know. The mind is like a gate. The more tightly it is closed, the less the chance that the enemy will gain entrance. That is what faith is. It is believing in a thing, even though you don't understand it. Understanding is the gateway to heresy."

"Understanding is the gateway to knowledge," Heloise said.

"And where has your knowledge gotten you?" Tone asked. "Did it save your village? If you had cried out to the Order when your wizard friend had first confessed to you, none of this would have come to pass."

She pictured Clodio, his body cast off like a rag as the devil stepped through. Her friend, killed, and here this man who had taken her eye blamed her for it. The rage came hot and fast and she opened her mouth to respond.

But Samson spoke first. "You're right." Her father sounded exhausted. "It didn't save Leuba. It didn't save Hammersdown. But your precious worship didn't save your army outside the walls of Lyse, or from the devils.

"Knowledge. Faith. None of it ever saves anyone."

They rode in silence after that for a long time. Heloise was surprised that Tone was the one to break it. "I am . . . sorry for your wife. I never wanted that."

Samson shrugged. "Doesn't matter. It won't bring Leuba back."

When Tone finally spoke, his voice broke. Heloise was shocked by the raw edge of it. "Do you think I like this? Do you think I do this because it gives me pleasure to kill and to burn?"

If the pain in Tone's voice moved her father, he gave no sign. Samson merely shrugged again. "Doesn't matter."

"I do what I do"—Tone sounded angry now—"because I know what is at stake, and now you do too." He gestured at the woods, and presumably at the devils that might be lurking there.

Samson's exhaustion gave way to anger. He pounded a fist on the pommel of his saddle. "We always knew. We always knew and it didn't frighten us so badly that we tried to burn the world."

Those last words killed all talk between them, and they rode on in silence. Heloise stole a glance at Tone, could see the lines on his forehead, the trembling of his jaw. This was the man who had laughed as he took her eye, who had sworn he would take her father's life. Heloise had thought him a devil himself, maybe worse. And yet now, looking at him, he looked only another man. Wan, hungry, miserable.

And then he spoke. "There is another book."

The silence that hung across the group was total, as if they feared that by speaking, they would frighten Tone back into silence. "Apart from the Writ. One that only the Order reads."

"What is it?" Heloise asked.

"The Book of Mysteries," Tone said. "It relates the deeds of the Emperor after he drew the veil shut. It speaks of where the devils dwell, how they come forth, and how they are sent back."

"They come forth from wizardry," Heloise said.

"They do." Tone nodded. "But only singly, not so many as attacked us."

"How then . . ."

"For the veil to be rent so . . . A wizard alone may admit a single devil. Perhaps two. But two or three wizards together may rend the veil wide enough."

The rage came so suddenly that Heloise nearly choked. "It was you. At Lyse. You sent three of them against us."

"Those were not wizards," Tone said, but his voice was uncharacteristically soft.

"What were they, then?" Heloise growled.

"The Mysteries also tell us that the Emperor chooses his instruments, passes his power into them."

"Do they tell you that?" The lie was so plain that Heloise was staggered by the ease with which Tone told it. "And is this power from the Emperor the same as the power wizards wield? Sacred Throne!"

"How convenient." Sir Steven laughed. "When Imperials use wizardry, it's suddenly a gift from the Emperor."

"It is written!" Tone's cheeks colored. "I will not excuse the Emperor's own deeds to heretics!"

"I was at Lyse," Heloise snarled. "I heard the Song from outside the walls, as loud as if he were standing next to me. I saw the wall come apart. The Traveling People can feel wizardry when it is used; they say they felt it then."

"What they felt was the hand of the Emperor on his chosen people, if they felt anything at all. Heretics say what they will."

"And so do you," Heloise said. "You had us Knit Hammersdown for doing something you do every day."

Tone swallowed hard, stared at his horse's mane. "Tell me . . . did you see . . . a light?"

Heloise's stomach turned over. "We did. It was . . . wrong. Sick."

"A killing light. The Book of Mysteries speaks of it. Those touched by the Emperor should not have rent the veil so."

"But it *is* rent," Heloise said, "so how do we Knit it? With an army of devils out in the world?"

Tone looked at his horse's mane. "I will appeal directly to the Emperor. I will call upon him to save us."

"Can a mere Pilgrim appeal to the Emperor?" Samson asked.

"Perhaps. The veil has never been rent like this before. I have . . . I have seen devils before, but never more than one."

"And you killed them?"

"No one but a Palantine may kill a devil." He met Heloise's eyes, but could not hold them. "Most times, a single devil would not walk the sunlit world for long. They spend their rage and return of their own free will. Only once did one remain, and then we appealed to the Congregation to send it back."

"Are they wizards, too?" Heloise tried to keep the anger out of her voice—vexing Tone might make him reconsider his choice to speak with them—but she couldn't help but choke on the enormity of the lie the Order had told for so long.

"They are singers." Tone's answer was defiant. "They are chosen by the Emperor himself, through his Song, who leads them. He raises the glorious shout that sends devils back into hell, and smooths the veil behind them."

"The Song . . ." Heloise could picture the cruel, beautiful face going slack as she pressed the machine's unyielding metal into his throat.

"The same," Tone said, "the one you killed."

Heloise looked down. "I didn't . . . I didn't know . . ."

"You lie," Samson muttered. "You lie because you have no way to help us, and so you want to blame my daughter for—"

"I do not lie!" Tone said through clenched teeth.

Samson opened his mouth to reply and Heloise gestured him to silence. "Is there no one else?"

"The Song had yet to choose his successor, but his predecessor still lives, I think. The Emperor's Nightingale. But she is an old woman by now. If she lives, she can help us."

"Have you seen this Nightingale?" Heloise asked.

"Only once, when a devil remained in the sunlit world. Ten winters ago, when you were still a little girl."

"What are these monsters?" Sir Steven asked. "What do they want?"

Tone shrugged. "Why ask these questions? Devils are not creatures to be understood, only destroyed. The only thing you must know of them is where they are."

"And you are certain this . . . choir of yours will work?" Sir Steven asked.

Tone's expression was theatrically certain. "Congregation. If the Nightingale still lives? Absolutely. The Emperor's will is always done."

"Like it was just done against your army?" Sir Steven asked.

"The Emperor's will is a mystery. He may be testing us, or perhaps luring the hellspawn out for a final reckoning. I am not so proud as to flatter myself that I can perceive his grand design."

"This is very pretty talk," Sir Steven's tone was sharp, "but I need you to answer my question, Pilgrim. Does this singing of yours work? Have you *seen* it work?"

"It will work," Tone snapped. "I know it . . ."

Heloise's stomach had cinched into a tight knot at Tone's words. She realized that for all these years, even as much as she had despised the Order, she had still *believed* them. And now . . .

"You lie," she said suddenly. "You lied that you don't use wizardry. You lied that wizardry is always bad. You lied that you were good and that what you want is to protect people. And when you're not lying, you're just wrong, and you always have some fine story for why up is down and black is white and you're not really wrong at all. Why should we believe you now?"

Tone was silent for so long that Heloise wondered if he would refuse to reply, but at last he straightened in his saddle. "If I am lying"—he turned to face her, his face shadowed by the peak of his hood—"then you will have no choice but to face the devils in the field."

"We have done that already." Sir Steven's calm was forced. "You can see we survived."

"You fought a handful," Tone said. "I have faced their full strength."

"And what can you tell us of them?" Sir Steven asked.

Tone eased his hood back and faced the First Sword. Dried blood crusted black alongside a huge gash that ran from the ruin of Tone's ear and up over the back of his head, leaving a ragged red furrow through the matted spikes of his golden hair. "I can tell you that I speak true that the Congregation can send them back, and that we are all lucky that I do."

After that, they rode in silence until the sun sank below the treetops and the gathering dark forced them to give up the march. Sir Steven ordered the kindling of fires. "Those monsters know where we are. If they're coming, then they're coming. We'll not hide from them by going cold. If we're to face them, we'll do it with warm bodies and full bellies."

The order certainly lightened the mood, and Heloise could hear voices lifted in song as villagers and Traveling People mingled around the campfires, close to the flames and one another for warmth. The Imperials did not sing, but Heloise could see them clustered around Tone, heads bowed, the flickering flames sending shadows crawling up their chins as the Pilgrim led them in prayer.

Heloise didn't bother with her own fire. She'd have to leave the machine to get close enough to feel its warmth, and there was no way she would do that. Barnard did not return to her side, huddling beside Wolfun, Guntar, and Chunsia, hands stretched out toward the flames. Only Samson stood with her, and Xilyka of course, quiet as a shadow, bundled in her cloak.

Heloise jerked her chin at Tone, the machine trembling as she stirred the control straps. "I am surprised . . ." She trailed off, unsure of how to finish.

Her father looked over at Tone. The Pilgrim had raised a hand in benediction, a single finger pointing arrow-straight toward the night sky. Embers rose in a funnel, as if he had directed them.

"At him? At me?"

"At both you and him, and at Barnard, too. That you didn't try to kill him."

"You think I don't want to?"

"I know you do. I do, too."

"So, why don't you?" he asked her.

"You heard my reasons when I addressed the army. But . . . I saw what you did to Sigir, Father. You knocked his teeth out."

"Aye." The firelight had made her father's face a thing of weathered stone. "And you burned him alive."

She was quiet at that, and her father's expression softened. "Should I take vengeance? For your mother? She wouldn't have wanted that. She liked life to go easy. She never stood on honor, or justice, or any of those things that didn't put food in your belly or fix the thatch."

He paused, took a deep, shuddering breath. "Suppose I loved that about her most. She saw the world as it was, didn't worry about how she wanted it to be. Men burn nations, kill each other by the thousands for some mad vision of the future. Your mother wasn't like that. She just wanted to cook good food, and sit outside in the gloaming and watch the fireflies come on. Don't think I ever realized how much that helped keep my feet on the ground until now."

"I feel like I never knew her," Heloise said. "I feel like I wasn't like her."

"Aye, you weren't. Your mother never knew what to do with you. Always said if she hadn't pushed you out of her own body, she'd have guessed you were someone else's." He chuckled, cuffing at his eyes.

Heloise laughed, then felt badly for laughing, then laughed again. She realized she was crying, too. "Mother would never say something like that."

Samson laughed all the harder at that. "Oh, aye. Your mother said that and worse more times'n I can count. Not to you, mind, but she was a levy serjeant's wife, after all."

"I never knew," Heloise whispered. The hot tears pattered off the inside of the gorget. "I never knew."

Samson reached inside the frame and gripped her knee. "Ah, but she loved you, my dove, she loved you like she loved the dawn and the strawberry harvest and the birdsong at morning. You were her precious little girl and she was never happier than when she knew you were fed and warm and curled up beneath your blankets. She always told me that of all the gifts I'd ever given her, you were the greatest one of all."

"How? How could I not have known that?"

Samson stepped up onto the machine's knee, reached for her hand. She slipped her fingers out of the control strap and twined her fingers with his.

"Remember what Tone said of faith," Samson whispered fiercely. "Sometimes you don't have to understand, only believe."

·    ·    ·

One moment there was only the unbroken curtain of the falling snow, and the next, the capital appeared, black spires suddenly piercing the gray-white.

Crenelated turrets, black stone towers filled the horizon, cutting toward the clouds. The capital's skyline reminded Heloise of a devil's teeth, black, long, wickedly sharp.

Heloise could see the smoke rising even through the driving snow, could hear the distant shouts of fighting, the clash of metal and stone. The eagle-shrieking of the devils pierced the air so thick that it sounded as if a giant flock of predator birds were circling the black stone parapets half-visible through the weather.

"We have come too late," Sir Steven said.

"No." Tone practically spoke over him. "Those are the calls of fighting men. The Emperor will not let His city fall."

He reined his horse around, looking toward the knot of Imperial troops that stood staring at the smoke on the horizon. Sir Steven seized the reins. "Where are you going, Pilgrim?"

Tone yanked on the reins, trying to free them from Sir Steven's grip. "Release me. The Sacred Throne itself is besieged. I must go to its defense!"

Sir Steven tightened his grip. "And you will. But because of the friendship between us, I will not let you go alone, to be cut down by the devils with ease. Instead, you will go with all of us, and our combined force will strike the monsters from behind. Then, *we* will have the victory, and *together*, we will liberate the Sacred Throne."

He let go of the reins and the horse shied, forcing Tone to take a moment to get it back under control.

"There is no need to thank me," Sir Steven said. "I do this for the love I bear you."

Sir Steven sent outriders to scout the enemy position, and drew up his archers while they waited. Florea assented to draw the Hapti knife-casters up on their flank, and Heloise nearly gasped at how few they were, a knot of rabble alongside the disciplined line of the Red Lords' troops.

When the outriders returned, they looked frightened. "The garrison cannot hold, First Sword," their captain said. "The gate is breached."

"Do the monsters have pickets out?" Sir Steven asked.

The captain looked confused. "They are like hungry dogs, First Sword. They only have eyes for what is before them."

"How many are there?"

"It is difficult to count, with all those arms, sir. More'n a score, I'd wager. Perhaps twice as many."

The news wasn't precisely a surprise, but Sir Steven was still silent for a moment while he took it in. "Scorpions would help here," he said at last, "but there is no time to build them."

"The garrison will have them," Tone said, "and catapults besides."

"He's right, First Sword," the captain said. "We saw them on the battlements. But the monsters are too close to the wall for the crews to man them, and the rest do not have a line of sight."

"Then we must draw the monsters away," Sir Steven said, "and give the garrison time to man their siege engines again."

"First Sword, why?" one of his knights, a big man made even bigger by his red enameled armor, asked. "The creatures have the city invested. Let them have the run of it, and we will come behind them after the Imperials have softened their ranks."

The captain shook his head. "We didn't see much, sir, but it didn't look like there was much softening being done."

"Sir Tobias"—Sir Steven turned to the knight—"do you believe that I serve the will of the Senate?"

"Of course, First Sword." Sir Tobias's face fell. "It's just that—"

"It's just that the Senate's will is best served by a *whole* city delivered into their hands, with a grateful Imperial government willing to make favorable terms. It is worst served by a city leveled to the ground, depopulated, and overrun by an army of monsters we presently have a chance to strike unawares."

"Yes, First Sword," Sir Tobias said. "Of course, sir."

Tone nodded, turning to his troops again. Sir Steven stopped him with a hand on the Pilgrim's shoulder. "You," he said, "will also serve the will of the Senate. And it is the Senate's will that you ensure the garrison's siege engines are turned *only* upon the monsters, and not upon us."

"Of course." Tone looked offended.

"Sir Tobias," Sir Steven said.

The big knight saluted. "First Sword."

"You will take a squadron of your best and ride with Brother Tone at all times. If he forgets his promise to ensure our safety from the Imperial garrison, you will remind him."

Sir Tobias lowered his visor and tapped his sword hilt. "I have never more dearly wished for a man to prove false."

"My faith is the Emperor. All else is dust." Tone kicked his heels and trotted off to rally his men, the Red Lords escort close behind.

Heloise moved just behind the line of archers as they prepared to march. Xilyka rode out to join her.

"Come back," Samson called. "No need to be in the thick of it now."

"Your father is right," Sir Steven said. "My men know their business. We need only draw them off."

"There is one person in this army who has killed a devil," Heloise said, "and she is speaking. I haven't fought in many battles, but I've fought in enough to know that things . . . go wrong. And when they do, you'll be glad I'm there."

Samson's reply was lost in the sound of the horn and the serjeants bellowing their orders to set the army marching again. Heloise was surprised to find that she felt no fear, only a burning impatience. The promise of the devils had more power over her than the creatures themselves. The sooner she came to grips with them, the sooner she could break their power to frighten her.

The sound of the battle was nearly deafening by the time they finally crested the rancid-skim of a rise and the capital wall came into view. It was made of thick black stone, the huge blocks interlocking perfectly, making the wall at Lyse look like a child's lark. The towers soared into the air, and would have reminded Heloise of a devil's horns save for the gold-stitched banners that fluttered from them. The massive front gates were made of thick beams of fire-blackened wood, banded with even darker strips of iron. A portcullis lay in the slime before them, twisted by the force that had ripped it from its anchoring chains.

The walls were far too thick for the devils to breach, but the gates had been smashed apart, one of the huge doors sagging askew from a single massive iron hinge.

The devils surged outside the gates. Heloise nearly gasped at their numbers. How many had she thought they might face? She could scarcely imagine a score. There were at least twice as many swarming at the base of the walls, a tangle of purple-white limbs, a bobbing throng of black, corkscrewing horns. *Just six of them nearly destroyed us. We cannot hope to fight so many. No army can.* The devils stretched and scrambled, climbing over one another like ants striving for a bit of fallen fruit. The fruit here was the garrison, falling back from the parapet walk that topped the gatehouse. Heloise could see the shattered remains of two scorpions, the broken winches and crossbars hanging between the crenellations of the battlements. As she watched, one of the devils leapt and managed to grasp the edge of the parapet with one clawed hand, only to hang for a moment before giving up and dropping back to the ground. *The walls are too high for them, why don't they just go through the gate?*

An instant later, one of the devils stumbled back, and she saw the answer. The garrison had built a barricade of overturned wagons, bits of broken masonry, sacks of meal probably dragged up from larders across the city. Pikemen stood in packed ranks behind it, presenting a hedge of bristling points to the enemy. The devils surged forward, and she could hear the shafts snapping as the points caught on scales, stopped cold before they could do damage. A devil swatted down with one claw, knocking the points down, snapping more of the weapons. She could see soldiers passing fresh pikes forward, flights of arrows arcing up through the open gate into the devils' faces. They did little to bring the monsters down, but more than a few of them fell back, raising hands to guard the clusters of their white, stalked eyes.

Heloise could see a handful of Pilgrims just behind the pikemen, flails in the crooks of their arms, texts held out before them. "They're reciting the Writ."

"Don't seem to be helping," Wolfun said.

A moment later he caught his breath. "Don't seem to have helped at all."

Heloise looked over at him, followed his gaze to the base of the wall.

Pilgrims and Sojourners lay in heaps beneath the towers astride the broken gates. The red and gray of their cloaks were streaked with blood and the black slime that marked the devils' passage. Flails were tossed among them, broken like so much matchwood. Horses were strewn across the field around them, piled here and there in places where it was plain the Order had tried to use their corpses as barricades. It had done them little good. There were more cloaked dead than all the losses the Red Lords, villagers, and Traveling People had sustained combined. Perhaps a thousand in all. Heloise wouldn't have been surprised to find that it was nearly every ordained Pilgrim and Sojourner left in the Emperor's service.

She wanted to look to Tone, but she couldn't tear her eyes away from it. *The fight is already over. The devils did our work for us.*

"Stupid bastards." Wolfun gave voice to Heloise's thoughts. "They must have ridden out to face them."

"Of course they did," Heloise breathed. "The Order was made to fight devils."

Wolfun shook his head. "Doesn't look like it was much of a fight."

"We can't win this," Heloise said, taking in the thronging devils. "We have to find another way . . . Sir Steven . . ."

She turned to the Red Lords' commander, but he had already drawn his sword, held it over his head. "Captain! Loose shafts by ranks! Stay wide of the gates! And someone get that Pilgrim up here!"

"Sir Steven!" Heloise shouted. "No!"

But his orders were already being relayed down the line and the First Sword was turning to face his army. "On your guards, Free People! The fight is about to begin!"

She took a step toward him, banging her knife-hand against the shield's edge to get his attention. "No!"

But the first flight was already away, a great rush of wind as the feathered shafts rose, arcing up and out, and began falling among the devils, plinking against the hard scales and spinning off into the black scum the devils' touch made of the snow. The archers fired true. Not a single arrow fell within the confines of the gatehouse, where it might harm the men of the garrison. The devils were not harmed, either, but she could see them staggering slightly as the stronger shots landed on them, letting out their eagle screams as they spun to face their tormentors. They hissed, crouched, spread their clawed limbs.

"Captain!" Sir Steven shouted. "Have your men fall back by ranks! Prepare to . . ."

Heloise did not hear him finish his order. The devils moved so quickly that it seemed they simply blinked into existence among her troops. Her mind vaguely reported them turning from the walls, charging toward them, but it was a thin thing, a wisp of a dream. Her waking mind only knew that one moment they had been gathered outside the ruined gate, and the next they were among the army, throwing the archers screaming into the air with great sweeps of their huge arms.

All semblance of order vanished, and the careful ranks of the Red Lords became a chaos of shouting men. Heloise saw Sir Steven knocked from his horse, rising to one elbow, eyes dazed. His bodyguard raced for him, only to be bowled from their saddles by a huge devil with one broken horn and a scorpion bolt protruding from its side. It snarled, pounding the ground with one of its fists, Sir Steven just managing to roll to the side before he could be crushed. Xilyka threw a knife at it, but the creature paid it no mind, reaching for the First Sword.

Heloise leapt over him, swatting the monster's hand aside with her shield, punching the protruding bolt with her knife-hand, ripping the wound wide. The devil shrieked and fell back, but Heloise couldn't see it fall. It was instantly replaced by two more, raising sparks from the heavy shield with swipes of their clawed hands. The sound of battle was suddenly a roar around her, so loud and so close that she felt as if she stood in a cave made entirely of screeching noise—the clanging of blades against armored scales, the screams of terrified men.

"I have him!" Xilyka's shout cut through the din as she helped Sir Steven to his feet.

Heloise caught a claw on her shield's corner, counterpunched, was rewarded by the feel of something giving way and an eagle scream that nearly deafened her.

"We have to run . . ." Sir Steven slurred. His face was ashen and blood trickled from his temple. ". . . Buy time for the garrison to man the engines . . ."

Heloise spared a glance at the army. It was riddled with devils. She could not see a single unit formed and fighting. Two of the Hapti wagons lay on their sides, a third smashed into splinters. She could see her villagers mixed in with the Red Lords' troops desperately trying to strike at the enemy, succeeding only in tangling themselves up with their allies, ill-timed strikes fouling spear thrusts, or worse, missing entirely, hitting their comrades. The shouts of alarm were hysterical.

Tone's voice alone rang out clearly, chanting verses from the Writ, riding through the maelstrom as if the people about him were stalks of grain, bending aside to admit him. He lashed out with his flail, drawing sparks from a devil's side, ripping some of the scales away from the creature. It lashed out with two arms, but Tone had already dug in his spurs and rode out of range, circling back for another pass.

"Come on!" Sir Steven had found his wind, was bellowing at the Pilgrim. "We have to run!"

"No," Heloise said, knowing that he couldn't hear her, but past caring, "we will never outrun them now."

She raced to Tone, reaching him in two strides and snatching him out of the saddle. His horse shrieked and she bulled it aside.

"What are you doing?!" he shouted at her. He kicked, twisted, but Heloise had him wedged between her shield arm and the machine's breastplate, and there was nothing he could do. "Let me go!"

Heloise turned to the army and shouted so loud that the muscles in her sides cramped. "Into the city! Follow me and live!"

She turned and raced toward the gates, not waiting to see if the others would follow. She could see the faces of the garrison staring, dumbstruck that the army of devils had been distracted by a rabble of enemies. It didn't take them long to close ranks and present their pikes at the girl in the war-machine racing toward them. She could hear the bowstrings of the archers behind them stretching taut.

She gave Tone a squeeze. "Now would be the time to tell them about our arrangement."

"We have no arrangement," the Pilgrim grunted as the lurching machine jostled him.

"Of course we do," she said, squeezing in with her shield-arm, crushing him against the machine's breastplate. "You know, the one where I don't crush you to paste, and you tell the garrison to let us in?"

Another squeeze, and Tone was shouting the moment she relented enough to let him draw breath. "Stand aside and let us enter! I am the Emperor's Own! Make way for the Righteous Hand!"

The garrison pikemen cast uncertain glances at one another, but held their ranks, points leveled as Heloise came on. It was the two or three remaining Pilgrims who pushed their way into their ranks, yanking on their shoulders and tapping their helmets, prying them apart. At last the pikemen fell back, making room for Heloise to race past them, releasing Tone as she went. He hit the ground running, matching her pace as they moved past the remains of the shattered gate and turned to face back the way they had come.

Precious few of the army had followed her. None of the Hapti wagons had made it, and Heloise could only see a few of the Traveling People sprinting free of the flailing devils still outside. All the men of her command were with her—her father and Barnard, Sir Steven still leaning hard on Xilyka, Wolfun. They had been close to her when the fighting had started and were saved by their proximity. But most of the Red Lords were out there, somewhere, with the villagers who had sworn themselves to her banner after Lyse. Some streamed past the bewildered pikemen in ones and twos. Heloise could see more through the broken gates, running away from the walls, trying their luck with the devils. She watched as an infantryman in a red tabard tried to race between a devil's legs, eyes fixed on the gatehouse. He looked as if he might make it, when suddenly the monster dropped onto its knees, crushing him to the ground, then reached back with one of its hands, ripping his head off.

The creature turned, saw the pikemen milling about uncertainly, the Pilgrims gawking at Heloise and her people among them. It hissed, stalked slowly forward. Some of its kin followed its movements, closing in on the gate. Samson's levy instincts reacted instantly. "Form up!" he bellowed. "They're coming again!" He was a villager issuing an order to Imperial troops, but they instantly complied, driven by his serjeant's voice.

The last shreds of her army raced past the devils and into the city as the monsters finally tired of chasing the routed villagers and Red Lords' troops, and turned their attention back to the gatehouse.

Heloise gaped. There were so few. *The rest aren't dead . . . we're just separated. Maybe they've escaped.* But she had seen the devils' incredible speed, their terrible numbers.

She searched the faces of the Traveling People, saw no one she recognized. *Florea.* She glanced at Xilyka, but if the knife-caster was worried for her mother, she gave no sign. She caught Heloise's worried glance. "My mother is the strongest among us. If any can escape them, she can."

Heloise nodded and scanned the crowd, found Guntar. He'd thrown his mother over his shoulder as he dashed into the city, and gently set her on her feet. She stared at the ruins of the gates, blinking.

The garrison pikes were trained men, disciplined and efficient, but even they could not match the devils' speed. They were still desperately trying to re-form when the first of the monsters crashed into them, its six arms flailing like threshing blades, felling the garrison like ripe grain.

The pikemen tried to fall back by ranks, keeping their points steady, but it was useless. Together, they could at least create a barrier solid enough to present an obstacle, but in ones and twos, they may as well have faced the devils with sharpened broomsticks. Heloise charged at one of the devils in their midst, dropped the machine's shoulder, and slammed into it. The creature looked up just as she collided with it, its head whipping back, feet leaving the ground. Heloise didn't wait to see where it landed, taking advantage of the brief reprieve to look back into the city, desperate for an avenue of escape.

Inside the gatehouse was a broad cobblestone plaza, vast beyond Heloise's imagination, big enough to fit all of Lyse inside it with room to spare. It was lined with shuttered market stalls, thick curtains drawn across the fronts, bulging from the wares behind. Beyond them were tall row houses, blackened beams crosswise between plaster smoothed over stone. Glass windows were veined with leaded designs—scrolling patterns of scattering flowers or vines bursting with fruit. Broad streets marched off in all directions, deserted now, save for handfuls of soldiers racing into the square with fresh pikes, sheaves of arrows, or beams for the barricade.

Heloise stared, open-mouthed. The walls above her were nearly empty, the garrison troops racing across the square to join the fight so few. The Imperial capital, the great city that had ruled her all her life, was practically empty. *They lost two armies. One to us at Lyse, another to the devils on the road. The Order lies dead outside the walls. There is no one left to fight.*

When Heloise had taken Lyse, the townsfolk had stood in the common, watching as her people came on. Here, the citizens were shut up in their beautiful houses, faces pressed to the windows. Heloise could catch flashes of jewels at heads and throats, bonnets and lace collars. She thought of the muddy lanes and leaking thatch of Lutet, of playing among slopping pigs and tanning pits. The huge houses rising about her were so clean they seemed to glow.

But they were nothing compared to the palace.

Of course it was the palace. What else could it be? It rose among the beautiful houses, so lofty and refined that they looked like flies on the flank of a prize horse. It was hewn of the same black stone as the outer wall, but planed so smooth and polished so brightly that it reminded Heloise of a still lake at night, reflecting the moonlight. The spires rose so high that Heloise had to crane her neck to follow them up, and eventually gave up when the machine's helmet cut off her vision. She lowered her gaze, but not before she saw the gold scrollwork chasing the eaves—the Emperor surrounded by his Palantines, their heads haloed by glowing suns, their hands held palms-outward in the traditional pose, writhing devils crushed beneath their feet.

And something more.

A ringwall, topped by high battlements, stone embrasures pierced with arrow slits. And siege engines—huge wooden machines that looked like giant crossbows, straining wooden arms laden with throwing stones. Manned and waiting.

"You . . . you saved us," Tone said. He was pale, his jaw tight.

"It was madness to stay out there."

"It was," Tone said, then looked down at his feet. "And none saw it but you. I have been such a fool."

"What?" Heloise asked.

When Tone looked up, his eyes blazed with certainty. "The

Emperor's hand is on you, Heloise. How else could we have fought through to here?"

Tone sounded so much like Barnard that Heloise felt her skin crawl. Religious men were so determined to make a saint of her. *If I made water on my feet you would call it divine providence.* But Heloise's eyes were fixed on the siege engines attached to the ringwall. Tone might be mad, he might be determined to make a Palantine of her, but they both wanted to go in the same direction, at least.

"To the palace!" she shouted, and started running.

Xilyka followed her immediately, and she could hear Sir Steven cursing at the sudden movement before he looked up and realized where they were heading. "The siege engines!" he shouted. "Captains, get your . . ." His voice trailed off as the loss of his army struck home. A motley of infantry and serjeants ran along with him. His knights were gone. There were no captains to order.

As Heloise drew closer, the tiny remains of the shattered army behind her, she could see giant bolts being loaded, engineers working winches on the machines, lowering them to aim directly at her.

"The devils, you fools!" she shouted at them. "Not us! The devils!" But her words were lost beneath the war-machine's roaring engine, the pounding of its metal tread. Arrows whisked past her, a few plinking off the machine's shoulders. She heard Xilyka curse as the girl dodged aside.

Heloise heard a shout from behind her, risked a glance back and was rewarded by the sight of the wall of garrison pikemen dissolving. They ran now, abandoning their useless weapons, taking cover in the market stalls or racing down the broad streets. The devils surged through, rushing into the vacant square. Two, twelve, thirty.

Heloise turned back to the palace steps just as the first of the giant bolts struck mere handspans from the machine's leg, hitting the cobbled street hard enough to split the stone and lodge quivering in the earth beneath. She could see the engineers loading the next bolt, winching it back. She stared at the cracked stone. The bolt's head was sharp iron as wide as the machine's metal helmet, the shaft thick as her arm. The war-machine would not stop it, of that she was certain.

She turned back as the engineers locked the next bolt in place and trained the siege engine on her. Behind her, she could hear the devils' eagle shrieks coming closer.

And then Tone's voice split the noise. The Pilgrim ran past her, hands cupped over his mouth. "Let us pass! They are with me! Let us pass!"

Tone. The man who had taken her eye. He could have run, joined his people in the fight for the gate. But here he was, calling for her safety. His gaze was fixed on the massive arching stone doors and the scattering of guards who stood before them. A handful of men in gaudy armor, black chased with gold, the ridiculous false wings worn by the knights at Lyse spreading from their backs, only greater. The huge wooden frames were painted with golden letters proclaiming verses from the Writ, jewels sparkling from the tip of each long feather. They leveled gilded halberds at Heloise, paused at the sight of Tone. *So few*, Heloise thought. *Here now at the palace, the seat of the Emperor, and there is almost no one left to stop us.*

"I am a Holy Brother of the Emperor's Own!" Tone shouted. "Stand aside and let us enter!"

"That . . . that is the heretic," one of the guards said, gesturing at Heloise with his weapon, "with the hounds of hell behind her." He swept the weapon down again to indicate the knot of Traveling People, villagers, and Red Lords trailing behind her.

Tone hammered his flail haft against the halberd's head, knocking it so hard against the black steps that it rang. "The hounds of hell"—he jerked his chin at the devils—"are behind all of us. We must appeal to the Throne directly. Only the Emperor can save us now."

"Heloise!" Wolfun called. "There isn't much time."

She turned. The square was full of devils now. The garrison had given up all hope of fighting them, and fled. The creatures raced toward them, snarling, arms spread, slowing as they closed, the stalking behavior that Heloise had seen them repeat when they felt confident their prey was helpless and cornered. The last of the army had gathered around her, scores winnowed out from thousands. Most were wounded, lacking all semblance of order. She could feel them edging backward up the steps. They were broken and terrified. They wouldn't stand a chance.

Heloise moved up beside Wolfun and Barnard. Xilyka joined her. Sir Steven had found his wind and stood with them, Samson at his side. "If you are going to speak to the Emperor," Heloise called to Tone, "then you should hurry. I will do my best to give you time."

"That is poor comfort," Sir Steven muttered, then called to his men again. A few of them came forward to join the line at the base of the steps, but most backed further up behind them, toward the huge doors.

"It is all the comfort we will get. Our faith is in the Emperor, and His in us," she quoted from the Writ, "and He will be a mighty fortress and the bane of our enemies."

"Yea, though mine enemy is vast beyond counting, ten thousand before me, and twenty thousand behind," Barnard added.

"Yea, though my foe bears a glittering sword, and his countenance is terrible to behold. He shall not come nigh to me, or to my family," Samson said.

"For a mighty fortress is my Emperor, and none shall pierce His walls," Heloise finished. "Go, Tone. Go and do what you can."

A bolt shot down from the battlements, slamming into one of the devils' shoulders and sending the creature spinning before it fell to the ground. A moment later two huge stones arced past them. The first flew wide, bouncing harmlessly across the square before crushing an abandoned cart. The second struck a devil full in the face, sending the creature staggering back into the monsters behind it. The devils paused, wary of the engines on the palace parapets and Heloise in her machine.

"No," Tone shouted to her. "The Emperor has sent you to me for this, of that I am sure. I do not know His plan, but I will see it through. We go in, all of us, together."

"You do not wear the red," the guard shouted, raising his halberd again. "No mere Pilgrim takes audience before the Sacred Throne."

"He does when the veil is rent!" Tone shouted.

"He does no—" The guard's words were cut short as Tone hammered the flail haft into his head, knocking his helmet askew and sending him clattering down the steps. The guard beside him had no time to react before Tone reversed the weapon, bringing the head into a rising loop that caught him in his stomach with such force that Heloise could see his breastplate dent. The man pitched forward onto his knees gasping for breath, his helmet slipping off his head to tumble down the steps until it was stopped by his comrade's body. The rest of the guards backed away as Tone raised the flail over his head.

"The veil. Is. *Rent*. I will appeal to the Throne if I must kill each of you to do it. The Emperor sent this girl and her people to me. They saved me, they brought me here, and they are coming in with me. Now are you going to open the gates, or are you going to die?"

They did neither. Their weapons rebounded off the stone and they ran, their false wings shaking as they vaulted the stone balustrade and disappeared around one of the buttresses.

"Heloise!" Tone shouted to her.

She turned, leapt up the steps, wedged the corner of her shield into the gap between the stone doors. They were the biggest doors she had ever seen, huge slabs of stone bigger than even the Imperial shrine in her village. She was shocked at how easily they opened. They swung smoothly, so silent that she would have believed they had not moved if she hadn't been able to see it, the darkness beyond so complete it swallowed the light.

More bolts were raining down among the devils, more stones. Their stalking advance had broken apart, their arms raised over their heads. Two more knelt, clawed hands covering wounds. One braved the hail of missiles and rushed toward them, and Heloise leapt from the stairs, hammering down with her knife-hand. The devil turned the blade aside with a sweep of its hand, but the weight of the machine staggered it back, and it wrapped its arms around her to keep itself upright. Heloise felt the machine tipping forward, kicked out a foot to hold herself upright. It came down hard on the devil's ankle, and she could hear a crunch that told her she had hurt it, followed by a scream so loud it made her eyes water. She jerked her elbow back, ripping the knife-hand free of the devil's grip, then sent it swinging up into the monster's side. She felt the hard scales resist it, then the engine drive harder to compensate, rewarded by the feeling of the hard surface giving way and a second scream, near silent now, barely audible over the ringing in Heloise's ears. She brought the knife down and up, again and again, and again, until at last she felt the devil's hold on her slacken, and she shoved it away, turning back to the palace.

Her people were streaming up the steps, disappearing into the hungry darkness that held like a curtain across the open doors, forbidding the daylight to enter. Xilyka and her father were the last of them to race through, and Tone stood beside the open doors, waving Heloise in. "Come on!"

Heloise leapt up the steps, slowing just enough to let Tone run in, and then she was inside, the cool darkness swallowing her. She could see nothing, but heard Tone straining at one of the doors. She ran to him, felt with her shield until she found the door's edge, and slammed it shut. The devils were nearly upon them as she found the other and pushed it closed. She braced the machine against the doors, expecting to feel the weight of the devils at any moment, to hear their shrieking and feel the weight of their numbers as they tried to push their way inside.

But there was nothing. Whatever force forbade the light to enter forbade sound as well. There was only the faintest hint of the battle outside, the quiet darkness all around them broken only by the panting of her people, the gentle puffing of the idle war-machine.

"Where are we?" Samson whispered.

"You are in the center of the world." Heloise could hear Tone working a mechanism, and a locking bar falling into place inside the doors. "You are in the heart of all you have ever known. And soon you will meet your savior."

# 10

## SACRED THRONE

*Like the ranger, the wizard is a solitary creature, plying his trade in darkness, away from the light of the Emperor's grace, and from the gaze of those who might cry out to us. While this makes the work of finding them harder, it is fortunate. For if but one wizard might rend the veil enough to let a devil through, I shudder to think of what two or three together might do.*

—Letter from Brother Witabern
to the Secretary of the Pentarchy

The doors shuddered. Heloise could hear the faint scratching of claws. She leaned back, braced the machine against the doors, realized it wasn't needed. The massive portal was at least as heavy as the city gate, the shuddering gentle. The scratching reached her ears faintly, muffled by the thick stone, but also by something else, a closeness in the air around her. Whatever mechanism Tone had engaged was holding for now.

Heloise stepped away from the door, trying to take in her surroundings, but her eyes stubbornly refused to adjust to the darkness. She squinted hard, but the black was so complete that she had to blink to make certain her eyes were open. "Xilyka?"

"I'm here, Heloise." The Hapti knife-caster's voice was muffled, as if she were speaking through a scrim of cotton. Hearing Xilyka's voice pushed some of the fear down.

"Can you make a light? I can't . . ."

"I have it." Tone's voice came from some distance away. "Your tinder will not catch in here."

Heloise heard the scraping of flint and steel, and a small flame blossomed. By its soft light, she could see Tone at the base of another set of stairs, so broad their edges were swallowed by the darkness. The tiny light illuminated only the space just around him, leaving Heloise and the rest of them in the pitch black.

"It's not enough to . . ."

"Wait." Tone held up a hand.

Heloise waited as long as she could stand, opened her mouth to speak again.

The flame danced, sparked, spread. It seemed to follow tendrils in the air, twining and untwining and then breaking apart until it danced about them, like a storm of fireflies clustering overhead. The flickering light fell on all of them, lighting the huge space brighter than a dozen torches. Heloise felt herself smiling as she looked up to see tiny motes dancing above their heads. They drifted as they burned, bouncing against new motes, kindling them. They lit and burned, lit and burned, and Heloise felt the gentle sprinkle of ash as it fell around her. It was as if they stood beneath a billowing cloud of tiny burning stars, a night sky on fire just above them.

"Only the sacred oil can light the nave," Tone said.

"It's beautiful," Heloise said.

"It is but a taste," Tone said. "The Emperor is the light of the world."

The room was smaller than Heloise had thought, dominated by a wide spread of stairs rising up to another set of doors, smaller cousins of the ones they'd just entered. These smaller doors were made entirely of gold, their faces chased with the image of two Palantines in the traditional pose. Above the Palantines' heads were etched two halves of a throne, joining at the seam between the doors.

Two ancient Sojourners sat before the golden doors, so thin that Heloise at first thought them skeletons. One of them shifted, his ragged red cloak shaking off dust. The edges of the old fabric were trimmed in a silver pattern that mimicked chains. The man stood, leaning on his flail, more crutch than weapon, and extended a hand to them, palm out.

"I am the Emperor's Left Gate. Who comes to stand in the shadow of the Throne?"

"I am Brother Tone, the Emperor's Own." Tone mounted the bottom step and inclined his head.

"Brother, not Father?" the Left Gate asked. "Come closer; my eyes are not what they once were."

Heloise was shocked. Was the Sacred Throne truly beyond those doors? The seat of the Emperor Himself?

Xilyka caught Heloise's expression, and the corner of her mouth lifted. "Something wrong?"

"It's just . . . to guard the Sacred Throne itself . . . just a couple of old men sitting in the dark."

Xilyka chuckled. "It's always old men with you villagers. It's all you will have to lead you."

The doors shuddered gently behind her, and she could hear a whooshing and then a thud as one of the siege engines fired a bolt down into the devils. An eagle-scream told her the missile had found its mark. The doors ceased trembling. "Will these doors hold?"

Samson looked up at them. "They'll have to. Nothing in here to brace them with."

"They will not need bracing," Tone said as he moved up the

steps. "The Emperor Himself will help us soon." He continued approaching until the Sojourner stopped beckoning with a withered hand. He was so close that the old man could have reached out and touched him.

"Your cloak"—the Left Gate squinted—"is gray. Where is your chapter father? Did he send you under his seal?"

"Father Harace," Tone said, "stands at the Emperor's right hand now. The chapter is scattered, and I will appeal to the Throne for an elevation."

"That is why you are here, to make your case that you should be raised up?" The Left Gate sounded angry. "Have you forgotten the command of the Writ? Pride . . ."

". . . is the Emperor's alone," Tone finished. "I know the words, Holy Father. I do not seek the elevation for myself. That is to the Pentarchy to decide, if they still live. I saw many red cloaks among the dead at the gate, and at least one trimmed with gold."

The Left Gate frowned. "What dead?"

Tone gestured at the shut doors, seamless in the gloom. They were still and quiet for now, as the devils regrouped from the siege engine's missiles, Heloise guessed. But even if the devils had been pounding on them, she doubted the ancient Sojourners would have been able to tell. "The veil is rent, Holy Father. The devils are here. That is why I have come, to appeal to the Sacred Throne for aid."

Heloise thought of the thick silence in the room, the unyielding dark. Anyone here would be ignorant of what happened outside, but only if they never left.

"The Emperor speaks through me," the Left Gate said. "If the devils were here, I would know."

Heloise's frustration boiled over. "They *are* here! They are beating on the doors of this place right now! Enough of this, we have to . . ."

Tone cut her off with a glare.

"Who is that?" The Left Gate squinted down at Heloise.

"She is a villager—the Emperor's instrument," Tone said. "When the devils would have taken me, she delivered me. She took me through them and into the city. She must come with me before the Throne."

"A villager? I deny her and you, Pilgrim. You may not pass. We have admitted only Pentarchs for as many winters as I can recall."

"How many winters can you recall, Holy Father?" Tone asked. "The veil is rent, I do not have time for formality now. Stand aside. I am going before the Throne."

The Left Gate's pale face turned even paler. "You dare! You will be cast out of the Order! You will be made heretic! Your life and soul shall be—"

"All our lives and souls are forfeit should the devils win through, Holy Father," Tone said. "Stand aside."

The other Sojourner rose slowly to his feet, leaned heavily on his flail. "I have heard enough. Spears! To me! Take this heretic in irons!"

Heavy silence swallowed his words.

"Spears! Spears . . ." His voice trailed off.

"I am sorry, Holy Father." Tone sounded stricken. "They are all . . . gone."

"What do you mean . . ." The Right Gate sagged against his flail.

The doors vibrated. Heloise heard the faint screeching of claws against stone.

"Tone," she said, "there is no time!"

Tone sighed and nodded. "I am sorry." It took Heloise a moment to realize he wasn't speaking to her.

He strode to the golden doors. Both Gates threw themselves at him, but the ancient men were barely able to hold themselves up. Tone gently disentangled the Left Gate, pressed him back down into his chair. The Right Gate beat his withered fists uselessly on Tone's back, his flail head jingling over his shoulder. Finally he too sank back into his chair, exhausted. "Your soul," he panted, "is damned."

"Aye, Holy Father," Tone said as he pulled the first door open, "and I will pray to the Emperor for deliverance."

Heloise realized that she had stopped breathing, forced herself to suck down air. Barnard sank to his knees, and she could hear her father's muttered prayers. The door, unlocked, swung smoothly open. There was no clap of thunder, no bolt of light. Just a door moving on well-oiled hinges, like any other. Perhaps this wasn't the right door. Perhaps it was an antechamber, and the Sacred Throne was further beyond.

Heloise squinted. There was no thick darkness behind the golden doors. The massive chamber inside was lit from above with a gray half-light. The floor was thick with dust, broken only by a few footsteps trailing off out of view.

Heloise took a step, pulled along as surely as if a rope were tied to the machine. She was terrified by the prospect of seeing the Emperor, but the burning curiosity, the sudden spike of hope, was too strong to deny.

Barnard got to his feet, and Samson took a step with her.

"Back!" the Left Gate shouted, but his voice was weak from the effort of trying to stop Tone. "None of you may come before the Sacred Throne!" *It is no antechamber.* Heloise's heart fluttered, leapt. *It is the Throne, and I am about to see it.*

Tone turned back, beckoned to her. "Just the girl."

Xilyka, Samson, and Barnard shook their heads in unison. "She is not going anywhere alone with you," the Hapti girl said.

Heloise quieted them with a gesture. "We will leave the door open."

The two Gates looked up in awe as she approached close enough for their weak eyes to see. "Sacred Throne protect us."

"Your eminence . . . Heloise, please!" Barnard voice's was thick through his tears. "Take me with you! Let me see . . ."

"Come on, Heloise." Tone beckoned to her.

The palace doors shook gently once again, went still.

Heloise turned back to the doorway, but not before she saw Samson's steadying hand on Barnard's shoulder, holding him back.

"At least . . ." Barnard sobbed, "at least tell me if my children are there. Tell me if they stand in the Shadow of the Throne. Tell them how much I love them."

"And Leuba," Samson added, his voice breaking. "I'd like to see her if I could, one more time."

The few remaining villagers added other names, children and spouses lost. Heloise did not listen. Her mind trembled as she confronted what she was about to see, and she was sure that to add the weight of their expectations would crush her utterly. "Guard the main doors," she said, if only to give them something to do. "Put your bodies against them."

Beyond the golden doors was the Emperor himself, whom she had been raised to worship, whose Writ had guided her life. She had faced devils from hell, she had fought against armies that outnumbered her ten-to-one. Still, at the thought of finally approaching the Throne, her knees shook so badly that she wondered if she would be able to move the machine forward.

She remembered her speech at Lyse, the one her father had quoted to her on the way to the capital, repeated it to herself. *Just one more impossible thing.* With that thought, some of her strength returned, and she ducked the machine low, walking carefully through the golden doors.

The room beyond stank of dust and mildew, of rotting mortar

and wet stone. All was cast in a thin gray half-light, filtering down from a circle of dirty windows in a huge cupola that capped the room hundreds of feet above her, perched atop decrepit stone ribs, hung with tendrils of long-dead moss. She let her eyes drift down to take in the room, so vast and empty that she felt a brief sense of vertigo. Dust carpeted the floor, stuck to the walls.

She glanced around for anything to break the emptiness and finally found it—a pedestal in the center, reached by three steps, plain stone worn smooth and concave over time. Atop them sat a throne of simple gray stone, speckled with tiny flakes of moldering gold paint, still clinging to the surface despite the ravages of eons, caked with dust and mold.

It was empty.

Heloise wasn't sure what she should have expected. She had always pictured the Emperor as he was described in the stories—a stern-faced man in golden armor, shield and hammer in his hands. Could he be something else? Something she couldn't see?

Heloise had no idea, but she was sure of one thing: if this was the Sacred Throne then the Writ had lied. It did not glow with the holy radiance of the divine presence. The souls of her beloved dead did not stand in its shadow; indeed the whole room was so cloaked in shadows that it was impossible to tell which one was cast by the throne. Her mind desperately fumbled for an explanation, an expectation that any moment the Emperor would make himself known to her.

But no, she could feel it. There was nothing, the room was *truly* empty. No holy presence occupied the space, no blessed odor scented the air. There was only the rot, the dust, the detritus of years. A simple chair as ancient and moldering as the men just outside the doors who'd been set to guard it.

Rage and grief warred within her. *They tricked us.* They had groveled to the Order for nothing. There was no Emperor, no great power to fall on them if they disobeyed. Only this moldering, ancient city, barely defended, its rich inhabitants hiding behind their leaded-glass windows, its most sacred spaces guarded by withered old men.

She thought of Barnard and her father outside. What could she tell them? That everything they believed, every rule they lived by, was a lie?

She looked over at Tone and could see that he, too, felt the truth. The Pilgrim stood silently staring at the throne. As Heloise watched, his flail fell from his limp fingers to clatter in the dust on the floor. He gave no sign that he'd even noticed, sank slowly to his knees, letting out a muffled sob, shoulders shaking.

Heloise was shocked that after all he had done, the sight of his grief tugged at her, calling on her to comfort him.

"Perhaps . . . perhaps he has moved to another chamber," Heloise ventured, but she felt the yawning gulf in her gut, knew it wasn't true. Still, her mind scrambled for a reason to believe. *No. It can't be. The devils are real, so the Emperor must be real as well.*

But if he was, he was gone from this stretch of empty dust. He would not be coming to their aid. Not today. Heloise swallowed the rage, the doubt, the boiling questions. If the Emperor was a lie, the devils were not, and they were still outside the palace gates, in possession of the city. If her father, the villagers, the city's cowering residents, if any of them were to live long enough to grapple with the truth of the Emperor, the devils had to be defeated. Heloise was grateful for the thought. Even a task as great as defeating an army of devils was simpler than facing the questions that mounted until she thought her mind could not contain them all.

"Tone," Heloise called to the Pilgrim, "what about the Congregation of the Faithful? Where is it? How do we find them?"

But Tone only knelt and wept. She strode to him, nudged him

with the machine's knee. He shrugged the touch off, gave her no answer.

"There is no time! Where is the Congregation?" Nothing. She considered thumping him with the corner of her shield, but what good would it do? She could not beat the words from him. Somewhere deep within her, a cry was welling up, a bubble of sick horror at the lie she had been told, had believed. A part of her demanded that she stop and grapple with the truth she had witnessed.

She pushed the thought away. *Later.* The devils *were* real and they *were* outside the palace doors. She would deal with them first. The thought of having to speak with her father and Barnard and the rest of the villagers terrified her.

And so when she left Tone and returned to the antechamber, she did not meet their eyes, motioned instead to Xilyka, jerked her chin back toward the Pilgrim. "Bring him."

Xilyka alone still stood at the foot of the stairs leading to the golden doors. She didn't question the order, just ducked her head and darted through the doors, emerging with Tone a moment later. The Pilgrim was still weeping, head hanging. He went as meekly as a child, Xilyka leading him by the hand, his flail left behind.

But Samson, Barnard, and Wolfun all raced from where they had stood with their backs bracing the palace doors. "What did you see?"

*They lied to us.* She wanted to weep. *All our lives, they lied to us. We didn't have to Knit Hammersdown. We didn't have to hurt anyone. All we needed to do was stand up to them, and we didn't.*

But instead Heloise shook her head. "Nothing. The Emperor is not here."

Barnard rushed forward, and Heloise moved the war-machine to block his path. She thought of what Leahlabel had said when they had left the Sindi camp to seek out the war-machine, one of the few times Heloise had been outside it since they had ambushed the Order. *Men have ever been weak. The same loss that makes a woman into a Mother and leader of a band will drive a man mad. They shrink from pain. Could you imagine one of them having to bear a child? This is why all mothers strive to spare their sons from grief. It takes so little to break them.*

Tears sparkled on Barnard's cheeks as he tried to get around her. "Please, your eminence. I have to . . ."

"No, Barnard. It will only hurt you more."

"Please!" he shouted, dodging left, then right. But Heloise had grown skilled at handling the machine's controls, and she matched his movements until Barnard was forced to stagger back.

He sank to his knees, weeping. "At least . . . at least tell me if you saw Gunnar and Basina. Tell me if you saw my children . . ." Behind him, Heloise could see Guntar holding his mother, sobbing into his shoulder.

It took Heloise three swallows to pull down the lump in her throat. The lie came easily to her lips, though it made her sick to speak it. *For you, Barnard, because I know you need it, and because you have hurt enough for one lifetime.* "They are surely in the Shadow of the Throne, Barnard. They are surely with the Emperor. But wherever that is, it isn't beyond that door. Do you trust me, Barnard? Do you believe I work in the Emperor's name?"

He sobbed, nodded.

"Then trust me now. There is nothing in there for you." She raised her voice. "There is nothing in there for any of us."

She turned to the Gates. "Where is the Congregation of the Faithful?"

The Left Gate raised his head to her, rheumy eyes squinting. "Who are you, villager girl?"

"I am not a devil," she forced herself to answer patiently, "and because of that, I forgive you for all the harm you have done to me and mine. I will save you, if I can. Where is the Congregation?"

"And if I do not tell you? Will you kill me?"

"No. The devils will do that soon enough, and if they don't, then time will. Tell me because we both know what is in that room. Tell me because Barnard Tinker has lost his children. Because I have lost my mother. Because all of us have lost someone coming here, and because you can still do some good with the little life that is left to you."

The Left Gate squinted at her without moving for so long that Heloise began to wonder if the ancient man really had died, but then he let out a sigh and stood. He made his way, leaning on his flail, down the wide staircase. Beyond him, the palace doors were still again, and Heloise could faintly hear the flight of missiles from the siege engines driving the devils back once more.

"What are you doing?" the Right Gate called after him. "You cannot . . . This is not right!"

"I have never done good or ill, right or wrong," the Left Gate answered. "Only what the Emperor asked of me."

Heloise started to call him back, but then a line of shadow caught her eye, and she saw why the Right Gate was so furious.

The Left Gate's narrow body had concealed an alcove. In standing and walking away, he had revealed a silver statue of a Palantine that stood on a pedestal inside, its silver wings folded back into the wall behind it. Heloise leaned the machine at the waist to get a closer look, succeeded only in scraping the machine's helmet against the wall. It was simply too big. If she wanted to examine the statue, she would have to get out. The thought sent a spike of panic shooting through her, and she walked the machine back. "Xilyka . . ." she managed.

The Hapti girl rushed to the alcove and ran her hands over

the statue. "It's . . ." The Right Gate walked toward her, and she paused long enough to pull one of her knives from her waist and point it at him. "No closer, old man. I don't revere your Emperor, and unlike Heloise I have not had my fill of killing yet. If you wish a test of faith, then keep coming, and we shall see if your Emperor intervenes to save you."

The Right Gate froze, took a step back, sat back down in his chair.

Xilyka turned back to the statue, and after another moment, gave a low whistle. "I have it."

She pulled the statue forward, and it moved with a grating of stone. Heloise heard a deep, metallic thunk and then the wall beside the golden doors began to shudder.

Heloise staggered back as it rose, shedding tiny bits of stone, sending up thick puffs of dust.

"Sacred Throne," Samson muttered, his eyes rising to watch the wall as it lifted up to disappear among the motes of light that still burned and died overhead, sending them scattering.

Even Barnard forgot his weeping at the sight of the most incredible tinker-work Heloise had ever seen. The raised wall revealed vast iron wheels, each big enough to fit on a Sindi wagon, driving thick metal rods. If there was a seethestone engine, Heloise couldn't see it.

At last the mechanism ground to a halt and the wall shuddered and stopped its ascent. Behind it was another staircase, much narrower than the one leading to the golden doors, but still wide enough to admit three men abreast. It wound sharply upward into darkness. Beneath the staircase was another corridor, and Heloise could see it running to a huge door that must have been on the far side of the throne room. She could see tiny shreds of daylight filtering in beyond it and knew it must lead out of the palace, a secret postern door.

Heloise turned to the Right Gate, motioned with her shield to the staircase. "The Congregation is up there?"

The man only stared at his lap, as senseless as Tone.

Heloise shook her head and moved to mount the stairs, then realized the machine would not fit. She turned it sideways and took a crab-step into the darkness beyond. Xilyka raced past her. "Let me go first."

Heloise turned to the tiny fragment of the army that remained. "Come on."

"Where does it lead?" Sir Steven asked.

"Away from the devils, and . . ." She regarded the ancient vastness of the room about them, the thick layers of dust, the withered old men. It was death. Not the quick, bloody death of the devils outside, but death all the same. "And . . . and this."

Progress up the steps was maddeningly slow. She had walked the machine sideways before, but never at such a steep angle. Her people crowded behind her until she told them to back off, to make room in case she lost her balance and the machine toppled onto its side. They followed at a respectful distance after that, all save Barnard and her father, as if they would somehow catch the machine and support its massive weight on their own. She thought of ordering them back down to brace the doors, but knew they wouldn't comply. She would simply have to hope the thick stone held for as long as they needed it to. Sir Steven steered Tone up the steps with them, guiding him by his elbow. The Pilgrim's eyes were dry now, but he stared at his feet, not speaking.

The staircase wound steeply around, and Heloise realized that they were inside the great dome that capped the room with the empty stone chair, were working their way toward the cupola with its few dirty glass windows. The corridor was wide enough for her companions to move, but the machine was so constrained as to be useless. Visions flashed through her head of Imperial soldiers pouring into the corridor, and she standing powerless to help.

They continued their steep, winding circuit for what felt like an eternity, and at last the corridor grew lighter ahead of them, opening out into a vast gallery. Heloise began to hear a faint susurrus, somewhere between a mutter and a whisper. Xilyka raised a hand, ducked around the latest turn in the corridor. A moment later, she stepped back into view, still looking around the corner, face slack with shock.

The corridor gave out into a vast archway, and Heloise was able to move the machine up beside her bodyguard. The cupola had looked small from the throne room below, but up here it was enormous—a vast ring capped by a massive dome. The dirty glass windows admitted the thin light, washing all in pale gray. An ancient and corroded iron railing ringed the gallery, scrolls of metalwork that looked like a vicious thorn bush run wild. On one side of the room was a vast tinker-made instrument, rows of huge metal pipes rising to where the curve of the dome began. They were covered in rust and moldering flecks of paint, so dust-choked that Heloise could tell they hadn't been used in hundreds of winters.

Seated before them was another withered Sojourner, as ancient and decrepit as the Gates, but broader in the shoulders and chest. His cloak was lined with a silver pattern that imitated the pipes in the mechanism behind him. He held a lash in his hand, the only thing in the whole room that looked carefully maintained.

Before him were twenty men and women, standing in two orderly rows. They looked so familiar that Heloise caught her breath, a spike of panic lancing through her gut. They could have been the twins of the three wizards the Order had brought against her outside Lyse. They were shackled hand and foot, starved, filthy, their stick-thin limbs draped in rags. Their eyes had the same vacant, defeated stare. They chanted, a constant tuneless mutter, too garbled and soft for Heloise to make it out. Even in the wide space of the gallery, with open air all around them, Heloise wrinkled her nose at their stink.

This Sojourner's sight was better than that of the Gates. He stood, eyes widening as Heloise rounded the corner and her people trailed in behind her. He raised a finger to his lips, moved quickly across the gallery, giving the chanting prisoners a wide berth. He shook out the lash as he came, and Heloise moved the machine forward to meet him. He winced at the clanking step on the stone.

"Softly!" he whispered. "If you wake them from reverie, it will be on your head! Who are you? How did you get in here?"

Heloise stabbed her knife-arm toward the row of chained prisoners. "Is this the Congregation?"

"By the Throne, you will turn around or I will—" The Sojourner froze as his eyes fell on Tone. The color drained from his face. "You! Gray-cloak! Aspirant! You have no business here! Out! Out in the name of the Emperor!"

Tone only stood, eyes cast down. The Sojourner pushed past Heloise, his face so incandescent that Heloise's party drew back from him. He managed to keep his voice to a harsh whisper. "Do you not hear me? I am the Keeper of the Congregation! I am raised above the red! I command you to answer me!"

Tone raised his head, but Heloise could see in his eyes that the shock of seeing that empty, moldering chair had not yet worn off. He stared at the Sojourner, silent and uncomprehending.

The old man exploded with a speed and fury that Heloise was shocked to see in one so old. He threw himself at Tone, the lash rising and falling. Tone threw his arms up to protect himself, staggering backward. Heloise watched as the crowd around them drew back, allowing one hated enemy to beat another.

Tone was driven back to the railing. The Sojourner followed

him, continuing to rain blows down. Both men were silent, the only sound the slap of the leather lash on Tone's arms, punctuated by the old man's grunting. Tone offered no resistance, and the Sojourner did not tire. Heloise turned to Xilyka. "That's enough, can you . . ."

Tone's eyes finally lit, and he swatted the lash aside and seized the old man by his neck. His eyes were focused now, cheeks red, breath coming fast. He spun, slamming the old man against the railing, bending him back so far that Heloise could imagine she heard his spine creaking.

"Enough!" Tone forced the whispered word out through gritted teeth. "I will wait no longer! I will not leave! I have served the Emperor faithfully!"

The old man sputtered, coughed. Tears escaped the wrinkled corners of his eyes and tracked their way past his ears. He tried to speak, but all that came out was a pained wheeze. Tone released his grip enough to allow the man to breathe, but not enough to let him break free.

"Please . . ." the old man managed, ". . . don't kill me."

"You damned coward!" Tone whispered. "If you die, then it is the Emperor's will! Where is the Nightingale? I will not ask you another time!"

But the Sojourner had shaken off the initial shock of the reversal. "The Nightingale? It is the Song who—"

"The Song is dead. Where is the Nightingale?"

The Sojourner's jaw went slack as he processed this news, then wrenched back into a snarl. "You lie. I will do nothing for a rogue member of our Order. I will not damn my soul for the likes of you!"

"The devils are here!" Tone said. "They are within the city, around this very building! There is no time!"

Xilyka alone was not impressed by the struggle unfolding

before them. She wore a slightly bemused smile. "I don't see why we need a Nightingale to wake them. I can just go over there and clap in their faces . . ."

"Do not dare!" The Sojourner struggled against Tone's grip. "Wake them incorrectly and they will rend the veil asunder . . ."

"It is already rent!" Tone shook the Sojourner like a dog worrying a fresh-caught hare.

Heloise remembered the captive wizards the Order had unleashed on the walls of Lyse. She remembered the wood going slick, the metal crumbling to rust, the structure sagging in on itself like the lips of an old man who had lost all his teeth. She could picture that happening to the huge dome around her. "No," she said, "we must wake them properly."

"You lie!" The Sojourner shook free of Tone's grip, stood, holding his hand to his throat. "The devils are not here. Now, get you gone, and take your . . . companions with you. Leave your cloak. I strip it from you. I cast you out. You are no Pilgrim of the Emperor."

Tone's face hardened. "I am a greater servant to the Throne than you will ever be." He seized the old man's wrist, began tugging him toward the stairs. "Come, look upon the devils, and we will see if that wakes *you*."

"No!" The Sojourner struggled, but it was useless.

Tone spun on him, stabbing an angry finger at the staircase. "All the devils in hell are right on the other side of these walls, you old fool, and this Congregation is the one thing that can send them back again."

The Sojourner's face twisted in horror, and Heloise felt sudden sympathy for the old man. She, too, knew how it felt to be frightened to leave the safety of familiar confines, to confront the too-close sky and the too-vast earth. "I cannot leave the shrine," the Sojourner whined. "Please. Don't—"

Tone dragged the Sojourner almost close enough to kiss. "Then tell me the truth. Does the Nightingale still live?"

Heloise felt herself sweating despite the chill air as the Sojourner licked his lips, eyes darting around the room.

Tone shook him again. "Does she live?"

The Sojourner nodded.

Tone's shoulder's went slack with relief. "Where is she?"

"The Nightingale is . . . in its cage."

"Then tell me where I may find this cage!" Tone squeezed the old man's wrist tight enough to make him wince.

The Sojourner groaned, fell to his knees, but said nothing.

"Old fool," Tone said, "tell me or I will drag you out into the light and throw you to the devils."

The old man nodded, weeping now. "East! It lies to the east! Past the silver mines! Follow the tow-path for a day or two!"

Tone released his wrist, stood glaring at him. "Perhaps you lie. I should take you with me as a surety."

"No! I swear I speak true. Let me stay here. I must tend to the Congregation. They cannot feed themselves. They need me or they will die."

Tone leaned down, pulled the old man to his feet. "I will be back, and if I find you have lied, you will pay."

The Sojourner nodded and backed away, leaving his lash where it lay.

"We must go." Tone turned to Heloise. "We must retrieve the Nightingale and bring her here."

"And you are sure this wizardry will work?" Heloise asked.

"It is not wizardry," Tone said. "They are blessed by the Emperor Himself. His power flows through them."

Heloise swallowed bile. The Order used wizardry even while they murdered others for it, only they called it a blessing from the Emperor. *The Emperor who does not exist.* She wanted to leap at him, beat him with her metal shield until the lies ran out of him and her anger was spent.

"Tone." Heloise lowered her voice. "You saw that empty chair the same as I."

Tone said nothing, and Heloise bit back her rage. It would do no good to argue with him now. "This will work? This will send the devils back?"

Tone nodded, but he looked chastened.

The sight filled Heloise with doubt. "How can you be sure?"

Tone looked down. "I cannot. But the city is already fallen, Heloise. Your army is scattered. We cannot beat these monsters by force of arms. Not now. If the devils are to be driven back, it is the Emperor's hand that shall drive them. This Congregation is our one hope."

Heloise looked back at the prisoners and sighed. "Slim hope."

"I am going to find the Nightingale," Tone said. "Alone, if I must."

"And when you have found the Nightingale"—Heloise whirled on him—"when this works and the devils are driven back, you will face the world and tell them that it was *wizardry* that wrought their salvation. That the Order trucked with wizards all along. You will never raise a hand to anyone again, so long as you draw breath."

Tone was silent for a long time. When at last he looked up and met Heloise's gaze, his eyes were wet. "I will. Help me to do this, and I will. I swear it in the Shadow of the Throne."

Heloise stepped close to him. "We have *stood* in the Shadow of the Throne," she whispered, low enough that only they could hear. "It is cold, and it is dark, and it is *empty*. You swear it in *my* shadow now, in the shadow of my war-machine. And I accept your oath and swear my own, that if you ever break yours, I will make you pay."

# II

## TO THE CAGE

*The road to salvation is long, and beset with troubles. The wolf shall assail thee, the wanton tempt thee. Thou shalt know the privation of storm and hunger, of sweltering sun and piercing cold. But I am thine Emperor, and the harder the step, the closer it taketh thou unto me.*
—Writ. Lea. IV. 2.

The Gates had resumed their seats by the time Heloise and her party returned to the bottom of the hidden staircase. They were silent, shoulders slumped, not even bothering to raise their eyes as Heloise finally ceased her sideways-walking and stepped the machine out into the wide open space.

The great doors to the outside were still sealed, motionless.

"Perhaps the devils have given up and gone home," Wolfun said.

Heloise was surprised to find herself laughing. "That is unlikely."

She turned back to the people gathered around her. "Stay here. I'd rather sneak out than fight, and that means a small group who can move fast. I will go, in case we have to fight devils, and Tone, in case this Nightingale's cage is guarded by the Order. Might be his cloak will get us in without a fight." *And I am not leaving him alone with Barnard,* she added silently.

"And I will go," Xilyka said, "because I am not leaving your side."

"You don't want to seek your mother?"

"Mother would never forgive me if I left you to look for her. We will find her when this is done."

Heloise moved the machine close to her father, bent it at the waist. For once, Samson did not plead with her to stay, only reached in and placed a hand on her foot. "Do not die, Heloise. My heart could not bear it."

"Lead the villagers until I get back. Barnard will be your strong right hand."

Sir Steven surveyed the few troops he had left to him. "He will have a score of strong right hands."

Samson nodded, too choked with emotion to speak. When he finally mastered himself, all he said was "Hurry back."

Heloise turned to the long passage that led to the postern door. "Find some way to brace the doors."

Wolfun nodded. "Might be we can scavenge some of that iron from up top, though that red-cloaked bastard is like to screech like a bag of cats."

"We'll keep him quiet," Sir Steven said. "Heloise, you need to get going."

Heloise nodded, motioned for Xilyka and Tone to go before her down the dark passage. Tone rushed past her, and Heloise saw his hands were empty.

"Your flail?" Heloise asked him.

"It will not serve against this foe anyway," he called back over his shoulder.

He approached the postern door and reached into a niche beside it, yanking on something inside. The door shuddered and the locking bar slid aside, drawing out of the iron brackets and into the wall. Tone pushed the door wide with the same smooth silence that had so startled Heloise when she'd first entered. The light washed across her face and she blinked it away, stepping out behind the palace, shield raised, anticipating a blow, the scraping of iron sharp claws across the shield's surface.

There was nothing. She heard growling, but it was distant. She slowly lowered the shield, blinking at a wide boulevard that shot arrow-straight toward the other side of the capital and its outer wall. The sight was breathtaking. It was as if all the chaos and violence Heloise had just witnessed had taken place in some other world. Here, the city was pristine and deserted, the cobbles recently swept. The houses and storefronts were shuttered but otherwise untouched. The stone and wood was in good repair, the leaded glass unbroken.

"Come, Heloise." Tone was already moving. "Perhaps the devils have not found the postern gate. It will not be manned now. We can get out right under their noses."

They jogged down the central boulevard unmolested, the thick silence nearly as frightening as the sound of the devils had been. Not a single soul stirred. Heloise didn't see so much as a stray dog or a bird perched on a rooftop. The postern gate was, as Tone had predicted, abandoned. The thick gates were shut fast, the massive locking bar across them, the iron portcullis down. Looking at the clean surface of the stone, the empty cobbles around the gatehouse, Heloise could almost believe the devils had never come, that they had been an invention of her fevered imagination.

Tone disappeared inside the gatehouse, and moments later, the clinking of the great iron chain that lifted the portcullis snapped her out of her reverie. "The bar is too heavy for me to lift," the Pilgrim called to her from inside.

As soon as the portcullis had winched up high enough, Heloise advanced the machine and set the tinker-engine to the task of raising the massive piece of ironwood, a mighty trunk carved down into a single beam. She let it thud against the cobbles as Tone emerged panting from the gatehouse. The doors drifted open under their own weight, and Heloise pushed them wide enough to admit the machine, joining Tone and Xilyka on the other side.

A cobbled road ran straight from the postern gate through a village of tents and shacks cobbled together from cart wheels, blackened timbers, and branches. It was as squalid as the houses inside the city were beautiful, and like the city, it was utterly deserted. Heloise felt anger rise as she considered the ravaged slum around her. Right outside their walls, people had lived here, in this filth. The people inside, with their fancy jewels behind their leaded-glass windows separated by a simple wall, had done nothing.

Tone set off down the road, heading toward a pillar of black stone where signs had been affixed.

"Come on," Tone said, following one of the signs onto a dirt track that led off the main road, "it's this way."

"Shouldn't we close the gate?" Heloise asked.

Tone shook his head. "We cannot set the locking bar from outside, Heloise. And there is nothing out here that can trouble our people more than what is in there."

"It is better to leave them open," Xilyka said. "Folk might be glad of a quicker escape, should things go poorly before we return."

*She's talking about Father. About Barnard.* Chastened by the thought, Heloise hurried after Tone. "Then we must return quickly."

They ran.

The dirt track meandered some, but mostly ran straight to the east, finally falling in beside a river, where it became dotted with hoofprints and piles of dried mule dung. They pushed on in silence until Heloise realized that the sound of her companions' footfalls had grown quieter, and she slowed the machine, looking behind her. Xilyka and Tone were stone-faced, jogging along behind her, but they were panting, and Heloise knew they wouldn't be able to keep pace with the machine unless she slowed it to a jog. Panic creeped its way up her spine. "We must hurry. If we don't make it back in time, the congregation could be lost." *And Father.*

Tone and Xilyka ran on, but far too slowly, and Heloise at last could stand it no longer. She ran the machine to them and scooped Xilyka up, setting her on the machine's shoulder. Tone she held to the breastplate, nestled behind the table-sized shield, as she had carried him into the gates of the capital.

"Heloise, put me down!" the Pilgrim said. "This won't work!"

"It has to," she said. "We're moving too slowly. We don't know how long it will take the devils to break into the palace!"

She set off at a run, and knew right away that it was useless. The machine shuddered and bounced as she lengthened her stride, and within moments, both Xilyka and Tone were shouting as they held on for their lives. After a moment, she heard Xilyka's boots crunch on the snow as the Hapti girl leapt from the machine's shoulder. "I'm sorry, Heloise, I can't hold on at this pace."

Heloise set Tone down and let out a frustrated growl before she could stop herself. The image of the Congregation lying slaughtered rose in her mind, her father's corpse gray and blood-streaked among them. "We have to move faster!"

"Not if it kills us," Tone said. "Give me a moment."

Heloise gritted her teeth while Tone stripped off his armor, leaving it in a pile as he refastened his cloak.

Xilyka laughed as he settled the cloth on his shoulders and raised the hood back up over his head. "You look . . . smaller."

"I'll move faster this way," he said, then hunted around on the ground until he'd found a solid-looking branch, nearly as long as he was tall. "Lend me one of your knives."

Xilyka's eyes narrowed. "That is an . . . intimate request to make of a Hapti caster."

Tone fought to keep the frustration off his face. "I'll give it back."

Xilyka exchanged a glance with Heloise and shrugged, handing it to him. "I don't have time to teach you to cast, priest."

"What are you doing?" Heloise asked. "There's no time!"

Tone ignored her, kneeling, and placed the branch across his thigh. Using Xilyka's knife, he stripped it of its branches and knots. He worked quickly, muttering under his breath. Heloise didn't need to listen to know they were verses of the Writ. Her father and Barnard were not here to overhear. She needn't protect their faith. "How can you . . . after what you . . . what we saw?"

"I saw nothing," Tone said.

"That's right," Heloise said. "It was an old, empty chair."

"The Emperor is more than a chair, Heloise."

"Stop lying! I know you felt it too! You were struck dumb until that Sojourner beat you!"

"I was shocked, yes, and my faith was tested. But I have found it again."

"How can you say that? Maybe the Emperor lived once, but he is gone now!"

Tone never took his eyes from his work, but the knife moved more quickly, his cuts becoming savage. "I do not presume to know the Emperor's will in all things, Heloise, and neither should you. His will is like . . ."

". . . like unto the wind, unseen, yet touching all. It rippleth the wheat in the field and draweth the wave across the still water. I know the verse, Tone. I am a factor's daughter."

Tone stood, tossed the knife back to Xilyka, spun the branch in his hand. Bark still clung to it in patches, but it made a passable staff. "A factor's daughter may recite the Writ word for word, but that does not mean she divines its meaning. It does not mean she understands. You are brave, Heloise. But you lack the humility you will need if you are ever to truly work His will."

"Why should I believe you?" Heloise felt heat rising in her cheeks. "You, whose army I destroyed. You, who I found cowering in a ring of carts on the road. You, who wept at the sight of that empty chair you claim means nothing. You, who would still be stuck behind the postern gate without my help."

Xilyka made a great show of testing the edge of the knife Tone had borrowed. "This will need sharpening."

Both Tone and Heloise stared at her, until at last Tone said, "*Now* I can run. Let's go," and set off running again.

Xilyka was right, he did look smaller. Without his armor, Tone was of a height with her father, but nowhere near as broad, practically a child beside Barnard. The stave, too, without the black iron head of the flail, made him look more an old man than a warrior. But Tone's pace gave the lie to that thought. No old man could run this fast. Before long, Xilyka's breath was coming in tense, tight puffs as she struggled to keep up.

It was then that Heloise realized that the unseasonal snow had broken. It hadn't fallen since they'd arrived at the capital. The wind that lifted the leaves and stirred the branches around them was still unseasonably cool, but not nearly as biting as before.

·　　·　　·

They found the cage the next morning.

It was a small fortress, even smaller than Lyse, with a wooden wall instead of stone, made of logs stood on their ends and sunk into the earth, sharpened at their tops. There was a tower, standing not much higher than the palisade itself, a rickety thing, leaning so precariously that Heloise wondered that it didn't fall when the wind blew.

There had been a fight here. An Imperial banner lay trampled in the grass, and Heloise could make out a mound of fresh earth. She had seen similar too many times since she had left Lutet, the kind of hasty pile that came of burying many dead quickly. Here and there, the grass was marked with the tacky brown of blood dried not too long ago.

"The devils made it here . . ." Xilyka began.

"Not devils," Heloise said, pointing with her knife-hand to where the back end of a wagon was visible drawn up behind the fort. The edge of the Sindi trefoil could be seen on its canvas housing.

Xilyka frowned. "Traveling People . . . here . . ."

"It must be Onas," Heloise said, "and those who went with him."

As she spoke, a man appeared behind the palisade, walking along some hidden parapet. It was Poch Drover, his thick paunch held in by a stolen Imperial cuirass, his big head squeezed into a plumed helmet with a visor tied up with a leather thong. He had a halberd over his shoulder, and he kept switching it from side to side, unsure how to carry it.

"Of all the refuges for them to find, it had to be here," Heloise said.

"The Emperor tests us," Tone said.

"There is no Emperor," Heloise said. "This is the world, Tone. It is the world where the wolf eats the rabbit, where lightning splits trees, where a bad winter leaves a village to go hungry. The world doesn't care about any of us, it only wants to devour everyone in it. That's why it put you over us, why it put Onas and his people here. The world wants to eat, and by my knife-hand, I will see it starve."

Poch turned and called something up to the tower, the distance too great to make out what it was. Heloise followed the direction of his eyes and saw Giorgi, leaning out over its rickety railing. Beside him was an old woman in a black gown sewn to fit her, the high collar rising all the way to her ears. Her face looked younger than her withered body, and Heloise realized that it was because she was smiling, delighted by something Giorgi was showing her. The Sindi man gestured and Heloise followed the path of his movement to where two of his flame men danced beside the fort, pirouetting around a small fire that must have been built to provide the fuel for them.

Giorgi spread his fingers and the flame men threw their shoulders back, raised their heads to the sky, growing brighter, larger. Giorgi stood back, tugging his forelock and bowing to the woman, who laughed and set her hands to the railing. Her face grew serious, brow furrowing. She bent at the waist, her knuckles tightening on the wood. A wind picked up, whipping through the grass around the fire, so that clumps of it were uprooted, flung into the air. The wood scattered, embers swirling, dancing like fireflies. The flame men were pulled apart, flickering pieces of them torn away, but they bent back toward themselves, reforming. They reached out to the remaining pieces of burning wood and drew from them, their fiery bodies regrowing as they were reduced, becoming whole as the wind cut them apart. The woman bent deeper, thrusting her shoulders out over the railing and gritting her teeth. The wind rose higher, howling now. Heloise could see the edges of a funnel, drawn by the embers, the tufts of grass, the burning fragments of twigs. The flame men swirled within it, shrinking as the rising wind cut across them, fighting to reach closer to the ground. For a moment, Heloise thought they might be snuffed out, but at last the old woman slumped against the railing, panting. The wind died as quickly as it had come and the flame men settled back onto the ground, burning brightly. Giorgi clapped, laughed, and placed a hand on her shoulder.

"No Traveling Mother would ever dress like that," Xilyka said.

"No villager, either," Heloise agreed.

"That must be your Nightingale," Xilyka said. "She seems to be getting on well with Onas and his ilk."

"Where is Onas?" Heloise asked.

"If Giorgi is there, then so is he," Xilyka said.

"No matter her allegiances, if that is the Nightingale, she must come with us," Tone said. "Let us go speak with her."

"Are you mad?" Heloise asked. "That is Onas and Poch and the rest of them. They left because I took up with you, Tone. They will not be happy to see you."

"Perhaps," Tone said, "but the Nightingale is the Emperor's servant, and we must trust in Him to deliver her unto us no matter who surrounds her."

Xilyka looked at him as if he had sprouted a second head. "Your Emperor's will seems a fickle thing, and that woman seems quite happy to be in Giorgi's company. It would be best if you stayed out of sight until we figure out their mood."

"I am the Emperor's Own," Tone said. "She will answer to me."

"You're a man in a gray cloak, leaning on a branch," Heloise said. "You shouldn't even be wearing the cloak, anyway. That Sojourner stripped you of it."

"That was not—"

"Tone. Please. We are bringing the Nightingale out of there one way or another. I brought you along because I thought we'd be dealing with Imperials. But those are villagers and Traveling People. They hate the Order, and you most of all. Giorgi is a powerful wizard, Onas is the greatest knife-dancer in his band, and if all the rest of them are there, they outnumber us at least ten to one. We don't want a fight. Xilyka and I will go and speak with them."

Tone's cheeks went red, his eyes flashed. Heloise gestured to the woods behind him. "Tone, please. You can watch from hiding here. The moment we need you, I will call for you."

Tone had faced down Heloise willingly enough on horseback, in his armor and with his flail in his hands. But the man before her now was different, stripped not only of his arms and armor, but of something far more important. It had gone from him the moment he had set his eyes on that empty chair, and without it, he was just another man standing before the might of the war-machine and the steel-eyed Hapti knife-caster beside it.

Tone ducked his head. "Very well. I will wait here."

"Thank you," Heloise said, turning toward the fort. Giorgi and the woman had left the tower, and Poch was no longer visible on the walls.

"What do you think?" she asked.

"I think they're going to kill us." Xilyka shrugged.

"So we should go back empty-handed?"

Xilyka laughed. "The question, Heloise, is where would you rather die? In the streets of the capital, shivering in the dirt as you flee from the devils? Or outside these walls, trying to fix this broken world?"

"Asleep in my bed," Heloise said, "so old that I must mash my food."

She looked down at her feet. "And next to you."

Xilyka grinned, rapped her knuckles on the side of the frame. "Well, then, our way is clear."

The Hapti girl started for the fort, and Heloise was so surprised by her sudden departure that she had to hurry the machine along to keep up. Xilyka stopped them close enough for a parley, but far enough from the walls that an arrow's force would spend itself before it struck home. "No sense in making it easy for them. You are the saint and the leader of our ragged band, no? It should be for you to open the parley."

Heloise nodded. Unbidden, her mind began to compose a prayer to the Sacred Throne, begging for guidance. She squashed it angrily. *No. There is no Emperor. There is only what I can do.*

The thought was oddly comforting. What had the Emperor done for her? Heloise, on the other hand, had done much herself. *Just one more impossible thing.*

She tilted her head back, and had drawn breath to call out when Onas appeared at the top of the wall. He looked older somehow, as if years and not days had passed since she had last seen him. His head was bound in linen, stained yellow by some unguents. It covered his eye and ear, and Heloise could tell by the set of the cloth and the red stains on it that he had lost both.

"Hello, Heloise." His voice was thin, rasping. "It seems we are both one-eyed now."

Heloise was shocked at the sorrow she felt at the sight of him, this boy who would have taken her for his own, who had ripped her army in two when she had refused. He was a fool, and selfish. And for a short time, he had been her friend.

"I am . . . sorry, Onas. I hope you are healing."

"I am healing as well as I can without my mother's help. I never thought to see you again, and certainly not without your army. Where are they, Heloise? Why have you come here?"

"The army is gone, Onas. The devils are in the capital."

"I am sorry for that, Heloise. I know that must grieve you, but it is nothing to me."

"It is not nothing to you. I know how to beat them. I know how to send them back to hell and keep them there."

"And that brings you to me? Do you think a single knife-dancer, or even twenty, will make a difference against creatures who scattered your entire army?"

"I do not need knife-dancers. There is a wizard here, called the Nightingale. I need her."

"I do not know about Nightingales, but the Order was keeping a wizard here. My people have liberated her. She is quite unharmed, I can assure you. She is practicing the Talent with Giorgi. I'm afraid it keeps her much too busy to go anywhere."

"She is the only one who can send the devils back, Onas. Whatever you think of me, you cannot be a friend to them."

"No more than you could be a friend to the Order, surely? Tell me, did your precious Brother Tone put you up to this?"

"Onas, don't. So long as the devils are in the world, you will never be safe."

Onas spread his arms, indicating the palisade, the rickety tower. "Oh, I think we are well enough defended here."

"Lyse didn't stand, and it was stronger than this rat-trap."

"Lyse was assailed by an army, trained and provisioned. The devils are . . . like wild dogs, animals. They cannot organize a siege. And at Lyse we did not have this new wizard. She can summon storms, Heloise, you have never seen the like."

"I have already seen the like. A little squall that couldn't even blow out two of Giorgi's living candles. She won't save you, Onas."

Onas's smile fell away. "That may be, but it is no call to return her to the Order to be destroyed. We protect wizards here."

It was too much. "Damn you, Onas," she said. "You *know* I hate the Order. You *know* I am no friend to Tone. You know, and you don't care, because you are still a boy. Because your mother was right. She said men were weak. She said that the same loss that makes a woman into a Mother will drive a man mad. She said you shrink from pain. She said it takes so little to break you."

Onas pounded his fist on the top of the palisade. "My mother is dead!"

"And I mourn her," Heloise said, "but we both know she would be laughing at you right now. She would slap your head and curse you for a fool. Leahlabel knew what it was to put aside foolishness when something more important was at stake. Your mother knew how to fight."

"Do not speak to me of my . . ."

"I *will* speak to you of your mother, Onas. She was my friend. She saved me and spoke for me when your people wanted to turn me out. And she would have told you what we both know, that this has nothing to do with the Order, or Tone. You are angry because I will not love you. You are angry because I will not be your wife.

"You are angry and you have let it sour inside you until you are willing to give the world to the devils rather than swallow your pride. And if your mother sits astride the Great Wheel and is watching this, then she is surely wondering what she did wrong to raise a boy who will not grow into a man even though it is past time that he did, that it is the world, and not me, who is standing outside this gate and asking him to."

Heads began to appear along the palisade, Sindi and villager alike, men and women she recognized. Her old friends and traveling companions. They glanced from Onas to her and back to him. Heloise felt the moment hang on a knife's edge, waiting for him to explode.

Heloise watched the rage and grief mingle in his face and remembered the night she had kissed Basina. She remembered her best friend, her love, pushing her away, her hands coming up, the shock and horror on her face. She remembered fleeing into the woods, the thorns and branches cutting at her face like an echo of consequences. She remembered how it was to love someone, and suffer for it.

And just as quickly as the anger had come, it was gone. "Onas, please. I have lost my mother. I have lost my Maior. I have lost my best friend. I cannot bear to lose anyone else. I *need* you."

Onas's shoulders slumped, and his head hung, but he said nothing.

"I am tired of shouting from outside a palisade," Heloise said. "At least let me in so we can talk face-to-face."

Shouts from the woods. Heloise turned to see Xilyka sprinting toward three figures. Squinting, she could make out Danad and Ingomer Clothier, dragging a gray figure between them.

Tone. They had circled around them, or had been out on patrol. They had found him, and they were bringing him to Onas.

She turned back to the boy, but his face was already shifting from recognition to shock to rage. "Clever words, and to think I nearly fell for them. Your precious Pilgrim comes to oversee your mission. Where are his troops hiding?" He cupped a hand over his mouth. "Danad! Ingomer! Slit the bastard's throat!"

"Xilyka!" Heloise shouted, but the Hapti girl was already picking up speed, knives fanning out in her hands.

"I've got him!" Xilyka called back, casting her first knife. It sliced past Danad's thigh, laying open the skin and sending him to one knee. Tone shook one hand free, but Ingomer seized it again, pinning his arms behind him. The clothier was young and strong, and much bigger than Tone, and soon he had the Pilgrim on his knees.

Heloise swallowed the urge to run to Xilyka's side. She knew what the Hapti girl could do. She would have to trust her. Heloise's task was clear.

She drove the machine forward, feeling the engine translate

her strides into a powerful sprint, the weight of the metal adding to the momentum. She hurtled toward the gate, lowering her shield as she came on, angling for the seam where the portal joined the wall.

She knew the gate was weak, but she was shocked by the ease with which it burst open. Heloise barely felt any resistance, only heard the splintering of wood, the squeal of badly forged iron hinges, and the sound of wood banging on wood as the portal swung wide and slammed against the wall. There was a scream as whatever sentry had stood behind it was pinned behind the weight of the wood, and Heloise heard a grunt as a man stationed atop it toppled to the ground.

The courtyard within was tiny, a wide circle of green dotted with dirty tents. A few Sindi wagons had been drawn up around a fire pit to one side. Opposite them stood a small stone structure, made of the same polished black stone as the palace.

There were people scattering, but Heloise was too fixed on her purpose to note them as anything more than flashes of color. She had to find the Nightingale and get her out, carrying her if need be. Heloise thought of the gusting wind she'd seen outside the fort, and prayed that was all the ancient woman could do.

Something banged off the machine's shoulder, and Heloise caught a glimpse of metal spinning away. A knife? *No. The Sindi are not casters.* A villager had thrown that, maybe one of the people who had come all the way with her from Lutet. Whether they were the people she had grown up with or no, they were coming for her. She had to keep moving. She leaned, and the machine leaned with her, tearing up the grass as she bolted for the black stone door. Perhaps the Nightingale was not inside, but it was as good a start as any.

She straightened the machine and pounded for the door. It grew in her vision, but not nearly enough, and Heloise was struck by the possibility that it would not be large enough to admit the machine. Heloise wasn't sure if she could . . .

Onas dropped in front of her, so close that she could make out the rippling edges of his cloak, the hooked blades of his silver-handled knives. Heloise knew she should simply keep going, let the weight of the machine run the Sindi boy down.

But she could not help it. She jerked the machine aside, felt it overbalance, take three sliding stutter-steps, and then she was falling, the horizon tipping sideways. She staggered as she fell, covering the short distance to the tower, the helmet banging hard enough against the side to dig a splintered furrow in the wood. Heloise's teeth clicked together, her head rattling against the leather pads inside the metal helmet. She cried out as the machine slid down the tower wall and landed on its shoulder, propped up by the reliquary box.

She shook the fog from her head, saw Onas racing for her. Her head still swam, the horizontal horizon making it look as if the Sindi boy were running across a wall of grass. *Get up. Get up!*

Heloise pushed off with the corner of the shield, managed to get the machine onto its knees by the time Onas reached her. He leapt, stepping lightly on the machine's knee, thrusting the point of his blade into an eye slit. Heloise jerked her head aside, felt the flat of the hooked blade slide against her cheek, the point sinking into the leather cushion behind her head. Shock mixed with the shreds of fog left over from the fall. Onas was really trying to kill her. The thought brought the anger back, and she clung to it, so much more useful than the confusion. The damned fool would kill her for not loving him.

"Damn you!" she screamed, lifting the shield across her chest. Onas sprang backward as it swept past, turning in the air and landing on his feet. "You'll kill me for this? Because I wouldn't be your wife?"

"I will kill you," Onas panted, darting left, then right, looking for an opening as she lurched the machine to its feet again, "because you are in league with the Order, who have hounded my people for as long as any of us can remember."

The lie stoked the anger hotter, and Heloise gave it rein, goaded by the slash in the pad beside her head. She crashed the knife-hand into the shield's edge. "Come on, boy! This isn't a dance and I am not some Imperial murderer. I am Heloise Factor, knife-handed, devil-slayer. I do not love you, and if putting you in the dirt is the only way to prove it, I will do it gladly."

Onas sprang at her, reaching for her shield. He had spent enough time around the machine to know that he could not take it head on. He would try to climb up on top of it and thrust his blade into the frame from behind her. But Heloise was ready. She swept the shield up and caught him mid-leap. He grunted as the metal slammed into his chest and sent him tumbling. He fell into a roll that saw him up on his feet, blades still in his hands.

Heloise charged toward him, determined to strike before he could get his bearings, but another Sindi knife-dancer appeared in her peripheral vision, a villager at his side. Heloise was sure that she recognized them, but she didn't allow herself to register their faces. Her blood was up, and she knew that was the thing that was keeping her alive. If she let it cool now, it would mean the end of her.

She turned at the waist, swinging her knife arm. She was grateful when the blade missed, but the metal hand still caught the knife-dancer in his hip hard enough to send him spinning, the cracking of bone loud enough to be heard over the engine. The villager chopped at her with a scavenged Imperial halberd, its edge ringing off the machine's metal arm. Heloise ignored him and turned back to Onas, who had spun on her and was sprinting around to come at her from the side. The villager tried a thrust as Heloise turned to track Onas, but she already had his measure. Whoever he was, his heart wasn't in the fight. He was seeking to show others that he had tried, without actually putting himself at risk. It was the sort of thing Jereb Mender might do, or maybe . . . She pushed the thought away. His name didn't matter. That he was an enemy was all she needed to know.

Onas saw her tracking his movements and switched back to come at her from the other side, moving so quickly that Heloise could feel the frame shudder as she moved to match him. *He is so much faster than I am. If I let him keep doing this, he will get behind me, and then I am through.*

With a shout, she charged him, making a great show of leaning to her right.

Onas let her approach almost to striking range, and suddenly switched directions.

As Heloise had known he would.

She threw the machine in the opposite direction, letting its weight carry it, sending it stumbling as she had when she had fallen into the tower's side. It overbalanced as it had before, and this time, she leaned into the fall. Onas tried to dodge backward, but it was much too late. The machine collapsed onto him, catching his outstretched leg with its shoulder as it fell, pinning him to the dirt.

Onas cursed, slashed at the machine's helmet, drawing sparks and dulling his blade in reward. The ground was soft enough that Heloise doubted the limb was broken, but she could tell from his frantic flailing that he could not move. She reached out gently with the knife-hand, hovering it over his face. "That's enough, Onas. You are beaten. Let me speak with the Nightingale and no one needs to die. All I want is to—"

A brief glimpse of flickering limbs, and suddenly she was burning. The leather and wool batting of her straps and padding smoldered, saved mostly by their sweat-soaked dampness. The thin fabric of Heloise's shift caught fire almost instantly, her skin beginning to register the heat. She rolled off of Onas, the machine flailing as she tried to free her limbs from the control straps to beat at the flames. She caught a glimpse of the fire then, man-shaped, long, sinuous limbs wrapped around her, curled up close around her like her mother had done when she was little and had nightmares. One of Giorgi's creatures, his wizardry turned against her.

She freed a hand from the strap, felt the shield-arm go slack in response. She swatted at the fire, at the skin where it touched her. It did nothing. The flames clung to her as if they were made of oil. She pawed through them as if through jelly, a thick, viscous feeling like fresh tallow. And like tallow, it stuck to her, the fire coming with it. The burning became maddening. She felt her hair smolder, smelled greasy smoke. The world began to dissolve in pain. She recalled the gusts of wind attacking Giorgi's flame creatures, remembered how they blazed and held true despite the roaring funnel. The Imperial troops at Lyse had been helpless against them. There was nothing she could do.

She rolled the machine onto its knees and then its feet; the brief rush of air from the movement brought no relief. She could see Giorgi now, the Sindi Mothers standing around him, watching her burn. She remembered the contempt on their faces as they turned her people out of their camp, as they tied their dead to the wheels they would use to send them on to the next world. The rising smoke and her watering eyes obscured their faces now.

Then she remembered the Black-and-Grays fighting them in the forest outside the Sindi camp. One of them had fled for her fallen machine as the flame men attacked his comrades. Heloise had sought to head him off . . . before he could get . . . what?

The water.

How could she have been so stupid? She reached behind her head for the waterskin and yanked hard. The thong that held it to its hook was nearly cooked through, and it came away easily. She upended it and squeezed, the cool water squirting out over her head. The relief was instant and so overpowering that she sagged in the straps. The driver's cage filled with smoke, greasy and stinking of cooked meat. The instant the water sluiced off her skin, she felt the heat rising back to the burned surface. *Don't look down.* Heloise knew she was burned, but she didn't dare to examine how badly. There would be a reckoning, she knew, but as when she lost her eye, it would come after the threat had passed.

The thing of flame that Giorgi had made may have been able to survive wind, but it was powerless against water. What was left of it huddled on the grass before her. The flames still flickered, but they were lopsided now, misshapen, sodden embers struggling to hold on to their light. Smoke rose from it, greasy and dark.

Heloise stepped on it. The thing threw up its arms as the shadow of the machine's metal foot covered it, and then it was gone as the metal smothered the air and it vanished in a wisp of smoke. She blinked, felt the hot tightness of her burned face. Her vision came clear, and she could see Giorgi stepping back, Tillie and Analetta at his side. The Mothers turned and ran, and Giorgi waved a torch, gesturing at it. A new thing of fire began to detach itself from the flames, stepping off the brand and onto the ground, careful to steer clear of the scattered droplets where the water still dripped from the machine.

Heloise ignored it, moving toward Giorgi. "Onas is a stupid boy, but you are a man-grown. You know better. I will step through your fires, Giorgi. They will burn me, but not before I reach you. But before I reach you, I want you to tell me why you are burning a girl you once called your friend. Why, when you set your wheel turning with mine, you turned it away just as quickly. What did I do to you? To your people?"

Over Giorgi's shoulder, the Sindi Mothers pressed themselves against the palisade wall. The few remaining knife-dancers clustered around them.

She glanced at Onas. The Sindi had gotten to his feet, but would not put any weight on his injured leg. He did his best to look ready to continue the fight, but she could see his hips trembling, and she knew he would not be coming for her soon.

She turned back to Giorgi. "I don't want to hurt you, Giorgi, but I will, if you make me. I will because I cared for Leahlabel too. And unlike you, I will do something to avenge her death. I will stop the devils who killed her. I will not sulk like a child, then run and hide in a pile of sticks to await the hungry world. I will fight the real enemy, and I will do it over your dead body if you make me."

Giorgi stared at her, his face grief-stricken, but he made no more gestures and the flame man did not move.

She turned back to Onas. "No one needs to die. You cannot walk, Onas. You are beaten. I only want to talk with the Nightingale."

"Your pet Kipti," Poch's voice came from behind her, "has killed Ingomer Clothier. I suppose *some* people need to die, eh, Heloise? So long as they were your own."

Heloise swallowed the ball of frustration that rose in her chest. Xilyka would not have killed Ingomer unless he had given her no choice, but it didn't matter. He wasn't much older than she was, just promised. The wedding had been planned for that spring. She remembered his braying-donkey laugh, the way he'd chewed his lip when he'd been deep in thought. Every step of the way, someone had to die—as if the world were a thing that turned only on the promise of blood, the only currency it would accept. No matter how stupid, no matter how small the need, the blood-toll would be taken.

What could she say to Poch? What could she say to any of them? Fatigue replaced the anger in a rush. "The Nightingale," she managed, "the wizard. Let me talk to her and this fight is over."

Onas took a limping step toward her, brandishing his knives. "I do not need to be able to walk to kill you, Heloise. And if you kill me, the rest of my people will—"

"Enough." An old woman's voice, high and thin. "Stop it, all of you. What do you want of me, girl?"

Heloise turned to see the wizard from the tower. Up close, she looked even smaller, older even than Florea, but straight backed for all that. She wore a fine black gown, a boned and quilted bodice with a high collar, long skirts embroidered with black thread over black cloth so that it hinted at patterns every time the woman shifted.

"You are the Nightingale?" Heloise asked. "The one the Sojourners spoke of?"

The woman caught her breath. "I must say that I am very surprised to see a villager girl in the Procurer's great commission, the one he entrusted to the valley's finest tinker, and to hear her call me that."

"Then it is you."

"Why do you ask?"

"I am Heloise Factor, and I come from the capital. I have seen the Congregation of the Faithful . . ."

The woman looked frightened now. "No villager has ever seen the Congregation. No villager knows of it."

"Then I am no villager," Heloise said. "The capital is taken. The devils are in your streets. The Order is dead before the gates. I do not know how many Pilgrims still live, but I have one of them

with me. The veil is rent, ma'am. I need you to help me knit it
back again."

"Where is the Song?" she asked.

Heloise looked at her feet, her cheeks flushing. "Gone."

The woman swallowed, swayed. She put a hand to her forehead. "Please tell me that you lie."

"I do not. Come with us. There is no time."

The woman sighed, mastered herself, then turned to Onas.
"Did you know?"

The Sindi boy said nothing, kept his eyes locked on Heloise.

"Tell her, Onas," Heloise said.

"I did not know that the devils had taken the capital," Onas
said slowly, "until just now, when Heloise brought word."

"That they had taken the *capital*," the Nightingale said, "but
you knew the veil was rent? That they roamed the sunlit world?
Why didn't you tell me?" The Nightingale's voice shook.

Onas looked at his feet, said nothing.

The Nightingale took a step, and Heloise wondered if she might
not strike him. She swallowed again, turned to Heloise. "If you
are lying . . ."

Heloise reached up to the reliquary box, realized with a start
that Barnard held the only key. The frustration boiled over and
she forced her knife-blade into the lock hasp, wrenching down
hard. The tinker-engine bellowed with the strain. Barnard had
made the lock well, but he had made the war-machine better. The
blade began to bend, and for a moment, Heloise feared it would
snap, but at last the lock tore open with a shriek of metal and
her arm came swinging free. She could see the blade was bent
badly. *Doesn't matter. Tone was right that we will not beat this enemy
with weapons.*

She reached up again, using the bent blade to hook one of the
horns on the devil's severed head. She drew it out, tossed it at the

Nightingale's feet. "I am Heloise Factor, knife-handed, devil-slayer. I am telling the truth."

The Nightingale bent, lifted the head, examined it for a long time. At last she spoke, trembling. "Where is this Pilgrim? Take me to him."

*If he is still alive,* Heloise thought. She gestured to the battered gate. The Nightingale nodded, gathered her skirts, and strode toward it.

"Wait!" Onas shouted after her.

"I will not," the Nightingale shouted back to him. "Send your dancing knives to cut down an old woman while her back is to you. Do you know what devils are, boy? Do you know what they do?"

She kept walking, her eyes fixed on the gate. Onas shot an angry glance first to Heloise, then to Giorgi, then to the knife-dancers where they stood in a protective ring around the Mothers.

No one moved.

Heloise turned and found herself face to face with Poch.

"I . . . I am sorry for Ingomer," Heloise managed, then pushed past him, the old Drover having to stumble sideways to keep from being crushed by the machine.

For the first few steps, Heloise's back itched, as she waited to hear the sound of knives whistling through the air, or footsteps pounding after them. But there was nothing. She cleared the gate just behind the Nightingale, and the two walked out into the field beyond.

Tone stood beside Xilyka, unharmed. Ingomer lay on his back. Heloise could not see the wound that had killed him, for Xilyka had removed the knife and folded his arms across his chest. He looked like a man sleeping.

Danad had dragged himself clear and was crawling toward the gate, casting terrified glances over his shoulder at the Hapti girl.

Heloise joined Xilyka in ignoring him. "Are you all right?" She scanned Xilyka for wounds. Apart from a small bruise on the her wrist, the knife-caster looked perfectly fine.

Xilyka shrugged. "He told me either he or the Pilgrim was dying today. Figured we needed the Pilgrim more."

"Oh good, I was . . ."

"Heloise, are *you* all right?"

Heloise followed the look of worry in her eyes, traced it to her skin. At once the pain of it hit her, the deep fire under it, the dry, stretched feeling across her bones. She looked down, caught the angry red patches across her belly and thighs. White blisters were beginning to rise in the midst of them, pale, numb islands in a sea of fiery crimson.

"I'm . . . I'll be all right." As she said the words, heat swamped her, followed by chills. A fever pulsing. She could feel sweat beading on her forehead, sliding down the waxy surface of the red skin.

Xilyka climbed onto the machine's frame, reached in, touched a red patch on Heloise's thigh and jerked her hand back, hissing. "This will need a poultice. We need to put her into a bath."

"There is no time for that," Heloise began.

"We will *make* time for—"

"She is right," Tone said. "We must return at once." He turned to the Nightingale. "You must return with us to the city. The Congregation must awake."

"The girl says that the Emperor's Song is gone—"

Tone looked away. "He . . . he fell in battle. I am sorry."

Heloise stared at him, but Tone did not meet her eyes, and he did not say more.

"Who are you?" the Nightingale asked. "Where is your flail? Your seal?"

"I am Brother Tone of the Cygnus Chapter. Though as far as

I know, I am the last of our convocation. My flail lies in the ruin of our capital. It is invested by the enemy, too numerous to throw back on our own. But my heart is true to the Emperor's purpose, and I will see His will done here. The veil must be knit, and you must help me to knit it."

"A Pilgrim with neither flail nor armor," the Nightingale said, "a Kipti and a villager in a tinker-engine. And you tell me the capital is invested by the Great Enemy, and the Song is fallen. What am I to believe?"

"What your eyes show you," Xilyka said, gesturing to the devil's head in her hands. "I have no great desire to travel in the company of an old woman in her mourning clothes, let alone this preaching-head. I am here to guard Heloise, and the sooner we get this veil closed back up and the devils knocked off back to where they came from, the sooner she will stop romping around after you fools. So, if I could trouble you to believe us, and quickly, I would appreciate it."

The Nightingale gaped at her, and Xilyka nodded, turned on her heel, and jogged off toward the woods.

"Where are you going?" Heloise called after her.

"To find spaderoot," Xilyka said. "Helps with the burning. I'll catch up. I'll eat one of my knives if that crone can move faster than a lame dog."

# 12

## YOU KEEP IT

*For what is a devil but a reflection of ourselves? It is our face in the mirror when the candle is spent, our soul laid bare in the instant just before it gutters out.*
—Sermon given in the Imperial Shrine
on the centennial of the Fehta

For the first league, Heloise kept turning to look behind her, shocked each time when she saw that Onas's renegades were not following. Her burns pained her, chafing against the scorched and ragged remains of her clothing and the unyielding leather of the control straps. The pain was not great, but it was endless, spread across the whole of her body under skin that felt stretched too thin. She was careful to avoid looking down at herself, but she could catch the angry red of the burned skin, the blossoming white blisters, out of the corner of her eye.

The Nightingale carried the devil's head reverently, her mouth working softly as she gazed into the gray clusters of its dead eyes, still as fresh as they were on the day Barnard cut the head from the monster's shoulders. Tone cast glances at her as they walked, the awe plain in his eyes.

Heloise felt the constant nattering of her burns. She just wanted to rest, to be *comfortable*, if only for a moment. The sight of the old woman gazing at the severed head like a lover sent a surge of sick anger through her. The pain and the tightness made it impossible to bite it back, and before she knew it she had said, "Keep it."

Both Tone and the Nightingale looked at her in shock. "What?" the old woman asked.

"Heloise," Tone said slowly, "you are the only living person in memory who has slain a devil and lived. That is your evidence."

"No, I'm not." Heloise fought to keep her voice down. "I bet some of your soldiers with the siege engines killed one. Maybe even two, but you don't want to talk about it because it spoils your stupid legend. If killing a devil isn't a great act, then maybe we don't need to be so frightened of them. And if we don't need to be so frightened of them, then why do we need an Order at all? Or an Emperor?"

Tone blanched. "That is heresy . . ."

"Yes, it is!" Heloise was shouting now. "What will you do? Hit me with your stick? Preach me a sermon? 'Heresy' was always a way to shut people up before you had to listen to what they had to say. Your stupid faith is like the capital—it looks impregnable, but once you've got something big enough to kick a hole in it, it goes over like a pile of sticks. The devils are strong, but they aren't special. Wizardry brings them in, but it also keeps them out."

"I am no wizard," the Nightingale said. "My gifts come from the Emperor."

"There is no Emperor!" Heloise felt her legs shaking. "The Sacred Throne is empty! It looks like it's been empty for a thousand winters! He's a made-up story! Just like the devils!"

"The devils are real!" The Nightingale held up the head as proof.

"So are bears! So is the pox or a dust-devil, or any other thing that can kill us! Doesn't mean you have to burn villages."

She could see Tone chewing on his bottom lip. A part of her wished he would try to strike her, so that she could repay it in kind. Her stomach roiled as she recalled the helplessness the last time she faced him, realizing that the war-machine alone was not enough, that mounted and properly armed, he was still a match for her. But not now, after he given up his flail and more, after the sight of the empty throne.

She leaned toward him. "You know it's true. You don't believe in the Emperor any more than I do. But you won't say it, and I know why. Because if you do, if you confess that you have been wrong all this time, then you will have to account for what you have done. You will have to pay for my eye, and my mother, and Gunnar, and for Austre and everyone at Hammersdown."

Tone blanched, his shoulders shaking. "The devils smashed your precious army just as surely as my Order. You cannot deny them."

"Not trying to," Heloise hissed back, "but neither am I using it as an excuse to be just like them."

She reached up, wedging the corner of the shield between the reliquary box and the machine's helmet. She pushed, was surprised to find the leather straps holding. She increased the pressure, feeling the engine gather force, roaring louder. Tone's mouth twitched, and she pictured him laughing at her as the Emperor demonstrated His power, the reliquary miraculously refusing to be budged.

But at last the straps sheared and the Nightingale stepped back as the metal box crashed to the ground. Its underside was nearly black with rust and mold where it had adhered to the metal beneath.

Heloise stepped on it, the machine's weight driving it into the ground. "Keep that." Heloise stabbed her knife-hand at the devil's head. "You. Keep. That." She bit off each word. "We go now to a final fight with the real enemy. And it will end either with their deaths or with ours. And either way, a severed head won't count for anything."

"Heloise, she is *helping* us," Tone said.

"She is helping us because she wants to see the enemy beaten," Heloise said, "because she wants to help everyone. *Everyone*. Traveling People, rangers, heretics, and Imperials alike. And if that's not why, if a few words of truth are enough for her to withdraw her help, then she can stay here on the road, and I will fight the devils myself."

"Heloise!" Tone began, but the Nightingale silenced him with a gesture.

"She is right, Holy Brother," she said. "I am here to defeat the enemy. And a few angry words will not change that."

"Still, I will—" Tone began.

"You will"—Xilyka's voice cut through the conversation as she emerged from the wood beside them, bundles of some uprooted plant clutched in both hands—"use that stick of yours to help me grind these. And you may gripe all you like while you work, but nobody is going anywhere or doing anything until we've a poultice for Heloise's burns."

•　　•　　•

Xilyka sent Tone to fetch water from a pond a few paces into the woods, cupping it in his hands for the short jog to a divot in a rock where he dumped it out. It made a shallow bowl into which Xilyka shredded the broad, green leaves. "Go on then, priest." She motioned to him. "Grind."

Heloise half-expected the Pilgrim to protest, but Tone leaned on his staff without complaint, churning the concoction into a bitter-smelling mush. Xilyka scooped handfuls of it out, slathering it across Heloise's skin. The relief was instant, a delicious coolness spreading through her, coupled by a tingling that felt oddly good. Xilyka then removed her cloak and cut it into broad strips, which she bound across Heloise's body.

"You must lance the boils," Tone said. "If you just cover them up, they will poison her."

Xilyka snorted. "You Pilgrims are great scholars of things you know nothing about. You have made a profession of being wrong. If we lance them, we put holes in her that are open to all the dirt of the road. That will surely kill her. Unless that was your intent?"

She turned a cold eye toward Tone, and Heloise, angry as she was, shook her head. "He is ignorant, Xilyka, but he isn't trying to hurt me."

Xilyka grunted and hopped down off the machine's knee. "Losing my patience with the ignorant. Come, let's finish this."

They went on in silence, faster now that pain no longer nagged Heloise. Still, the Nightingale was old, and Heloise endured her slow walk for as long as she could before finally insisting that she carry the old woman. She was careful not to jostle her too much, keeping the machine at little more than a fast walk, but it was a little quicker at least. The Nightingale endured it with something approaching dignity, cradled gently between the shield and the machine's breastplate.

It was then that Heloise realized that the Nightingale no longer carried the devil's head.

The old woman had set it down somewhere along the way.

·     ·     ·

The journey back was lost in a rhythm of anxiety, each step accompanied by a fresh worry. Foot up. *My father is dead.* Foot down. *We'll never be able to get past the devils.* Foot up. *The city will be destroyed, and the Congregation with it.* Foot down. *I will lose everyone who is dear to me. I will be alone.* After a league, Heloise stopped watching the horizon, bent her eyes to the broken gray-brown of the road, the blurring of it as she hurried along helping her to feel as if she were moving faster. She could hear Xilyka and Tone panting as they struggled to keep up. The world blurred by, Xilyka's poultice and the chill wind masking the heat of her wounds.

"We are close," Xilyka panted alongside her, and Heloise looked up to see the familiar widening of the track as it wound toward the slum outside the capital's postern gate.

The wind rose, whistling through the trees loud enough that Heloise couldn't be sure she heard the sound of boots crunching on snow until she saw two figures stagger out of the distance, jogging down the track toward them. Heloise stopped, set the Nightingale down. "Get behind me."

Tone drew up beside her, raised his staff. Xilyka fanned her knives out in her hands.

"Protect the Nightingale," Heloise said to her. "She's all that matters now."

But as the figures drew closer, Heloise saw they were unarmed, faces lit with fear. They wore torn red tabards over their metal armor, streaked with brown swipes of dried blood.

"Red Lords' soldiers." Heloise's stomach sank.

"That . . . does not bode well," Xilyka said.

"Turn around!" one of them was already shouting. "Go back!"

"What is it?" Heloise fought against the panic rising in her gut.

"All is lost," one of the soldiers said, not slowing as he drew close. "The devils have the city."

"They already had the city—" Xilyka said.

"What about the palace? What about my father?" Heloise cut her off.

The two men finally slowed to a walk, but did not stop. Up

close, Heloise could see the blood matted in their hair, smearing their clothing, some of it fresh. "The devils have the palace," one of them said. "Everyone is gone. I am sorry. If you're smart, you'll come with us."

"But you two are alive!" Heloise turned as they moved past her.

"We ran out the back when they breached the doors," one of them said. "We didn't stay for the end."

"Cowards!" Tone shouted after them. "You cannot just—"

Heloise stopped him with a wave. The panic was like a caged bird inside her, fluttering and slamming itself against the walls of her stomach. "Did you *see* everyone killed?"

"We didn't stay!" the soldier called over his shoulder. "There's no way they could have survived."

"Come with us!" the other man called to them across the growing distance. "There's nothing more for you to do back there!"

"We have the Nightingale!" Tone shouted. "We can end this! Come back, you damned cowards!"

"We will"—the soldiers were dwindling with distance now—"once you have ended it."

"Let them go," Heloise said, and the panic spasmed and died, giving way to resigned dread. "We don't want cowards with us."

"They didn't *see* everyone die," Xilyka said, but she did not sound hopeful.

"It doesn't matter," Heloise said, starting toward the city again. "Even if everyone is dead, we must still bring the Nightingale before the Congregation."

"If those men speak true"—Xilyka did not move—"then the Congregation is dead, too."

"Xilyka. There isn't time. Come on."

"No," Xilyka said. "If the palace is lost, then why should we go back in there? Why should we all die fighting our way through to an empty building?"

"Because we have to," Heloise said with sudden heat. "Because if there is even a chance for us to end this, to save everyone, we have to try. They didn't *see* the Congregation lost. And if they didn't *see* that, it means there's still hope."

She turned to go again, but Xilyka didn't move.

"Xilyka," Heloise began.

"No." Xilyka's voice broke, and Heloise was surprised to see her chin quivering. "There's no point."

"The Congregation lives!" Tone said.

"How can you know that?" Xilyka asked.

"Because . . . because they have to," Tone said.

Xilyka snorted, a tear tracking down one cheek. "The Wheel turns as it will. You saw what those monsters did to the army. What makes you think the handful left in that palace could survive them?"

"It's a smaller space," Heloise said with a certainty she didn't feel. "Maybe they built a barricade. Maybe if only a few devils can attack them at once—"

"You saw what the devils did to the other barricades people built," Xilyka said. "You can't go dragging this old woman in there for nothing—"

"This old woman," said the Nightingale, "is going on. Heloise is right. If the Congregation has been destroyed, then that is the Emperor's will, but I will see their corpses with my own eyes before I turn back."

"Xilyka. I need you with me," Heloise said.

Xilyka refused to move. "Heloise, please. You don't have to die."

Heloise felt tears prick at the corners of her eyes, shook her head to chase them away. "Then help me to live, Xilyka. Help us all to live."

Xilyka swallowed, nodded.

"Good," Heloise said, and then they were running again.

.   .   .

At first, the capital appeared as they'd left it. The ramshackle slum, the unlocked postern gate, the abandoned walls. Heloise felt her heart lift at the sight. Maybe the refugees they'd met on the road had spoken too soon, fled before they took the full measure of things.

Tone must have been thinking the same, for he whispered, "Throne be praised," and set off running for the palace.

Heloise followed, careful not to jostle the Nightingale as she lengthened the machine's stride. The beautiful houses whipped past her, but Heloise only had eyes for the long road, the pattern of cobbles leading arrow-straight to where the huge palace squatted, smooth and black, at the center of the city. Her father was there, and Barnard, all that was left of her old life now. All she had to love. She would not let herself pray, not to the false Emperor that may never have existed, but her hope was too powerful to deny, and so it became a repeating chant. *Please be all right. Please be all right. Please be all right.*

She made a promise to herself then, that when this was over, she would go to her father. She had not been able to be his daughter when she was leading an army, but with the devils defeated she could love him again. *I will tell him that I love him. That I am still his daughter. That I am sorry.* A mad image rose in her mind, all the more delightful for its impossibility—Heloise, returned to Lutet, living with Xilyka and her father, knowing peace and love for all her days remaining.

The thought lent strength to her legs and she ran all the harder, the machine eating up the distance, until Tone and Xilyka fell behind, and at last the palace reared up before them.

Heloise slowly jogged to a stop, the ember of hope sputtering, then finally going out.

The fleeing soldiers had not lied.

The palace was ringed with devils. Heloise could see the postern door shut fast, streaked with blood, the remains of two bodies just outside it. The cobbles leading up to it were cracked where one of the bolt-throwers' giant missiles had pierced it. Bolts and heavy stones cracked the cobblestone everywhere she looked, as if it had been cultivated, a garden that sprouted fruits of war. Scattered Imperial corpses showed that the garrison had attempted a sally to drive the devils back.

It was a fight the defenders had clearly lost.

Two sights froze her heart. The first was that so many of the devils were idle. They stood or sat, resting, mismatched nostrils lifted to scent the air, stalked eyes contemplating the gray sky. *It's because they've won,* her mind whispered to her. *It's because there's no one left for them to kill.*

The second sight was worse. One of the palace front gates lay on its side, the huge black door ripped from hinges and dragged all the way around to the back.

Which meant the palace was open. Which meant the devils were inside.

Heloise could hear the growling now, the eagle screams, muffled by the distance and the palace's thick stone walls.

*Father.*

Heloise was running again before she knew she'd moved.

"Heloise!" Xilyka shouted after her. "Not that way! Go through the postern!"

Heloise stopped, choking back tears. "That's one of the palace gates! The front way is open!"

"It's too long that way round, too many devils," Xilyka said. "We go straight in through the back."

"There's too many devils everywhere." Heloise could hear the whine rising in her voice, borne on the cresting wave of panic. *They are all already dead. You have already lost.*

"I will draw them off," Tone said, already moving away from them, away from the palace.

"Tone!" Heloise called to him. "I can't protect you!"

"The Emperor will protect me," Tone called back. "Get the Nightingale to the Congregation. You stand in the Shadow of the Throne, Heloise, truly."

And then he was running, bellowing at the top of his lungs. It took Heloise a moment to recognize that he was shouting verses from the Writ, calling the devils to him with the text that condemned them.

Heloise heard the familiar eagle screams as several of the creatures noticed him. A moment later they were on their feet and after him, not with the blinking speed with which they had struck the army outside the wall, but with the slower, stalking pace Heloise knew they used when they wished to savor the chase. At least five of them detached themselves from the palace, trotting after Tone, who was racing toward the ruin of one of the fancy houses, collapsed in on itself around a catapult stone.

But not all of the devils had given chase. At least a score of them remained around the postern door, eyes tracking their brethren, perhaps seeing too little sport in chasing a single man to warrant competing with so many of their own. As Heloise watched, one of them swiveled its head her way, gave its piercing call. It was joined by another, and another.

Heloise looked down at the Nightingale. The old woman was clinging white-knuckled to the shield's edge, pushing with her thin legs to brace herself against the machine's chest. *If I lose her,*

Heloise thought, *it will all have been for naught.* She bit down on her panic, on the desperate need to reach her father's side. *I can't lose you, Father. You have to be alive. You have to be.* "Hold on," she said, and set off.

Three devils raced to meet her. The others were rising now, their screams joining the chorus as they realized that there was more than just one fleeing man. She saw one of Xilyka's knives whisk past, striking one of the devils between the slits of its nostrils, making the creature scream and duck its head.

The Nightingale was groaning now, clinging desperately to the inside of the shield, bracing as hard as she could against the jostling of the machine. "Hold on!" Heloise shouted to her as she lowered her shoulder, raised the shield. She pressed her knife-arm behind it, bracing it to keep the pocket of empty space that was all that kept the Nightingale safe. The devils closed, and Heloise dropped her shoulder lower, so that she was stumbling forward now, only her run keeping her upright. The palace grew in her vision, and the cluster of devils converging on her grew with it.

Heloise glanced up, seeing the devils nearly upon her, aimed herself between the two closest, and dropped her shoulder even lower, jerking it up just as she hit.

She struck the devils with the sound of a hammer on an anvil. She pushed hard with her knife-hand, thrusting the shield out and up, feeling the metal corner slam into the devils. She could hear their screams, the screech of their claws against metal. The sudden impact made the frame shudder, and then Heloise could hear their screams over her head as they went flying. Heloise heard another chorus of screams as they slammed into their comrades.

Heloise staggered a few more steps, but she had overbalanced the machine, the headlong pitch too extreme to correct. *I'm going to fall.* She glanced down at the Nightingale. The old woman was still braced behind the shield, her eyes wide, face so pale that it nearly matched the white of her hair.

Heloise took three more staggering steps, watching the postern door growing in her field of vision, before the machine staggered onto its knees, and Heloise opened the shield to keep the Nightingale from being crushed against the machine's chest. The old woman tumbled free, rolling along the cracked cobbles. Heloise watched her rise to her knees, shoulders trembling, crawl the few remaining paces to the postern door. Xilyka raced to the Nightingale and stood over her, knives fanned out in her hands. Her head whipped left and right, unable to pick a single target out of the throng.

A weight slammed into in the machine's back, and Heloise threw her arm back, driving the shield's point behind her. She was rewarded with a shriek, and the weight lifted. Heloise staggered the machine to its feet, punched out with the shield corner, cracking a devil in the side of its head just as it made for Xilyka.

She staggered the last steps toward them, screaming. She didn't bother with her knife-hand now, swinging the heavy shield left and right, the devils so close it was impossible to miss, each stroke connecting, rewarding her with the shock of the blow reverberating up her arm. She lost sight of Xilyka and the Nightingale, vanished in the thickening forest of devils surrounding her. A blow struck the side of her helmet, sent her staggering into another devil, its body keeping the machine upright.

Heloise slammed it aside with the shield and took another step, felt the ground shift beneath her. She risked a glance down, saw she was standing on the long ironwood beam of the gate's locking bar, dragged by whatever devil had decided to pull it here. A blow on her back drove the machine to its knees again, and suddenly the beam filled her vision, the smooth grain of the petrified wood whorled like carved stone. *It's no use. There are too many of them to fight.* Another blow on the back of the helmet sent her face slamming into the inside of the visor. Heloise tasted blood.

She glanced up, saw movement through the forest of devils' legs around her. A glimmer of something white. *You haven't seen your father dead. You haven't seen Xilyka dead. Until you do, you have to go on fighting.*

Another blow on her shoulder sent the corner of her shield banging into the cobblestone beside the locking bar. The tip of a claw scraped past her face, slipping below the gorget to dig a furrow across her chest. She screamed, not from the pain, but from the frustration of having come so close, only to lose now. She remembered Xilyka swallowing her tears on the road. *You don't have to die.*

*Yes, I do,* Heloise thought, *if living means I lose everyone who matters to me.*

She tried to push off with her shield corner, but it slid sideways, scooping under the locking bar. Heloise watched the bar rise, felt the pressure of it against the shield. She reached out with the knife-hand, pinned the bent blade against the locking bar's opposite side, pinching it against the shield corner. She pushed with all she had, felt the machine translate the movement, the engine roaring in response.

Heloise screamed and stood, swinging the massive beam up. For a moment, she thought it would be beyond even the machine's great strength, but at last she felt it rise, swinging up and around. It was as long as a tree trunk, and Heloise let the momentum carry the machine to its feet. The beam's own weight carried it now, and it swung crosswise, slamming into the crowd of the devils, knocking them aside, sending them tumbling into one other. They screamed as they pulled back, shocked by the unexpected weapon in their midst. Heloise let the momentum of the swing carry her around again and again, feeling it shake as it found a devil each time. With each blow she feared it would break, but the beam shivered and held. A devil darted toward her and the beam caught it beneath its arm, sending it flipping sideways and landing on its face. Another tried to duck low, but Heloise caught its horns on the backswing, snapping them off and knocking the creature onto its face. She stepped back with each blow, the space around her clearing as the devils backed off to assess the new threat, their screams receding into the now-familiar stalking growls.

Somewhere in the distance, she could still hear Tone's mad chanting. They hadn't killed him yet.

Heloise took another step back and felt the palace wall scrape against the tinker-engine mounted to the war-machine's back. "Xilyka!" she shouted.

"The door is shut fast." The Hapti girl sounded dazed, but also close.

"You're alive!"

"For now, by the Wheel, but you have to get this door open."

Heloise glanced to her right and saw the knife-caster standing over the Nightingale. The old woman was curled up against the wall, an arm thrown over her face, panting like a rabbit with hounds on its tail. *Panting means breathing.*

Heloise swung the bar crosswise again, and the devils once again drew back, the palace wall keeping them from circling around her.

"Can you get the door open?" Heloise asked. "Can someone inside let us in?"

"I have tried." The resignation in Xilyka's voice made the panic in Heloise's belly surge. "It won't budge. I do not know that there is anyone alive inside to let us in, Heloise."

Heloise rested the locking bar long enough to ensure the machine's grip on it, and barely got it up in time to bat aside a charging devil, catching it across its face and knocking its head sharply to the side. It dropped like a sack of stones, and Heloise used the bar's momentum to swing it up over her head and down, smashing the creature's chest. She felt the crunching of bone, and the spray of black blood told Heloise the damage had been done.

The devils circled, wary, waiting for an opening. Heloise inched closer to Xilyka, making sure she and the Nightingale were inside the beam's range. Heloise glanced at the postern door. The ironwood beam would make a perfect ram if she could get a running start, if she could couch it behind the shield. But she watched the circling throng of devils and knew they would not give her the chance. She was trapped here, the palace at her back, until she tired enough to make a mistake, or the devils grew brave enough to rush her at once. She thought of fighting her way around to the open front doors, but she knew the moment she didn't have the palace wall at her back, she would be surrounded and overwhelmed.

"I . . . I can't, Xilyka," she said. "I'm sorry."

The knife-caster's voice was kind. "You've done what you could, Heloise. We all have. The Wheel turns."

A devil lunged for Xilyka and she flinched back, throwing a knife that skipped harmlessly off the creature's shoulder, but she did not budge from her position over the Nightingale. The devil reached for her, then spun away as Heloise swung the beam and bowled it aside.

"I never thought I would meet my end," the Hapti girl panted, "astride a withered old bag of bones beside a one-handed madwoman wielding a tree."

Heloise was shocked to feel herself smile, felt the tears come. "I'm sorry," she said again.

"Aye, me, too," Xilyka said. "Me, too."

The devils pressed in, the circle of them of them drawing tighter. They'd figured the bar's range now, stood just a handspan outside it, waiting for Heloise to tire. She could see the tension in their legs, knew they were readying for a final charge.

Eagle screams, loud and urgent, from the back of the pack of devils. Heloise braced herself for their onslaught, lifted the bar to swing again.

And then the circle was breaking apart, the devils turning away from her.

Smoke was rising among them. She could see flickering fire shapes, shaped like men, darting through them, waving their red-and-orange limbs in their faces. Heloise knew only one man who could make fire dance in the shapes of men.

She surged forward, swinging the locking bar again, clouting the devils on their backs now, sending them scattering. A few turned to hiss at her, swatting at the bar, but they were focused on a new threat now, the dancing flame men and the flesh ones Heloise could see now, down the cracked cobblestone street. Giorgi stood at their head, a torch in each hand. Heloise could not make out his face at this distance, but she didn't need to. He had come.

"Heloise!" Xilyka shouted, but she was already moving, resting the beam against the machine's knee, taking hold of it again, this time couched under the machine's arm. She jogged the machine a few paces out, then raced toward the postern door, throwing her weight against the beam as it struck.

The door shuddered. She could hear the cracking of stone inside, see fragments splinter away from the jamb. But it held.

Heloise stepped back, readied herself to try again, saw Xilyka's eyes widen. She dropped the beam and spun, her shield connecting with the face of a devil just as it reached her. It staggered backward, clustered white eyes going gray, stumbling. Heloise turned her back on it, snatched up the bar again, and charged a second time.

This time the door shuddered and groaned, and with a loud snapping of stone, swung open.

Heloise turned, heaved the locking bar into the devils, then bent to scoop the Nightingale back up again. The old woman blinked as Heloise lifted her. "Are we . . ."

But Heloise ignored her, stepping through the door and into the passage beyond. Daylight streamed in behind her, revealing the broad passage skirting the throne room to where it opened beside the dark staircase she would need to mount to bring the Nightingale before the Congregation. She took a step into the cool darkness, and froze.

The first thing she saw was the Right Gate, his face gray, eyes sightlessly staring, mouth frozen in an O of shock. One of Sir Steven's red-tabarded infantry lay across him, his face little more than a red hole the diameter of a devil's claw.

Heloise's breath caught. For a moment, the Congregation, the old woman nestled behind her shield, even the possibility that all was already lost vanished, replaced by a single, urgent thought: *Father.*

She took off running, the hallway rushing past her, Xilyka's hurrying footfalls behind her nearly drowned by the clanking of the machine's metal feet. She saw the first devil almost immediately, its purple back filling the corridor, its head bent to keep its long horns clear of the ceiling. Beyond it, she could see its comrades packing the nave, a wash of purple and yellow-white.

It was already too late.

*No,* she thought fiercely. *You haven't seen any other bodies. Maybe they're still alive.*

"Hold on!" she said to the Nightingale for a third time, then raised her knife-hand and leapt at the devil, slamming it into the monster's back.

As soon as the knife moved into her field of vision, Heloise realized she'd made a terrible mistake. The blade was still bent from when she had used it to pry off the reliquary lock.

Instead of a sharp point, it was a flat band of iron that struck the devil. The metal protested, sparked, and finally sheared off, her weapon going spinning up, tumbling end-over-end, until it bounced off the wall and went tumbling in the dust.

The devil shrieked, tried to turn, but Heloise used the momentum of her strike to barrel into it, letting the machine's weight wedge it behind the monster, pinning it against the wall. The devil flailed, threw two elbows hard into the machine's side, screamed as its bone collided with the metal.

The Nightingale groaned and Heloise looked down to see the old woman pressed flat against the inside of the shield. She was bleeding, though Heloise could not see from where. *She's alive, and you must keep her that way or all this will be for nothing.*

She tried to push off, to create enough space to slip past the devil and reach the staircase, but she couldn't do it without pressing the shield flat to her body, crushing her precious cargo. "Xilyka!"

"I'm coming!" Xilyka's voice sounded so close that Heloise realized the Hapti girl had charged in just behind her. She caught a flash as Xilyka leapt, springing off the machine's knee, grasping one of the devil's arms and vaulting over it, pinning her back to the wall, feet braced on the creature's chest.

"Xilyka, no!" Heloise shouted as the devil stretched its jaws and whipped its head forward.

But Xilyka was ready and thrust her hands forward, flat knives clutched tightly in her fingers. Heloise watched them plunge into the center of the mass of stalked white eyes. The devil screamed, the piercing cry thankfully directed away from her. It must have deafened Xilyka, but the Hapti girl showed no sign of pain, pulling the knives out and plunging them back into the creature's eyes again and again with such speed that her hands were a gray blur, arms coated in the fetid black blood up to the elbows. The devil's bite went wide, and it lurched back, four of its six hands coming up to claw at its wounded face. Xilyka dropped to the floor and plunged into the nave beyond.

Heloise felt the pressure of the creature's body threatening to press her shield arm flat, and punched out with the shield's corner, pushing until the engine coughed. At last, the devil rolled aside, flailing blindly down the corridor toward the postern door.

She turned, ran the last two steps to the entrance of the staircase. Xilyka was already up it, leaping over the bannister, stumbling as she touched down on the other side.

Beyond her, Heloise could see the nave, crowded with devils. Three had turned at the screams of their wounded comrade, were gathering their wits for a charge. Heloise ignored them, spared one glance for the Nightingale to ensure the old woman was still clutched against her, and leapt for the bannister.

She knew she'd misjudged the moment the machine's feet left the stone. She was not outside, and while the ceiling was not low, it still existed. Heloise prayed it was higher than she—a sharp ringing on the machine's helmet told her it was not. The machine's shoulders collided with the stone above her next, and she fell hard, striking the stone bannister with enough force to crack it, before flipping over and landing on the staircase beyond. She could see Xilyka scramble out of the way just before she landed. Her head rattled inside the helmet. She could feel her body wrench tight against the control straps. Her bandages slipped free, the heat blisters on her skin bursting. The fire in her skin, the nagging pain, made itself known to her again.

The machine was lying on its chest, the shield pressed flat against it. Sick with horror, Heloise pushed off with the corner to raise it up.

The Nightingale was not there.

Heloise levered the machine onto its knees and saw the old woman. She was stumbling, bleeding badly from her head. Xilyka had slung her arm around her shoulders, was dragging her up the steps.

Toward a barricade, a jumbled mass of severed pipes, lengths of rusted iron railing, and scavenged blocks of stone.

Behind it were people, *her* people.

She spotted the silver spikes of Sir Steven's hair, Wolfun's gray-streaked beard. But she didn't see . . .

"Heloise!" Samson shouted, standing up behind the wall of debris. He'd scavenged a pike from some fallen Imperial and pumped it over his head. "Heloise, come on!"

Her heart surged. She forgot her wounds, forgot her fatigue, got the machine to its feet to follow after Xilyka and the Nightingale, who had reached the barricade, were stretching for the hands of the defenders to pull them up.

Something heavy collided with the machine and Heloise was smashed back down onto the stairs. She could hear the devil scrabbling on top of her, could feel it raking at the machine with its claws. She pushed off with the shield corner, the old familiar technique to get back on her feet. She gritted her teeth as she felt the tinker-engine strain, and the machine began to rise.

Another weight was added to the first, then another. The machine was pressed flat again. She could feel the claws now, a flurry of sharp bone swiping at every exposed inch of metal. There must have been at least three of the things atop her. She would never be able to stand now. She looked left and right, trying desperately to see her enemies, to figure out some way to . . .

"Heloise!" Barnard's voice. The huge tinker had leapt over the barricade and run to her. She could see him looping his forge hammer up, swinging the heavy iron head with all his strength. She heard a sickening crunch as it collided with something, and suddenly the weight on the machine lightened as the devil he had struck jerked back.

She could feel its flailing arms reach out, scrape across the tinker-engine on the machine's back. They scrabbled for a moment, found purchase.

Suddenly the weight on the machine's back trebled, pulling with such force that the machine bent at the waist, lifting up so high that Heloise had a view of the barricade once more, could see her father had leapt it as well, was racing to Barnard's side.

And then there was a shrieking of metal as the devil's weight tore it off her back, taking the war-machine's engine with it.

The machine's strength died. The frame slumped back down to the staircase, lifeless.

The devil who had ripped the engine from the machine's back had flopped down the stairs, taking its comrades with it. Heloise could hear them shrieking and hissing as they tried to disentangle themselves.

Sir Steven was hauling the Nightingale onto the barricade's top. Heloise knew she had to get off the stairs before the devils found their bearings and returned to the attack.

But that meant leaving the machine.

She felt her father's hand snake inside the frame, push her knife-hand hard, popping it free of the control strap. "Heloise, come on! You have to come out!"

"I can't," she tried to say. The words came out as a soft croak.

Xilyka slithered under the machine's hip, and Heloise felt her fumbling at the chest strap buckle. "Heloise! Help us! There isn't time!"

Heloise knew they wouldn't be able to free her unless she helped, but even with the machine dead around her, the panic at leaving it was too great. Her limbs felt heavy, her head stuffed with cotton. Outside the metal frame, death was assured. At least if she stayed she would be safe for a little while longer. "I can't!" she screamed as Samson reached behind the shield and yanked on her wrist, ripping it free of the control strap. "I can't I can't I can't!"

She whipped her body back and forth, upsetting Xilyka's fingers on the chest strap, forcing her to withdraw from the buckle.

Xilyka's sounded sad. "Very well, we will defend you as long as we can."

"No!" The panic curdled into grief. "You'll die!"

"Aye," her father said, "but if I am to lose you, then I have nothing left to live for." She could hear him step back, retrieve his pike, make ready.

"What are you doing?" Sir Steven shouted to them. "Come on!"

She could hear the devils hissing as they untangled themselves behind her. It wouldn't be long before they returned. And they would find Xilyka, and her father, and Barnard. And they would kill them all.

She reached down with her arm and unfastened the chest strap, letting the buckle fall open. She was free of all the straps save the ones about her legs, but the panic seized her with a fury beyond anything she'd felt before, and her limbs turned to water. "Please, Father. Just go."

Samson knelt back down to the machine, reached in, grabbed her arm. "Not without you. Heloise, kick free and come on."

"Papa," she whispered. "Papa, I'm frightened."

"I know, dove, but now is the time to be brave. Now is the time to come out."

"I can't."

"You don't have to," Samson said, "only kick free of those straps, and I will do the rest."

"Heloise." Xilyka was kneeling beside her father, reaching out to grab her other arm, just above the elbow. "You do not have to be brave. You do not even have to move. Only kick free and trust us."

Heloise closed her eyes. The world outside the machine was a thing of claws and blades and broken stone. It hung over her, a storm on the verge of breaking, ready to thrust its dagger-lightning into her the moment her head peeked past the metal. It stank of swamps and rang with eagle-screams.

That terror closed in on her, and Heloise knew she wasn't strong enough to face it.

But Xilyka had said she didn't have to.

Her father had said all she had to do was kick free of the leg straps. That was easy, wasn't it? You didn't have to be brave to kick your legs.

Heloise tried it, felt her leaden feet thump against the metal frame. Had the straps come away? She couldn't tell. That was fine. She hadn't been brave, and that was fine too. Here, at the end, she had kicked her legs like the ones she loved most had asked.

And suddenly she was being pulled by her arms, so hard and fast that her shoulders cried out, so that her face and chest scraped against the gap between the chest plate and the machine's gorget. She snapped her eyes open and even the dim light of the stairwell seemed overpoweringly bright. The touch of the close, musty air was freezing, her father and Xilyka's grip on her arm rubbing her skin raw. *No. It's too much. I can't. I can't.* Heloise tried so hard to be good, to be still for them, but she couldn't, and her body shuddered and thrashed on its own, her jaw locked so tight that her scream turned inward, vibrating in her throat.

But if Heloise had been strong inside the war-machine, outside it she was just a girl of sixteen winters. Samson and Xilyka merely tightened their grip on her and ran, vaulting up over the wreckage of the barricade, dragging Heloise flopping along. Behind her, she could hear metal groaning as the devils pounced on the machine, shrieked in frustration as they found it empty.

And then her feet were under her, and Xilyka and her father were hauling her up step after step, and she was running to keep up with them, to keep from going down on her face again.

Ahead of her was the Nightingale, just cresting the top of the stairs and turning into the gallery, leaning heavily on one of the Red Lords archers. At the sight of the Congregation, she found her feet, hurrying on, already singing in a voice that sounded much younger than the throat it issued from. It was strong and clear, filling the gallery instantly. Heloise imagined she could see the dirty circle of windows brightening. The old Sojourner was nowhere to be seen, but Heloise could see that the Congregation were already awake, shuffling in their chains, blinking with stupid fear.

At the sound of the Nightingale's voice, they turned, began to drift back into rows, their mouths working.

Below them, Heloise heard shouts, then screams, then a terrible crash, the sound of stone and iron fragments being battered aside. *They're not stopping to fight at the barricade. They're smashing through it. They're coming for me.*

The Nightingale sank to her knees. The blood flowed freely from the cut on her head, soaking into the fine black fabric over her shoulder. The singing was growing louder, and Heloise realized the Congregation were adding their voices to hers, stumbling at first, but gradually finding a harmony that filled the huge space, echoed down the stairs behind her.

The devils shrieked a reply, their clawed feet hammering the stone as they came closer.

*Not me. They are coming for her. They want to stop the singing. They know.*

Which meant it was working. Heloise felt a surge of hope, the panic still upon her, but a smaller thing now, a cold stone in her stomach rather than a storm engulfing her soul. Her arms felt light, and she realized that Samson and Xilyka had released her.

The Hapti girl was pulling her knives from their sheaths at her waist, and Samson was turning to level his pike at the top of the stairs. He planted the butt spike against the smooth stone of the floor, cursed as it failed to find purchase. The long pike was meant to be used outside, braced against soft earth.

The first devil crested the stairs and raced toward the Nightingale. It screamed, but even its piercing cry was drowned by the rising chorus, ringing against the vaulted stone, making the glass shake. They had to stop it, couldn't let it interrupt the Nightingale before the song was done.

Heloise called to Xilyka, but the girl was already moving, stepping out in front of the creature, throwing her knives at its face. It didn't break stride, pausing only long enough to backhand her hard enough to launch her into the wall. The Hapti girl struck it with a grunt, slid down to her knees, collapsed on her side. Heloise cried out, but Samson was already moving, changing position just enough to put himself squarely between the monster and the Nightingale.

The devil snapped at his pikehead, mouth unhinging like a snake's, impossibly wide. Samson leaned into the movement, driving the metal head into the creature's open mouth.

The monster flailed toward the Nightingale, not even bothering to bite down. Heloise watched the pike shaft begin to bow.

Samson slammed one boot against the butt-spike, desperately trying to make it stick fast in the smooth stone. But he simply didn't weigh enough on his own, and the metal skittered and shifted along the floor, scratching a long line in the black stone. Slowly, her father was pushed back toward the Congregation.

The Nightingale's song rose higher, and Heloise could see the Congregation standing stock still, chins lifted, voices raised to the ceiling as if the song itself were pulling them up toward the rattling windows, just beginning to show a spiderweb of cracks spreading across their uneven surface.

Samson shouted, pushed down with his leg, slid back another few paces.

Heloise looked at Xilyka. The Hapti girl was still, and the thought that she might be dead was a hammerblow worse than the panic at leaving the machine. It made Heloise want to sink to her knees, to wail. *No. You must give them time to sing.*

She hurled herself at the butt-spike, draping her body across it. Her knife-hand was useless now, but she wrapped her elbow around the shaft, held fast with her other hand. Samson glanced back at her, saying something she couldn't hear, before turning back to the monster. They slid back another pace, and Heloise screamed. Her weight was not enough, it would make no difference. All these leagues behind them, all these dead, here at the end, for nothing.

She screamed, willed her body down toward the flagstones, to hold the pike fast. She flailed, kicking, trying to brace her feet against the smooth stone. The devil took another step and the butt-spike skipped along the floor, ripping up her toes to the top of her foot where it found the purchase it had so hungrily sought.

Heloise was no stranger to pain. She had been burned, stabbed, beaten. She had lost her eye, her hand, her teeth. But the pain as the pike's end punched through the small bones at the top of her foot was a new frontier of agony, and she screamed, her voice joining the Congregation's thrumming song. The butt-spike didn't care for screaming, it merely sank into her foot, punched out the bottom, dragging her body along, turning her into a fleshy weight, her mangled flesh giving it the soft purchase it needed.

With a sudden lurch that hurt her so badly she nearly fainted, the pike stopped sliding.

The devil came to a stop, arms flailing. The pike shaft bent nearly double. Heloise could hear the splintering of wood.

Over the monster's shoulder, through the red haze of pain, Heloise could see other devils pouring into the room, pausing only long enough to find the Nightingale, then shrieking, racing toward her, their path taking them right to where Heloise and Samson stood.

The Congregation's song became deafening. The stone walls seemed to throb with the noise, so powerful that Heloise forgot her pain.

Then suddenly, the devil they'd stopped with the pike was moving again, the weapon punching out the back of its head. The shaft straightened, and the creature slid down it until the monster nearly collided with her father.

And then, with a final sigh, the Congregation's song was done.

Their voices unfurled, a sudden burst of sound that Heloise could feel pass over her like a gale, making the stone walls shake. It was so loud that all other sound was drowned out, but she could see the devil's mouth opening in a silent scream, its field of black tongues vibrating so quickly, straining so far apart that she could see the purple skin between them.

The creature flailed backward, ripping free of the pike and swinging its head left and right, so quickly that Heloise thought it would snap its own neck. Black blood flowed from its scaled ears, its misshapen nostrils, its stalked patches of eyes starting to go gray. Behind it, Heloise could make out its brethren doing the same.

At last it threw its head back and screamed at the circle of windows above, shattering now, the sharp. fragments falling down around it as it finally slumped to its knees and then over on its side, black blood trickling from the corner of its mouth.

All around the room, Heloise could hear similar screams and the crashing of heavy bodies against stone, as the Congregation's song did its work.

The sudden silence was jarring. The song, the screaming, the sound of clicking claws on stone, all gone, and Heloise forgot her fear, forgot the pain in her foot even, all lost in the perfect stillness that followed the release of the Congregation's wizardry. *Did we do it?* Heloise thought. *Did we win?*

"Yes, my dove," Samson said, and Heloise realized she had spoken aloud.

Her father was looking at her, his face sad, his skin the color of fresh ash. "We have beaten them, praise the Throne."

Heloise reached for him, and the pain in her foot reminded her that she would have to pull herself free of the pike first. "Papa," she said, "set the pike down, I'm stuck."

But Samson only kept staring at her, as if he could drink her in with his eyes. "I love you, dove. I love you like I love the air and the turning leaves in fall. I have never known so great a love could be, but it can, and it is mine for you."

"I love you too, Papa, what are you . . ." Heloise began, dread overpowering the pain in her foot.

But Samson's eyes were already closed, and he was slumping to his knees, turning as he fell, so that Heloise could see where the devil's claw had unseamed him, cutting him open from throat to hip, letting his life run out onto the polished stone floor.

# 13

## THE END

*Therefore be bold and do not fear death. In taking the field today, each of you is like unto the glorious Emperor, who gave His life that the people shall know safety and peace. If it is His will that you fall, fall cursing the heretic enemy, and with a smile on your face, for like Him, you shall know life everlasting.*

—Pre-battle harangue at the Siege of Haraven

It was Xilyka who stirred first, shaking off the blow that had thrown her into the wall and gently untangling Heloise from her father's corpse.

She held Heloise's hand as they bound her wounded foot, and then led her down the stairs as they laid Samson outside the golden doors. Beyond them stood the moldering chair the Imperials had called a sacred throne. Heloise covered him with an old banner that Barnard scavenged, sable cloth embroidered with the image of a Palantine. Heloise knew it meant nothing, that they were symbols of a lie that had kept them prisoner their whole lives. But it was a lie her father had believed, and this was surely what he would have wanted.

Sir Steven and his last remaining men had gone to look for

Giorgi, but the Sindi had gone, fled back down the road to the cage, judging by the trail of devil corpses leading that way, dropped in the midst of their pursuit as the Congregation's song did its terrible work. "We found two dead knife-dancers," Sir Steven reported, "but not your Kipti wizard. The devils are . . . That wizardry does not appear to have spared any of them."

Barnard held Heloise as she wept. He was the last shred of her old life left to her, and mad as he was, she needed him.

When at last the tears were spent and she sagged in his arms he straightened, raised her to her feet. "It's all right, your eminence. Your father's body may be here, but his soul dwells in there"—he jerked a thumb at the throne room—"and his strength is added to the Emperor's forever. He gave his life to save us all. He would be glad of that, and you should be too."

But Heloise knew better now. She knew that there was no meaning, no pattern in life or death, merely the hungry world, devouring everything not strong or fleet enough to escape it. *Telling him that will do no good.* Worse, it might hurt him, anger him, make him leave her, and then she would truly have lost every shred of Lutet left to her.

Heloise looked at the devil corpses lying in the nave. They lay strewn across one another where the Congregation's song had killed them, fetid black blood leaking from their noses and ears. They'd dragged the one door off, and the other hung askew on its hinges, affording her a view of the wide steps and the place beyond. Devils lay there, too, scaled limbs outstretched, oblong mouths contorted in death screams. She could see the Imperial troops picking their way past them, a knot of garrison soldiers led by the winged guards who had quit their posts when Tone had demanded entrance. At their head was a reed-thin man, his skin so pale and soft that Heloise wondered if this was his first day of his life out under the sun. His scarlet cloak was immaculate, bor-

dered with gold thread, and with a stiff collar rising high about
his neck, much as the Nightingale's dress. His hood was thrown
back, pooling inside the collar, revealing soft lips and irritated
eyes that reminded her so much of the Song that she felt her skin
break out in gooseflesh. His flail was cut from fine gray wood, the
grain oiled until it shone. The iron of the head and chain were
chased with silver, sparkling in the weak light. Against the filth
and carnage, he looked as strange as a devil himself.

He looked up, saw that there were people in the palace, and
called out to his soldiers. They picked up the pace now, came clattering up the steps, weaving around the broken bodies of the
devils. Here and there, a guard stopped to thrust a spear or halberd into a cluster of eyes, ostensibly to make sure the creature
was dead. But Heloise could see the fury on their faces, and knew
they were really just venting their frustration. They had been unable to come to grips with the devils when they were alive, so
now they would strike them while they were dead.

The first of the winged guards reached the top of the steps and
leveled his halberd at Barnard. "Who are you? How dare you profane the palace of the Sacred Throne?"

Sir Steven put his hand on the pommel of his sword, turned a
weary head to regard the man. "You give me your name, and I
will consider giving mine."

"I am Alaric, captain of the palace guard"—the man's eyes
flashed—"and I will not see it profaned by Kipti and servants of
the Emperor's enemies."

"The Emperor's enemies," Xilyka said, drawing her knives,
"have done your job for you, Alaric. We have secured the palace
while you were . . . What were you doing exactly?"

"I'll not bandy words with a heretic girl . . ." Alaric turned, motioned to the throng of soldiers behind him. Heloise didn't have
time to count, but there must have been at least thirty, more than

enough to overwhelm the handful of her companions, all wounded and exhausted.

"You may not bandy words with a girl," Tone's voice rang out, "but you will kneel before a savior." The soldiers turned as the Pilgrim limped into view, leaning heavily on his staff. A long gash ran across his face, closing one of his eyes, puckering around the edges where it would scar.

"Who are you?" The Sojourner waved his flail at him. Heloise recognized the same irritated insouciance that she'd heard from the Emperor's Song.

"I am Brother Tone, Holy Father." Tone limped closer. "The Emperor's Own, and I bear witness to a miracle."

"A Pilgrim? Unarmored and unarmed? Nonsense. You stole that cloak."

"The Order is destroyed, Holy Father," Tone said, "but I remain a servant of the Emperor's will. I have seen that will worked through the hand of this child, scourged, wounded, stripped of all she has held dear. She has sacrificed all in the Emperor's name, to save us. To deliver us. The devils lie at your feet by her hand."

"I am still alive," the Sojourner said, "I am Pentarch Cleon, and the Order's authority reposes in me. It falls to me to restore order to this city. If you truly serve the Emperor, you will assist me in ensuring this rabble quit the palace immediately." He pointed a slender finger with a thick gold ring at Heloise. "And the heretic girl is to be set in irons."

Heloise froze, eyes moving to Tone, her stomach clenching. After all they had been through, it would be beyond cruel to fall prisoner to him at the end. She steeled herself to fight, but the exhaustion and the agony in her foot were too much. She could barely walk, had no weapons. The machine was a pile of dented metal on the stairway behind her.

But Tone only met the Sojourner's eyes. "No, Holy Father. I will do no such thing."

"You address the last living Pentarch of our—"

"And you," Tone spoke over him, pointing at Heloise, "are in the presence of the Emperor's anointed champion! The savior of us all!"

"You are no Pilgrim . . ." Cleon sputtered.

"Do you know who I am?" The Nightingale limped to Heloise's side. Her skin was so pale that Heloise thought she looked sculpted from the snow that was beginning to fall again, dusting the shoulders of the men outside. For all her frailty, her voice was as strong and as clear as it had been when she had led the Congregation in their powerful song.

The soldiers looked confused, but the Cleon's eyes widened. "You are the sacred charge. The Key."

"I am both of those things," said the Nightingale, "but I am also a witness. Brother Tone speaks the truth. Without flail, without armor, he is Pilgrim of the Order, perhaps the last one alive."

Alaric stiffened, blushing. He raised his halberd, bowed stiffly from the waist. "My apologies, Holy Brother, things are . . . turned on their heads at present."

The Sojourner tapped him on the shoulder with his flail haft. "What is the matter with you? This man is a mere Pilgrim. I have given my orders!"

The Nightingale spoke to Alaric, pointing at Heloise. "That is Heloise Factor, of Lutet. She fetched me from the cage when no one else would, she brought me here through hell itself to assign me to my sacred charge. It is by her hand, and by her hand alone, that we are delivered."

A few of the soldiers were kneeling now, doffing their helmets and tugging on their forelocks. "Savior," Heloise could hear them muttering. "Palantine." She had heard the honorifics so many times since her journey had started that they no longer meant anything to her. They wouldn't bring her father back to life, but if it would keep them from harming the few friends she had left in the world, then it would be worth it.

Cleon spun on them. "What are you doing? She is no Palantine! Get up! I speak for the Throne now!"

But the soldiers did not move, and Heloise took a dragging step toward him. "I have seen the throne," she seethed. "It is *empty*. It is just a story."

Cleon folded his arms across his chest. "I don't know what you thought you saw, heretic girl. The Emperor does not deign to reveal Himself to the likes of you."

"You lie!" Heloise took another step, and Cleon backed up to match her. "It is a story! Admit it! Say it's a story!"

Cleon took another step backward, nearly fell over another of his soldiers, still kneeling, despite his orders. "If it is a story," he whispered, "then it is one the people need."

Heloise ignored him. Instead, she spoke to the soldiers. "No more killing. There is to be no more killing, do you hear me?"

She heard wood clattering on stone as some of the soldiers dropped their weapons, louder as more and more followed their example.

Alaric looked at his men, at Cleon, then back to Tone. He kept his grip on his weapon, but he was outnumbered now, his own troops on bended knee, empty-handed before this strange and scarred little girl. Heloise could tell he was a man used to obeying commands, not giving them. "What . . . what should we do?"

"You should guard the palace," Tone said, "and look to the defense of your savior."

"That's enough!" Cleon shouted, his voice shrill. "You do not serve this false Pilgrim and his pet heretic!"

Heloise closed the remaining distance, grasped the fine flail by the haft, wrenching it away from him. It came easily, his thin hands unable to keep a grip on it. She held his eyes and threw the weapon away, watching it spin end over end, silvered chain jingling, to lodge in the dirty snow some paces away. "I said there is to be no more killing," she said, "and regrettably, that means you, too. Go get your bauble, Pentarch."

The man's thin lips worked silently, and Heloise could see that his lips were rouged, his pallor a thing of powder as much as soft living. He cast pleading eyes toward Alaric, and when he did not see hope there, at last he hurried away, snatching up the scepter as he went.

Alaric watched him go, looking even more confused than before. "What to do?"

"*We* will do as our savior commands," Tone said, "and she, I suspect, will mourn her dead and see to her wounds, and then she will rule."

"Rule?" Heloise turned to him.

Tone gestured at the golden doors, hanging open. "The door to the throne room is open to you, Heloise."

Heloise felt the room pitch, sick terror swamping her stomach. Barnard touched her elbow, held her straight. "He's right, your eminence. I cannot believe I am agreeing with him, but he is right."

"No." Heloise shook her head. It was too much, too soon. "You just heard that stupid vizier agree with me. It's just a story. I can't sit on that throne. I don't even believe in the Emperor."

Barnard gasped. "You don't mean that, your eminence. You are mad with grief."

"She does believe it," Tone said, "but she is wrong."

The anger surged in Heloise and she shook off Barnard's grip. "I am not wrong. You heard him say it was a story. You saw that empty chair the same as I did!"

"I did, your eminence," Tone said, slowly dropping to one knee, "and you saw that it cut me to my core. On the road to the cage, I found my belief again by force of faith alone. I believed through sheer strength. But it wasn't until we returned that the Emperor reached out and spared me from doubt. He showed me the way, through you. I watched you sweep hell aside. I watched the greatest evil I have ever seen reach out for your throat and be rendered powerless to touch you."

"It did touch me." Heloise gestured at the sheet that masked her father. "It took everything from me."

"Perhaps, but it has given you the power to build it anew. Because what I saw on the road, I know now is true. The truest thing I have ever known. There *is* an Emperor, your eminence. He was never gone from us. He is real, and He is divine, and most important"—Tone reached forward to touch the top of his staff against her chest—"He is here."

# EPILOGUE

## RULE

*From His seat atop the Throne, the Emperor sees all things, does all things, is all things. His hand is in the sunrise and the dew on the grass. He flows in the rivers and blows in the breeze. He blooms with the flower and churns with the earth, taking the spent shells of the dead back into its bosom. He is within us all, the seed that makes us people.*
—The Book of Mysteries, I. 1.

Xilyka helped Heloise to drag her father's corpse into the throne room, then shut the doors behind her. Through them, Heloise could hear her people working with the Imperial soldiers to drag the devils' corpses from the palace nave and throw them down the steps. She could hear Tone's voice chanting over them all, engaging in some ridiculous ritual he claimed was purifying the space defiled by the devil's presence. She could not hear Barnard, but she knew her old friend was standing guard just outside the golden doors, his hands folded over the butt of his massive forge-hammer, daring anyone to try to gain admittance.

The throne stood in the half light, showered with the fragments of the shattered glass from the cupola above.

Xilyka held Heloise while she wept for what seemed like hours, the stored grief slowly draining out of her, refilling even as she let it go.

"I was hoping . . ." she said, when she could finally speak, ". . . I kept hoping that we would win this. That it would all be over. And then I was going to . . . And now he's gone."

"I know," Xilyka said. She had entwined her fingers in the filthy ruin of Heloise's hair, was gently pulling the tangles out.

"I was so cruel to him, since we left the village. I wouldn't tell him I loved him."

"You were at the head of an army," Xilyka said. "You couldn't be seen mooning over your father."

"I was going to! I meant to. When it was over, and now it's over, and . . ." A fresh round of weeping doubled her over, and Xilyka held her until it passed.

"You didn't have to tell him, Heloise," the Hapti girl said. "He knew."

"How could he know? I was cruel to him, and I never told him what he meant to me, and he died knowing . . ."

". . . Knowing that his daughter had given the last of herself to save her people. Knowing that she had won the day. There could be no greater compliment you could have paid him, nothing he could have wanted more."

"I fought so hard to get here and now I don't know what to do."

"There is only one thing you can do." Xilyka pushed her back out to arm's length, her hands firm on her shoulders. "You must mount those stairs and sit that throne. You must rule, Heloise."

Heloise's stomach clenched, and suddenly the world felt every bit as close and threatening as it had on the staircase, when she had tried to exit the machine's dead frame. "What . . . how can you say that?"

Xilyka stroked her cheek. "Heloise, I *see* you. I know how much it grieves you to lose your father. I feel your grief, and I have seen how it hardens you, how it lifts you up to lead."

"Don't say that. I'm not a Traveling Person. I don't live as you do."

"That is not unique to us, Heloise. Loss lifts *all* up, it sets us all on high. You grieve your father, you are confused, bewildered. You just told me you don't know what to do."

Heloise nodded.

Xilyka pointed to the golden doors. "That is how it is for the people out there. All they have known and loved has been ripped from them. They move corpses and 'sanctify' that nave because they cannot think of what else to do. They are fumbling blindly.

"Think of it, Heloise. You want to heal the world? You want to make this right? Then climb those steps. You are the first person to have drawn all the peoples together, to make the Traveling People fight beside the villagers and the Red Lords both. You can be to all of them what your father was to you."

"Sir Steven would never stand for—"

"Sir Steven has no army, Heloise. He cannot stop you. And more, he respects you. You have shown him what you can do. He will treat with you."

Heloise stared up at the stone chair, the peeling flecks of paint so spare that they made the stone seem to glitter. The panic surged as Xilyka's words sank in, along with the realization that it was precisely what her father would have wanted. He would have stood at her side through it all.

"I won't let Tone make me into another Emperor. No more stories. No more lies."

Xilyka shrugged. "People will tell themselves whatever lies make them feel most at ease. You couldn't control that before and you won't be able to control it now."

"Still. I will always speak the truth."

"I know you will, Heloise. And perhaps the truth will set things right in time."

Heloise looked back at Samson's corpse, and despair replaced the panic, a wide gulf even vaster than the well of her grief. "Everyone is gone. What is the point of fixing things if I'm alone?"

Xilyka gave a rueful chuckle, shook her head. "The Great Wheel reminds all of three things—all people lose alone, rule alone, and die alone. Even now, even in your grief, you must look to *all*, Heloise. It is for *others* that the good must live."

Heloise felt the words like a hammer blow, felt her cheeks redden. "You're right, I'm selfish. I'm sorry."

Xilyka smiled. "You are not selfish. And you are also not alone. I am here, Heloise. If you take this throne, I will not return to the Hapti. I will remain here with you."

Heloise reached forward, cupped her cheek. She was painfully conscious of her missing eye and hand, of her burned skin, of her tangled hair. "But you are a Traveling Person. A throne is a chair, not a road."

But Xilyka leaned into her hand, kissing the palm gently. "It is a road, of sorts," she said, "and will it be an easier road, if I am with you?"

Heloise choked back tears. "You know it will be."

And then Xilyka took Heloise's face in her hands, and kissed her. It lacked the melting, the stomach-churning desire of her kiss with Basina. Instead it felt deeper, calmer. Safer. And for all of that, better. They stayed like that for a long time, Heloise's one good hand tangled in Xilyka's hair, devouring her kisses as if she feared it would be the only chance she would ever get. But when they finally broke apart to gulp down air, Xilyka did not pull away.

Instead, the Hapti girl pressed her forehead hard against

Heloise's. "And if it is a road," she whispered fiercely, "then it is *our* road, Heloise, and we will walk it together."

Heloise glanced over her shoulder up the stairs, worn smooth by the passing of so many feet, to the base of the ancient chair that had dominated her life. Had anyone ever used it? She doubted she would ever know, that anyone alive in the capital knew. Real or not, the people outside the door believed in it, and that the power it represented reposed in her, behind the thin scrim of bone Tone had pointed to with his staff, within her beating heart.

Just a chair, like any other, and nothing to be frightened of.

Anyone could sit a chair.

Even her.

# ACKNOWLEDGMENTS

With *The Killing Light*, I not only bring the Sacred Throne trilogy to a close, but I also put the finishing touches on a project that has deep, personal significance to me. I've made no secret that I set out to write this trilogy to prove, both to an audience and to myself, that I could write effectively outside the contemporary military fantasy subgenre (really a sub-sub-subgenre). I wanted to look in the mirror and know that people enjoyed my work not because it was an authentic military story written by a military service member, but because it was *good*. This book you're holding is me checking that box, marking that question answered, and dusting my hands. I said I would do a thing, and now I have done it, and that feels pretty darn good.

But the fact is that I almost didn't do it. *The Fractured Girl*, the novel that was cut down and reworked into the book that became *The Armored Saint*, languished for three years as I tried and failed again and again to make it saleable. I'd be lying if I said that I didn't almost give up.

It's ironic that I set out to write this trilogy to prove I could work *outside* the military subgenre, because the trilogy only came to exist via a very military phenomenon—a great team coalesced around me. They believed in me when my own faith failed. They held me up when I fell down. They fixed the things I broke. They "had my six" as we say in the service. If it weren't for them, I might very well be telling a different story, one where I threw myself at a task I wasn't equal to. And that story would simply have ended there, without you ever getting the other, more important one— Heloise's story.

I owe more to this small army of partners and supporters than I can express, and so these inadequate thanks will have to do.

First, to Justin Landon, who stuck with me through version after version and year after year, never flagging in his faith that it would see print, and who finally brought it over the transom and into the fold at Tor.com. Next, to Irene Gallo, who was willing to take a risk on an author stepping far outside his comfort zone. To Lee Harris, who took up the baton from Justin and the books across the finish line. And to the rest of the Tor.com staff, who worked tirelessly to bring these books to life: Katharine Duckett, Mordicai Knode, Caroline Perny, and Ruoxi Chen, and everyone else at Tor.com and the Tor mothership.

This book had extra editorial assistance from Karen Bourne and Betsy Mitchell, who helped point out errors, boosted my flagging confidence, and kept the book on track.

Thanks also to Joshua Bilmes and the staff at JABberwocky, who represented the whole series so ably.

Thanks again to Kevin Hearne, whose early belief in the project helped me to keep going on it as the early rejections came in. Thanks also to Sam Sykes and Chuck Wendig, whose Twitter antics have made the solitary writing life a little less lonely.

Of course, thanks to Chris McGrath, who was able to execute incredible jacket art that both set forward his own vision and held true to the tone Tommy Arnold set with the first two books. There is nothing more gratifying than seeing your own art reflected in someone else's. Thanks also to Greg Manchess, whose amazing design of Heloise's sigil has now been tattooed on two people that I know of.

And last, but certainly not least, thanks to all of you, who loved the series, told your friends, spread the word on social media, and most important, told me that it reached you. I'm no Emily Dickinson. I write to communicate, and closing that feedback loop—the reader telling me that my work has touched them somehow—is the whole reason I do this. Many of you took the time to let me know, and I will never be able to thank you enough.

Heloise's story is done for now. It's been a tough road for her, but I know she's grateful to have had you along for it.

So am I.